Hear Me Roar

by

Joy Smith

Hear Me Roar

Cover Art by *Kristian Norris*

The Wild Rose Press, Inc.
PO Box 708
Adams Basin, NY 14410-0708
Visit us at www.thewildrosepress.com

Publishing History
First Mainstream Mystery Edition, 2017
Print ISBN 978-1-5092-1296-5
Digital ISBN 978-1-5092-1297-2

Published in the United States of America

At first, she heard a wheezing sound,
and then a raspy voice. "Tell him he owes us ten grand."

"Who *is* this? How did you get this number?"

The phone went dead.

Tell him he owes us ten grand? Jan's hand went to her face. Of course. For the stash the police confiscated. She'd bet Jeff was supposed to deliver it, get paid, and share his cut with this character. Who were these people, and how far would they go to get their money?

Wrapping her arms around her body, she tried to shake off the cold fear that she and the children could be in danger. How had that sinister sounding man gotten their home number? Did he know where they lived? She shut her eyes briefly.

Would she ever be rid of the fear?

Jan had to do something, but she wasn't sure what. She ran to the living room and grabbed Detective Hoskins's card from the end table. As she turned, she caught the glint of headlights in her peripheral vision. It was past ten when few cars had reason to come down their street.

Jan edged over to the window, staying to the side where the drapery would hide her, and peered out. She sucked in a breath. A dark sedan had parked on the street in front of their house. If it hadn't been for the outdoor lights she'd left blazing, the car might've blended into the night. How odd. The car's headlights were off, yet a tiny glow from the interior indicated the vehicle was occupied.

Chapter One

The garage door groaned open.

Jan Simmons caught her breath, hating the dread that was sure to turn her into a blathering ninny. *The rat is home.* Gathering her inner strength, she rose from the couch, pulled back her shoulders, and waited as his footsteps grew louder.

Jeff stumbled into their living room and grasped at the back of the armchair to steady himself. Flinging his product case onto the seat, he dropped his suit jacket on the floor and ripped off his tie. "Why are you still up?" he snarled. Her husband's bleary gaze crawled over her. "And dressed like you were going out somewhere fancy."

Her nostrils flared, catching the sour scent of booze. The hands at her side tightened into fists and words spit from her mouth. "Somewhere fancy? Like we can afford to go out?" A tear washed down her cheek. "No, Jeff, like a fool I dressed for you."

"Fool, you're calling me a fool?" Jeff's eyebrows rose, and his face reddened. He stepped toward her, tripping over his feet.

Jan's hand went out in front of her, slamming him back. "You stink. How dare you go out drinking when you knew darn well I had dinner waiting for you."

"I forgot, so sue me."

Here we go again. Dr. Jekyll by day, Mr. Hyde at

night. Taking a deep breath, she swallowed her anger like a dose of bad medicine and spoke in measured words. "You could have had the decency to call." Brushing away the wetness on her cheek, she sniffed. "I grilled steaks and made scalloped potatoes, your favorites, and the children decorated a cake. I kept them up to see you past eight, but I finally had to put them to bed. Here." She handed him the cards nine-year-old Mae and four-year-old Billy made for him.

He clutched at them, wrinkling the art paper. "What are these for?" He appeared confused, and his words slurred.

"The children wanted to surprise you. They made you congratulations cards for completing the training for your new job."

"Aw, I'm sorry." He cast his eyes down for a moment then looked up. His blue eyes zinged darts at her. "Why'd you have to go and get the kids all riled up about the job thing? Now they'll be upset with me for not showing up." Shifting his feet to keep his balance, he pointed a shaky finger at her. "And it's all your fault."

"*My* fault?" she sputtered. "Because you chose to go drinking after your last class instead of coming home to your family, it's *my* fault?"

Jeff covered his ears. "Don't you shout at me!" Throwing down his hands, he came at her. "Listen, you. I can't be responsible for every little thing you think I ought to do. I'm in charge here, not you." His finger struck her chest. "Get it? Now, how about warming up those steaks and potatoes you said you made just for me?"

"Hah. You've already had dinner, in liquid form.

Wait." She grabbed hold of his shirt collar. "What's this red mark? Lipstick?" Her voice rose.

"You have a lot of nerve accusing me of fooling around." He grabbed the front of her shirt and brought her nose to nose with him. The sourness of his breath turned her stomach. "Whatever happened to you, anyway? You used to be so nice. Now, all you do is bitch, bitch, bitch." He released her so suddenly, she stumbled backward. "Never mind. I'll get something myself."

At his receding footsteps, Jan's shoulders relaxed into a slump. "Your plate's on the counter. Just nuke it for a minute."

Jeff didn't reply, which was good. Maybe it was over for now. She listened for the beep of the microwave. *Nada.* A cabinet door slammed, and she heard a thump, then the odious clink of ice hitting a glass.

Before she could stop herself, Jan dashed into the kitchen and grabbed at the back of Jeff's shirt. "No more."

He whirled around, eyes flashing fire. "I've had it with you." His hand lashed out and caught the side of her jaw.

A sob crawled up into her throat and released with a pitiful howl. She burst into tears and ran toward their bedroom.

Once inside, Jan quietly shut the door lest she disturb Jeff further. Leaning back against the cool wooden door, she pressed the sore spot on her cheek. He'd never slapped her before. Whatever was going on with him was getting worse. As she listened for movement and sound, her insides quivered with dread.

Good. He's not coming after me.

Rain drummed against the window, echoing the pounding of Jan's heart.

Only then did she process what she had seen. Lipstick on his collar. Was she a co-worker from his class? A sharp-looking beauty dressed to the nines, not a frumpy housewife in jeans like she was. Maybe it was a casual kiss, the see-ya-later kind, and she was getting all riled up about nothing. Besides, Jeff would never cheat on her. He loved her.

And I used to love him.

Despite the chill in the room, Jan's skin flushed with sweat that dripped down the inside of the body-hugging black shirt she'd worn to please Jeff, staining it with dark wet blotches. How foolish of her to hang onto the shred of hope that the caring, loving husband hidden inside the shell of this stranger would resurface and they'd be a happy family again.

Taking a deep breath, Jan caught the citrusy odor of Jeff's aftershave. Whatever happened to the sweet love they once had? Bending over, she picked up her husband's T-shirt and jeans from the floor and hugged them to her chest inhaling the scent of the man he once was.

Then, Jeff's last words played in her head. *I've had it with you.*

Jan squared her shoulders, allowing rage to trump her fear. "I've had it with you too." She hurled his clothes across the room, not caring where they landed or if he heard her. "Do your own darn laundry. I don't need you, and I don't need your insults. I'm out of here."

Grappling under the bed, she found the handle of

her roller bag, heaved it on top of the bedspread, and tossed in whatever she might need—jeans, T-shirts, underwear, and nightgown. She was headed into the bathroom for her toiletries when she halted her step.

Where do you think you're going this late on a stormy night with two young children?

A burst of pain welled up in Jan's chest and released as a guttural sob.

Trapped like an animal in a cage.

Even if she had the guts to rouse the children from their beds, pack their clothes, and stuff them in her rattletrap of a car, where could they go? To a hotel? Can't afford it. To her parents'? Three hours on slick roads and lots of explaining to do. Once her parents finished lecturing her on risking the children's lives, she'd have to tell them the truth about what's been going on with Jeff. They wouldn't understand. They'd blame her and send her home to make up with him.

I just can't win.

The suitcase, a black lump on the white comforter, glared at her, daring her to grab it and go. Its handle stuck out at her like a taunting tongue.

Hot tears flooded Jan's face. She pressed her fist to her mouth to stifle the sobs. Snatching a tissue, she blew her nose and then flung the disgusting thing at the bag.

The tissue landed at her feet.

Lightweight!

As if she needed a suitcase's judgment.

Jan jerked the offending bag off the bed. With a swift kick, she launched it under the bed and then fumbled in the dresser for the baby pink pajamas she wore whenever she was sick. She pressed the worn fabric against her cheek, comforted by its familiar softness, and then put them on.

Slipping under the covers, she rolled to the edge of their king-size bed, making herself as small as possible. With the quilt up over her ears and huddled in a fetal position, she shut her eyes, feigning sleep.

Jeff would be stumbling to bed soon. In the mood he was in, he'd try to paw her. No tenderness, just hard, fast, sloppy sex, leaving her feeling as used as a blow-up doll.

Her body tensed at the thought.

She waited.

****

Three weeks later, at five o'clock on a cool September evening—the kind when you can smell the crispness in the air—the garage door roared open.

Jan sucked in a breath. *He's home*. She never knew what to expect from Jeff these days. He could slam in with rage in his eyes or be as sweet as the frosting on the pumpkin bars she made for dessert.

The children heard him too. Mae and Billy sidled up to her ready to defend her against whatever mood their father might be in tonight. Jan hated the nights.

Her husband's footfalls, muffled by the carpet, brought him to their living room, where she and the children waited like a squad of soldiers. At his nib's command.

Jeff appeared with a grin and built up tension oozed out of Jan. While her wary daughter held back sucking her thumb, Billy ran to hug him around the legs, his superhero cape floundering about his shoulders.

"Up, Daddy."

"Whoa. Hold it Mr. Kryptonite, give me a minute."

Setting down his sample case, Jeff yanked off his tie, unbuttoned his collar, and tossed his suit jacket over the arm of the sofa. "Whew. It's hard getting used to being wrapped like a mummy in business clothes all day. Worth it, though. I made my first sale." His face glowed, his shoulders appeared broader, and it seemed to her he had grown an inch or two.

Jan smiled with relief and grazed his cheek with a kiss. "I'm so proud of you." Her stomach turned when she caught a whiff of his breath. He'd stopped for a drink on the way home.

"Yay. Daddy made a sale." Billy wiggled his hips in a little dance.

Mae moved closer to Jeff. Her face remained tight. "Does this mean you're getting a promotion?"

"Not yet, Maybug." He tweaked her braid and then ruffled Billy's hair. "Who wants a wheelie first?"

"Me, Daddy." Billy pushed at Mae. "You can wait your turn. I got here first."

Jan put a hand on her son's shoulder. "Be nice to your sister."

Mae stuck out her tongue at Billy. "That's because you're the baby."

Jeff's smile deflated. "Come on, kids. Cut it out." He glared at Jan as if it were her fault the kids were acting up.

Any happiness she'd felt moments ago drained out of her. "They're just excited, Jeff."

"Wheelie, Daddy."

"Okay. Just one, then I have to make a call."

"I'll get dinner going." Jan turned toward the kitchen.

Jeff whirled her around then put his hands on her shoulders. "You know, you're still pretty. You would be even prettier if you were a blonde."

She wrenched away, feeling as if he'd slapped her in the face.

He chucked her under the chin. "Come on, lighten up. I'm taking you and the kids out to dinner tonight to celebrate."

"We don't need to go out," Jan said with ice in her voice. "I've got Chicken Marbella ready to go in the oven, the kids have school, and you have a full day of work ahead of you tomorrow. Besides, we can't afford—"

He put a finger to her lips. "Not another word. Save that dinner for tomorrow night. Now, we'll have plenty of money."

Jeff, the dreamer. Jan didn't know the exact numbers—he hoarded the checkbook like an old lady with her memories—but with mortgage and car payments due, they had to be hurting.

"I want tacos," Billy said with a grin. "Can we, Daddy?"

Mae tucked her hand in Jan's. "I would rather get a salad."

She didn't, but she knew her mom did. Jan squeezed her daughter's hand in thanks.

Jeff's forehead wrinkled, and his mouth lifted to the side. "I was thinking of someplace nicer, where we can get table service and your mom and I can have a cocktail or two to celebrate. How about"—he drummed his fingers on his lips—"Georgio's Eatery in town."

"Yay. Georgio's," Billy cried, the prospect of a wheelie forgotten.

Mae glanced at Jan, checking.

She nodded. "Sounds fine. But, Jeff—"

"You guys put on some fancy duds, and we'll leave in ten minutes." Jeff pinched Jan's butt. "Wear those pants that make your ass look high."

"My ass is perfectly fine," she said to his back. She doubted if he heard her, and even if he did, would he care he sabotaged any good feelings she might've had toward him?

With Jan staring after him, Jeff headed to the small room off the family room he'd commandeered as his office. While the children scampered off to change, she went through her dresser, found a newish pair of jeans, and paired them with a sage green top that brought out the green in her hazel eyes. She checked her rear in the full-length mirror behind the bedroom door. Even *these* jeans hung low on her waist and sagged at the butt. Had Jeff even noticed she'd lost weight?

Ten minutes later, Jan and the children were ready, and Jeff had yet to surface from his office. Mae had put on the pink dress and ballet flats she wore to parties, but Billy hadn't changed from the jeans and tee he wore to Fun for Tots this morning.

"Come on kids, we'll wait for Daddy in the living room."

They settled on the velveteen sectional and passed the time playing I Spy with My Little Eyes, a word game Mae and Billy loved.

"What's taking Daddy so long?" Mae asked. "I'm hungry."

Jan checked her watch, almost six. Certainly, Jeff's had enough time to update his boss. And how much paperwork could he have with one sale? He must have lost track of time.

"Mae, go see—never mind, I'll check on him." It would give her a couple of minutes to talk to him alone.

Putting on a smile, Jan approached the office. The door was shut, as always. The hushed timbre of Jeff's voice wafted through. Something about his soft and caring tone made her press her ear to the door.

Her mouth dropped open, and her heart stood still. *No, I can't be hearing right. Did Jeff really say, I love you?*

A wave of sweat washed over Jan leaving her lightheaded. She stumbled backward, pressing her hand against the wall for support. Her quick pants became heavy breaths. How could he do this to her? There must be an explanation. His door had been closed, and it was hollow. Could he actually have said, *I'll see you*? She sounded the words, *see* and *love*. *Nope. Doesn't work.*

The truth. She needed the truth. Straightening her spine from a hunched over position, Jan burst into Jeff's office.

His head shot up, and a funny look crossed his face, one she'd come to recognize as guilt. Setting the handset in its cradle, he pushed back from his desk and stood. "What do you mean interrupting me when I'm talking to my boss?"

Jan narrowed her eyes until Jeff appeared to shrink before her. "Your boss? Right. I heard what you said." She did her best to keep her voice steady and assertive. "I'm done with pussy-footing around you." Her hands dug into her hips as she moved toward him. She stuck her face up to his. "Who were you *really* talking to?"

"None of your business. It's work." He spat out the words.

"Since when do you tell a business associate, *I love you*?"

Jeff's face paled at the accusation, and then his blue eyes went icy. "What the crap are you talking about? I don't know what you *thought* you heard while eavesdropping, Miss Nosey"—his lips curled into a sneer—"but you need to get your hearing checked. I would never cheat on you. Don't you trust me?" The tension in his face eased, and his eyes softened.

"Don't you dare pull that puppy-dog face on me. I'm not buying it." Whirling around with her back to him, Jan crossed her arms and stared at the rusty watermark on the ceiling. Waiting, wishing the stain would suck her out of the present and take her back to the good times when she trusted him with her heart, with her life. A tear trickled down her cheek and landed on her arm. She brushed it away. After coddling him for months while he lolled about the house waiting for a job offer to fall into his lap, this is the thanks she got?

Jeff's hand rested on Jan's shoulder, radiating heat into her body. If only it could take away the cold shivers racking through her, but it was too late for that.

With a twist, she shook off his hand and moved out of reach. "The kids are hungry, Jeff."

Hours later, after a tense meal out, Jan lay curled on the far edge of their bed listening to Jeff snore. As hard as she tried, she couldn't shut off those awful words playing over and over in her mind like a scratched record. *I love you, I love you* became *he loves her not me*.

Proof, she needed proof.

Flipping back the covers, Jan slipped from the bed, crept out of their room, and headed down the hall with

11

the glow of night lights showing the way. In the family room, she switched on the light, revealing Jeff's man cave. She only came in here when necessary. She spent her leisure time in their living room or the kitchen where she could read, bake, or do whatever she wanted without having to worry about saying or doing something that would set off a tirade between them.

Jeff had a thing about his office being private and worried the children would go inside and upset something. Jan never felt welcome in it either, but he accepted the carpet needed vacuuming, and the blinds needed an occasional dusting.

She opened the door, clicked the light switch, and peered inside. Cardboard boxes of brochures and plastic bags of sample products remained stacked by the closet door, where they eventually might be stored. On the cluttered, solid mahogany desk, the lid of the laptop that had come with his new job was open. She doubted a new computer would have anything incriminating on it, yet she couldn't resist checking. Stepping around a cardboard box, she slid behind the desk, eased into the plush leather chair, and punched the Enter key to wake up the screen.

Password. *Stink.*

She tried his birthday.

She tried Billy's

And then hers.

A nasty message came up. Three attempts. Locked out.

Okay, so much for that. Jan's gaze landed on the phone, an old-fashioned touch-tone model hard wired into the room, compliments of his former boss. With the new job, Jeff had reactivated it for convenience rather than necessity. She touched the sleek black handset where Jeff's hand had been this very evening, holding it to his ear and whispering sweet nothings to someone, a person he said he loved. She envisioned it with horns, like the devil.

Gripping the handset, Jan picked it up and held it to her ear. "I love you," she said into it, testing the words. Had he made kissing noises too? Had he had phone sex? "I don't know you anymore, Jeff Simmons." She slammed down the handset with a sob. "Darn you for making me cry."

Pull yourself together. Boo-hooing won't give you the answer you came for.

Kicking back Jeff's chair, Jan shot up, scanning the room. Maybe Jeff's briefcase, she'd almost tripped over it when she went around to sit at his desk. A perfect hiding place for—she wasn't sure what, but she would know when she found it. Unlatching it, Jan rifled through a bunch of samples and folders in search of something lacy or satiny. *Nada.*

Drat. There's got to be something…

She spotted Jeff's smartphone on the floor behind a stack of brochures, charging.

Gold mine coming up.

Jan bent to pick it up. Maybe a text message or email would prove…

"Mommy, what are you doing in Daddy's office?" Billy stood in the doorway, adorable in his superhero pajamas, clutching Bob, his boxy stuffed toy.

Bad timing.

She rose. "I, um…thought I dropped my watch in here when I came to get Daddy before we went out to dinner. You know the one I always wear. It's gold."

Billy looked down at the carpet. "Did you find it, Mommy?"

"No, sweetie. Now, tell me"—she knelt to talk to him—"what are you doing up?"

"I heard you go by my room. I'm thirsty. Can I have a drink?"

Jan kissed his cheek. "You know, I'm thirsty too. How about we go upstairs and have milk and one of those yummy pumpkin bars I made this afternoon?"

Chapter Two

Frank Di Giorno AKA Frank "The Lid" Carlucci wiped the glass of his high-powered binoculars with the tail of his dress shirt and then held them up to his eyes, his lips widening into an almost comical grin.

"Nice ass." He adjusted the focus for more clarity. Moving to the country was a good idea. All those pretty young things strutting their stuff outside his window. Frank twisted his lips and scrunched his eyes. "Yeah, man. Now this is retirement."

"Frankie, what's taking you so long to change out of your church clothes? I need some help out here," Tina called from the kitchen.

"Be right there, Lovie," he shouted.

Turning toward his dresser, Frank came eye to eye with the statue of baby Jesus. "Sorry," he said to it. When he stashed the binoculars in his top dresser drawer, his gaze landed on the stack of mass cards they'd received after his brother was murdered. The Camiglios lost one of their own for that. He'd seen to it. But he could never be as ruthless as Joe was.

Frank draped his custom-made gray pinstriped jacket over the matching pants on the wooden hanger and hung his suit in the closet. With a sigh, he tucked his shirt into a pair of tan slacks, and then followed his nose to a kitchen filled with Sunday dinner aromas of chicken roasting in the oven and pasta sauce bubbling on the stove.

Tina stood over the sink filling a large pot with water. Her chestnut hair was smoothed back into a neat chignon, and, as always, she wore a dress with hose and high-heeled shoes. She'd gained a little weight around the rump in the twenty-five years they'd been married, but he didn't mind at all.

Nothing like a woman with a big ass, he thought, admiring Tina's butt.

Grabbing her around the waist from behind, he nuzzled the velvety skin under her ear. "Dinner smells great," he murmured, "and so do you." He cupped her ample breast, and little Frank tingled in his crotch without even a dose of Viagra. Big ass, big tits, what more could a man want?

"How about we take a little break? Get you off your feet. You're working too hard."

"Stop, now, Frankie." Tina lifted the pot of water. "You'll make me spill this. Go out and pick me some lettuce and tomatoes from the garden. I want to get the salad put together before the kids get here."

"Oh, all right." Taking a few sheets of old newspaper with him to hold the vegetables, Frank punched in the code for the security system he had installed and pushed open the front door. He stepped outside into his yard.

Sure beats city living, he thought, surveying his property. Charming Way. What a dumb name for a street. He'd been embarrassed to tell the guys his address, but now that he was here, he'd stopped caring about the name. *Let them laugh. I have a nice little house and a garden. All they have to look at is tenements and traffic.*

Stooping to pull up a few weeds, he grunted at the stiff ache in his back. The lettuce was going to seed, and his knees weren't doing much better. It was sad the growing season was nearly over, and even sadder that the chick across the street wouldn't be bending over her flower bed much longer.

As he stole a glance, the woman rose and turned to wave at him. The sun shone on her, making the crown of her head glow like an angel's halo. Over her arm, she cradled a bunch of bright-colored flowers. Pretty woman, from what he could see of her. A small, towheaded kid and a little red-haired girl bantered in high-pitched voices over pushing the wheelbarrow toward the back of the house.

When the babe turned to settle things, he noticed her ass was skinnier than it had looked in his binoculars, but she had been bending over then. *Get your mind out of the gutter, Frank. You're in a classy neighborhood. The women here aren't sluts. They're nice ladies with families, the kind Tina should associate with.*

Turning away, Frank plucked a large ripe tomato and a couple of green peppers. He salvaged enough leaves from the top of the Romaine lettuce plants for Tina's salad. The entire garden would be going to seed soon. He made the sign of the cross. *Thank God, I got a gig going for the winter, or I'd go nuts home all day.*

The roar of an engine burst through the quiet of the neighborhood. Frank looked up to see his son-in-law's bright-red convertible bearing down on their home.

Hurrying inside, he dumped the vegetables by the sink for Tina to prepare. "The kids just got here."

Tina gave the sauce a stir, took off her apron, and

smoothed down the front of her dress. She liked to look nice for company, even if it was just family.

Moments later, Lucille and her husband, Vinnie, bustled into the kitchen. Lucille cradled a wailing baby Frank, whose face was as red as a ripe tomato.

"He's hungry, Ma." Lucille dug into her diaper bag and produced a bottle of milk. "Can you warm it for him? He likes it better."

His daughter paced and jiggled the baby, trying to calm him down. Frank was quick to notice the short skirt she wore barely covered her ass. *Christ. She looks like a Hartford streetwalker. Tina needs to talk to her about dressing like a proper wife and mother.* There would be trouble. Vinnie would never tolerate other men hitting on his wife.

"Hey, Vinnie." Frank dropped his arm around his son-in-law's shoulders. The man was in top condition, he noted, as his arm struck hard muscle. Until Frank stepped down as Don, Vincenzo De Luca was his top man in the collection business. When shop owners defaulted on their security program, he made them fork over the dough without breaking a sweat.

"Ya look good, Pops." Vinnie stood back and swiped at the dark strands of hair that had shaken loose from his comb-back. "Living in the country must agree with ya."

"Yeah, yeah, yeah. It's nice not to have everyone bugging me all the time."

"Come here, little guy." Frank opened his arms to take baby Frank. "Come to Poppa."

Lucille handed the kid over, shaking her head. "He's gonna cry till he gets his bottle, Da."

Frank jiggled his grandson up and down and cooed

at him until he was rewarded with a teary chuckle. An odious aroma assaulted his senses. "Pee-yew." He passed the baby back to his mother. "This kid ain't hungry. He's pooped his pants."

Frank and Vinnie's gazes followed the two women, their hips swaying in unison, as they headed for the spare bedroom to change the baby.

"You're taking good care of our Lucille, aren't ya?" Frank asked his son-in-law. "No other women?"

Vinnie arched his thick black eyebrows. "Pops, you know me. I wouldn't do nothing to hurt The Family."

"You're a good boy. Stay that way." Frank poured two glasses of Chianti and handed one to Vinnie. "Come on out on the porch. I got an idea I want to run by ya."

Leaning against the rail of the back deck, Frank lifted his glass in a toast. "*Saluto.*"

"So, Pops," Vinnie said, once they sampled their wine, "are you thinking of coming back into the business?"

"Nah, I'm done with all that rough stuff. Tina's making me live clean now and do everything legal. Ya hear that? Now that you're a husband and father, maybe you need to get out of the game, too. Find a safer way to make a living. Cousin Louie should be up to the job of taking over The Family."

Vinnie tipped back his head and broke into a loud guffaw. "You've got to be kidding. How am I gonna retire when your daughter has Fifth Avenue tastes? You see that skirt she's wearing?"

"Yeah. I've been meaning to talk to you about that…"

"Two-hundred clams, it cost," Vinnie continued,

"and that's just the beginning. You should see what she wants to spend on redoing the living room. She's already nagging me about moving out of the apartment into a house in the country like yours. I knew that was coming. To tell ya the truth, our neighborhood ain't no place to raise a kid." He shook his head. "But quit? I can't afford to quit."

Frank nodded. "Well, think about it some more. I want ya around to take care of me in my old age."

Vinnie set his glass on the railing and crossed his arms. "What's on your mind, Pops?"

Frank took a sip of wine, savoring the cool red liquid. "You know, when my father was around, me and my brothers would make this stuff in the fall. We'd do a trade for crates of grapes from Italy." He held the glass to the light. "Our homemade wine was never as clear as this stuff, but man, it could pack a wallop."

"Enough reminiscing, Pops. Get on with it."

The muscles in Frank's face went tight. He squinted at Vinnie until one of his droopy eyes closed. "How dare you talk to me like that?" He pushed at his son-in-law's chest. "You may be in charge of The Family, but remember who gave ya the job." He wagged his finger in Vinnie's face. "You respect me, hear?"

Vinnie's hands went up in the air, causing his jacket to spread open to reveal the holstered gun he wore.

"You bring a gun in my home?"

"I need to carry to protect us—Lucy, me, and the baby—you too. Tell me you don't have this house armed to fight off an attack. There's bad blood between you and the Camiglios."

Dropping his hands, Vinnie picked up his wine glass and took a healthy slug. "My father used to make wine too. The stuff tasted rank." He took a sip. "Nice stuff, Pops. Smooth."

Frank smiled, his tension easing. "Imported from the homeland." Taking his glass off the railing, he tipped it toward Vinnie's. "Sorry, I overreacted." He took a sip and smacked his lips. "Ah, nothing like good wine and a good Italian woman."

"Amen to that. Now, what's your idea? I'm all ears." Vinnie cocked his head.

"Promise me you won't laugh when I tell ya?"

"I'm laughing already. Go on."

"Well"—Frank rubbed his jaw—"I'm gonna open a little barber shop in town. I used to be a hairdresser, and I still got the talent. I have dibs on a perfect spot for the place. Give me something to do, you know. A place to go to get out of Tina's hair."

"I'm having trouble picturing ya all legit like that." Vinnie stifled a laugh with his fist. "But like I always say, if it yanks your chain, do it."

Frank put a hand on Vinnie's shoulder. "Someday, when you're ready to give up the business, I'll teach ya to cut hair, and you can take over the shop. We're *famiglia*, right? We take care of each other."

Chapter Three

Jan closed the front door after seeing Mae off to get the school bus. "Billy, where are you?" Quiet was never good.

"In here." His voice came from their bedroom.

"Don't bother Daddy. He's getting ready for work."

Or is he?

The persistent fear that Jeff had lapsed to his old way of ducking out of work made Jan hurry down the hall to make sure he was up and moving. True, he had no specific schedule except to be responsible for covering his territory, meeting appointments, and bringing in sales. Yet, the alarm had gone off at eight and, come to think of it, she hadn't heard the shower running.

As Jan neared the bedroom, she hesitated, noticing the room remained dimly lit.

I'd better be wrong. With a hopeful smile, she stepped into the room. The closed blinds shut out the bright sunshine, and undeniably, the large lump of Jeff's body remained huddled under the covers.

"Hi, Mommy." Still in his pajamas, Billy sat cross-legged on the bedspread watching Jeff sleep, she supposed.

Leaning over, Jan kissed her son's soft little cheek. "Thought you were watching your children's show, sweetie."

Jeff snorted and rolled over, covering his ears with the pillow. "Just another minute, hon," he mumbled. Sunlight streaming through the blinds turned the fine reddish hairs on his arms golden. Stretching his arms, he yawned and rubbed the stubble that had sprouted on his chin and cheeks. How could this man appear so innocent when only last night he professed love to someone else?

"Must've slept through the alarm," Jeff said with a lopsided grin that made the ice in Jan's heart thaw, just a little.

Now, in the morning, she wondered if she had been foolish to accuse him of cheating on her. To her knowledge, he'd always been faithful. Yet, he'd been a hard worker too, and that changed pretty quick. "No doubt, you're hung-over from last night."

Jeff's eyebrows went up. "What are you talking about? I just had a few. I'm fine." To prove it, he threw back the covers, sat on the side of the bed, and then rose. "I'm up. See?" He held out his arms. "Ta-dah!"

It was hard to be upset with Jeff whenever Jan saw a glimmer of the man he used to be, yet she couldn't help being disappointed in him.

"You should be ashamed of yourself for sleeping in the third week of a new job, and you know it. Now get going." She pointed to the bathroom.

"It's okay, Daddy." Billy climbed down from the bed. "I liked hearing you snore."

With a sigh, Jan cupped Billy's chin. "You, young man, need to get dressed for pre-school."

"Mommy, are you mad at Daddy again?" Billy said, trailing her to his room.

"I'm not mad, sweetheart. I had to wake up Daddy so he'll go to work to make money to pay for our house and clothes and food."

"And for Fun for Tots?"

"Yes, dearest. Daddy's money helps you too."

Once Billy had been dropped off at preschool and Jan had completed a few errands, she drove into their garage, almost sorry to be going inside on such a gorgeous fall day.

Jeff's car was missing. *Good. He's out selling.* Gathering the bags of groceries from the trunk, she carried them inside, hearing the house phone ring. She peeked at the tiny caller ID screen on the cordless extension in the kitchen.

Her mother.

Dumping the goods on the counter, she steeled herself before answering. She had to be careful. Mom had a sixth sense. It wouldn't do for her to suspect anything was wrong between her and Jeff.

She picked up the call.

"So Jeff is settled into his new job?" Mom said right off the bat.

No, how are you and the children? Just Jeff. It was always about Jeff.

"He sold an order yesterday." Jan cradled the phone between her ear and shoulder. With her free hand, she began unpacking the baking supplies. "He's going to bring you samples of his cleaning products the next time we come down to New Jersey."

"That's wonderful, honey. We're looking forward to seeing you and the children soon. How about this weekend?"

The pleading tone of her mother's voice made Jan

stop dealing with the groceries. She hated when her mom cornered her like this. Visiting them would entail an overnight stay. Right now, spending a large block of time with the parents was risky.

"This weekend isn't good. After being on the road all week, Jeff won't want to get back in the car and drive all that way."

"Maybe we could come up then?" The question hung in the air like a spider ready to trap its quarry. "It's been weeks since we've seen you. And we miss the children."

No. Not going to deal with the guilt trip.

"Mom, I'm sorry, but that won't work either. You know how it used to be when you were raising Will and me. Weekdays are filled with the children's schoolwork and game practices, and the weekends aren't much better. Mae's got a lacrosse game on Saturday, and Billy's invited to a birthday party."

Her mother sucked in a breath at Jan's slip of the tongue. Although she always thought about her baby brother, her parents never spoke of Will.

"It's not that we don't want to see you and Dad…" Jan went on as if she hadn't noticed.

"It's all right. Don't worry about us. You just go on with your lives. Dad and I will find something to do to while away the time."

Drat. Now she really felt like crap. Her parents could be overly nosy, bossy, and opinionated, but underneath it all, Jan knew they loved her. It hurt her to have to disappoint them.

After her mother's chilly goodbye, Jan disconnected the call.

Her eyes filled, blurring the bright green Formica

countertop. Until now, she hadn't realized how much she missed her parents. Had they lived nearby, it wouldn't have been so easy for Jeff to fool them into thinking he was still working at Lyco, when in reality he had been fired. It would have been harder for her to pretend Jeff was a good husband and father.

Yet, would anything have changed? Maybe it was best that they lived in New Jersey, continuing to think hers and Jeff's marriage was as solid as they expected it to be. She was such a scumbag for having lied to her mother.

Funny. All along, Jan thought she was salvaging Jeff's dignity by keeping silent when it really was her parents' feelings she was protecting.

Jan pulled out the items needed to make the cookies. As she measured out the various grains and blended the butter in a mixing bowl, she set aside her problems and focused on her latest attempt at perfecting the gluten-free chocolate chip cookie. Once she had dollops of dough lined up on a cookie sheet, she slipped them into the oven and set the timer.

With Jeff and the children gone, the quiet in the house echoed around her. Instead of wiping up the counter and doing the baking dishes, Jan went into the living room and glanced out their picture window, half hoping to see Rana or Diane milling about. It had become a Charming Way tradition for the stay-at-home wives to take a morning break over coffee, and she was ready for that break.

Jan loved this street. Charming Way lived up to its name with tall oak trees bordering concrete sidewalks, and picture-pretty homes with well-tended lawns and flowerbeds. Their home was set up on a slight slope on the right side of the *cul de sac*, which gave her an excellent vantage point for checking on the children, along with an overview of the street. Moving here had been a good choice, thanks to Amy's advice. "It's not the ritziest part of town," her childhood friend had said. "But the housing prices are reasonable, the street is loaded with families with young children, and the schools are the best in the state."

Amy had been right.

During the week, Amy taught school, so she wasn't around for their neighborly morning chats.

There's Rana now, pushing her stroller back down the hill.

Jan ran to the front door, stepped out onto the porch, and waved her over. "Hey, my turn today. Come on up."

With a grin, Rana turned up their driveway and parked the stroller at the base of the steps.

Rana, tall and slender with chestnut hair that rippled down to her waist, came inside toting four-month-old Carrie, trailed by Derrick, who was two and a half.

"Have you been outside today? That tree over by the Quigley's house is a brilliant orange already, and the humidity must be zero."

"I know. I hated to come inside." Jan beckoned her toward the kitchen. "I've got a fresh pot of coffee going."

"Where's Billy?" Rana's little boy said.

Jan knelt in front of the child. "Sorry, sweetie pie, Billy is at school. Would you like to play with his trucks?"

The little dark-haired boy nodded and handed her

the bunch of brightly colored leaves he apparently collected.

"Why thank you." She set them on the counter.

Once Jan found a few toys for Derrick, Rana settled him in the corner and laid a blanket on the floor for little Carrie, who gurgled and cooed as she gnawed at her teething ring.

"What's that sinful aroma? Oh Lord, tell me it's not a candle."

"Just some cookies. Ready to be a guinea pig? It's the fifth recipe for gluten-free chocolate chip cookies I've tried."

"Are they calorie-free too?"

"I wish." Jan set two mugs filled with coffee on the kitchen table and joined Rana.

"Are things any better with Jeff now that he's back to work?"

"Pretty good. I think. I hope. He was slow starting this morning, which concerns me, but he's out of the house. It's nice not to have him underfoot all day."

"I hear you. When Larry's home, he drives me nuts looking for lunch and starting projects. I can't get anything of my own done. Men."

Jan lowered her head, holding back tears. She couldn't let Rana see how miserable she was. She gripped her coffee cup, drawing comfort from its warmth. "I don't know what to do. I'm so frustrated with him."

When Jan looked up, Rana's brown eyes glittered.

She grabbed her hand. "I'm okay. Really." Jan hated using her friends as crutches. If only they could have known the cheerful, confident person she used to be before Jeff had been fired.

"Have you talked to him about it?" Rana asked, her smooth brow furrowed.

"I tried, but he ignores me. He gets so crabby that I don't even watch TV with him anymore."

"What about your parents? He respects them. Maybe they could have a word with him."

"I hate to worry them. They think I'm lucky to have such a nice guy. Jeff *used to be* a nice guy." Jan bit down on her lower lip to stop the trembling that could turn her into a sobbing mess. Turning away, she rose.

Keeping her back to her friend, Jan took her time sliding a few warm cookies onto a plate.

Rana came up behind her and rested her hand on Jan's shoulder. "It's okay. You're strong. You'll get through this." Taking the cookies, she set the plate on the table.

Settling across from each other, Jan sipped at her coffee, savoring its heady aroma and comforting warmth. "Thanks for caring."

"Now don't get all sentimental on me." Rana took a cookie and sampled it. "Hey"—she chewed thoughtfully—"you've got a winner here. This tastes like a regular tollhouse cookie. It doesn't crumble, except when I chew it, and it doesn't stick to the roof of my mouth like that other version you made."

"At least one thing in my life is going right."

Rana examined the cookie. "You could sell some of the great desserts you make. Lots of people can't tolerate wheat these days."

"I wouldn't know where to begin, but I'll think about it. You know, Rana, I traded the chance to go to Paris to learn pastry making to get married. Now, I wonder what else I could have done with my life." Jan lifted her shoulders in a shrug. "I became pregnant with Mae, and here I am. A mere housewife."

"I modeled for a teen magazine. I had an agent and everything. They said I was going to be the next Brooke Shields. You'd never know it to see me now." She drew forward a strand of shiny dark hair and examined it. "I'm already starting to go gray like my mother did at twenty-five. I love Larry and the kids, but by the time they're old enough for me to go back to work, I will have lost my looks." Rana took a sip of her coffee. When she looked up, her eyes were watery.

"Don't be ridiculous. You're not wearing any makeup, yet your skin is flawless. You've kept your figure, and so what about going gray? That's what hair color is for. Besides, it won't be long before the children are old enough for you to take on a few modeling jobs. You have your whole life ahead of you. Women are modeling into their sixties and beyond."

"A couple of years ago, my old agent called me to model maternity clothes, but I turned her down. Maybe I'll check in with her."

"I'll be glad to babysit." Jan looked over at Carrie, who had dropped the teething ring and dosed off. "Your children are adorable and so easy-going."

Rana's mouth widened in a smile. She clasped Jan's hand. "Wow, you'd do that for me?"

"Of course. Now, enough soul-searching for today." Jan leaned in. "Have you met our new neighbors? I've seen the man working his garden all summer, but the moving van just showed up last week. They must have been doing some major renovations inside."

"You must mean the DiGiornos next door? The husband stopped to talk to me when I was out in the yard with the kids. He seemed nice enough, grandfatherly, if you know what I mean. I hardly ever see his wife. I don't think she drives."

"They have company with fancy cars. They must be loaded. Makes me wonder what such people found appealing about our humble little street."

"Beats me. Diane told me Mr. D. bought Joe's Barber Shop on Wagner Street. I'll have to send Larry down to check it out."

"Jeff's hair's getting a little shaggy around the ears. He always went to Joe, but I'll pass on the news about the change."

Rana rose to leave and gathered up her children.

Jan walked her to the door, feeling better for having been able to verbalize her feelings without fear of reprisal.

"There's Mr. D now, in his garden," Rana said.

"The way it's all fenced in you'd think he was growing gold in there."

"Only vegetables, but you're right about them being protection-savvy. You probably couldn't see it from where you live, but a security installation truck was parked at the back of their house for days before they moved in. I forget the name."

"Yeah, what's up with that? Charming Way is so safe I never bother to lock my door."

"Me neither." Rana nestled her sleeping baby back into the stroller. "Just my luck Carrie will wake up when I go to move her to her crib."

"Derrick, wait. You forgot something." Jan ran to the kitchen for the child's leaves. "Here. Press these in a magazine, and you'll be able to keep them."

Derrick took the leaves. "Okay. What's a maga—"

"Zine," she finished. "It's a book."

He smiled and turned to Rana, "Mommy, I need a book."

Jan shook her head. Children were such fun. She once wanted a billion of them.

Once Rana disappeared into her home, Jan checked her watch. She had enough time to be neighborly before picking up Billy from school.

Digging around in a lower cupboard, she found a suitable container and layered in the remaining cookies. As she did this, she snatched a cookie and took a bite. It *was* good as Rana had claimed.

A baking business. Maybe it could work out.

Taking the cookies, Jan headed out the front door and ran across the street to the DiGiorno's gray cape. She rapped against the thick chain-link fence enclosing the garden. A gate faced the gravel driveway.

"Excuse me, Mr. DiGiorno?"

"What the fuck?" His head shot up, and he stood, his face tight, eyes focused.

Uh-oh. He's a grouch. Maybe this wasn't such a good idea.

At seeing her, the man's face relaxed into a smile. With a clink of the gate, he came toward her, removing his gardening gloves and shoving them in the back pocket of his grass-stained work pants. He walked with such purpose that she stepped back.

The man looked to be about Jan's father's age, but in much better physical condition—no beer belly on this man. His longish silver hair had been cropped just above his ears, but left in long layers, as if professionally styled.

"Welcome to the neighborhood. I live across the street. Jan Simmons. My husband's Jeff. You've probably seen the children playing outside." She shoved the container at him. "Here, I hope you like chocolate chip cookies."

He nodded, lips curling into a half smile that transformed him from fearful to friendly. His eyelids drooped half shut, giving him a sleepy, sexy look. "Yer a nice lady. Call me Frank."

When he took the cookies, Jan glanced at his hand. Perfectly manicured fingertips. Odd for a man.

Frank cracked the lid of the container and peeked inside as if he expected a cookie might jump out and bite him. "We'll have coffee. Come inside, meet Tina." He turned toward his house, expecting Jan to follow.

"I'd love to…uh…Frank, but I'm running late picking up my son at school."

"Another time then."

Chapter Four

"Ah." Frank waved his finger in the air and did a little dance. Music from the opera *La Traviata* bellowed through the speakers Louie's crew had installed in his barbershop.

Throwing his hands in the air, he announced, "The Men's Room is open for business."

His two beauticians looked at him, shaking their heads.

"Frankie, who's gonna want to sit and listen to that stuff?" Marilee said, one hand on her slim hip. "How about some real music?"

"Yeah," Irene chimed in. "Something we could dance to. You know, to entertain the customers."

"What do ya think I'm running here, a peep show? All you girls got to do is look good and schmooze with the customers while you use your talents to snip-snip their hair. We want them to come back for haircuts, not to watch a disco show." He pinched his fingers together, tent-like, and turned them upward. "*Capiche?*"

"Sure," said Irene, "I got ya." Taking the wad of gum she'd been chewing out of her mouth, she stuck it on the mirror at her station.

"Hey," Frank said. "Get rid of that. From now on, no gum in here."

"Yer tough, but yer cute." Marilee pinched his

cheek.

"Sure I am." Returning the favor, he pinched her skinny ass.

The door jingled.

"Ooh, we got a customer!" Irene exclaimed when a tall, auburn-haired man walked in. "Right here in this chair, sir."

Frank rubbed at his jaw. "Thanks for coming in. You're our first customer. Marilee, give this man the works."

"The works? What's that?"

The dude spoke with the smarmy tone of a salesman, the kind that would try to beat Frank out of his fee. Let him try.

"Well"—Marilee dug her fingers into his hair and kneaded his scalp—"I massage your head, and then neck, then your shoulders, and then…"

Frank held up his hand. "That's as far as we go with the works here, mister. Upper body only, *Capiche?*" He shot an evil eye at Marilee. *Dumb broad is gonna bring the cops in here and close me down if I don't control her now.*

"Say." Frank moved around where he could examine the guy. "Ya look familiar. Yeah. Ya live across the street from me. Your wife brought us cookies the other day. Pretty lady." He patted the man's shoulder. "You're a lucky bastard."

"That I am. She puts up with me. I'm not sure how." Frank's neighbor shook his head and offered his hand. "Jeff Simmons. Nice to finally meet you."

Frank took the guy's hand and shook. "Yeah, we'll see about that."

Word of Frank's new shop must've spread around

town. By lunchtime, they were busier than a hornet's nest. The girls stepped up to the job, handling shaves, shampoos, and trims like the professionals they once were.

Nice what a little spiffing up and a chance at a better life could do for street whores.

The problem was Marilee and Irene were so grateful they wouldn't leave him alone. "Frankie, come on in the back room for a blow job. Frankie, you look tired. How about a massage?" Frankie this, Frankie that.

He must be getting old because he didn't have the patience for being fondled by just anyone anymore. He had his Tina, and she made sure his sexual needs were taken care of, as long as he didn't piss her off. Man, that woman could be a bitch when she was mad. But that's what he liked about her. Feisty. She stood up to him.

Frank took a load off his feet and sat in one of the empty lounge chairs where four men waited their turn to be serviced. From his breast pocket, he drew out a cigar, lit up, and continued to watch his girls flit around in those tight little red shorts and low cut tank tops. Having them wear uniforms had been a good idea.

Next to him, a wimpy guy with hair down to his shoulders nudged his arm. "Are we allowed to smoke in here?"

"What do ya think? It's called The Men's Room, ain't it? Sure, light up."

"I love this place. I'm going to tell all my friends." The man pulled a joint from his pocket.

"Hey, none of that. Pot ain't legal in Connecticut yet, and I don't want no cops in here."

The man shrugged his skinny shoulders and pocketed the joint. "No problem, man. Thought I'd give it a go."

Frank nodded and stood when Louie pushed through the door. His second cousin was a hot-tempered gorilla who could overtake two, three men at a time.

"Good to see ya back in business, Lid." Louie slapped Frank on the back.

"Ya got me wrong, Louie." Frank hardened his gaze. "I told ya, I'm going straight. I promised Tina."

Glossing over Frank's comments, Louie said, "The music sounds good. I'm impressed with what ya done to the place. It used to be a pit." He glanced around. "Hardwood floors, new furniture, and the chicks are a nice touch. Maybe they got time to take care of your old buddy?"

"I owe ya, Louie, so anytime you need these ladies' services they're on the house. Here, have an imported Cuban cigar."

Louie took the cigar and ran it under his nose. "How'd ya get these? They're worth big bucks on the street."

Frank winked. "No way. These are my private stock." He took a puff, inhaling deeply, and blew the smoke in Louie's face.

Louie's bulldog of a face turned uglier as he drew back coughing. His chest puffed up, and his hand went to the gun holstered under his suit jacket.

"Chill," Frank said.

Louie's hand came down, and he appeared to deflate. "Sorry, boss."

Boss. I still got the power. If anyone else had

insulted Louie like he had, they'd be nursing a smashed jaw and drinking booze through a straw for a couple of months. Louie knew better, nobody messed with Frank Carlucci and lived.

But all that's history, Frank thought with a sigh. *No more dead bodies*, Tina demanded. *They killed your brother. You're next. Keep your head down and your nose clean. For me, for us.* She'd kissed him thoroughly, sticking her tongue down his throat, and then screwed his brains out right there on the living room carpet. What a woman.

To smooth things over, Frank draped an arm around Louie's broad shoulders. "Come in back where we can chat. I got a fine bottle of Italian Cabernet panting to be sipped."

While Marilee and Irene did their thing out front, they settled around the tiny table in the corner of the supply room puffing cigars and sipping aged wine imported from a Naples winery.

"This is gonna work out just fine," Frank said. "Thanks for putting the squeeze on Joe. I gave him more money for this business than it was worth. He would have retired soon, anyway."

"It didn't take much. We showed him the photos we snapped of him with some broad at the Siesta Motel. He caved in easy."

Frank snorted, causing one of his drooping eyelids to close in a wink. "Did ya keep the photos?"

Louie drew an envelope from his breast pocket and gave it to Frank, chortling. "She's not too bad for an old gal."

Flipping through the photos, Frank shook his head thinking, not much had changed since his retirement.

Instead of me doing the dirty work, I got mio amico, my brothers, to do it for me.

Chapter Five

Fall settled in with the trees flaunting brilliant reds, oranges, and golds and the children making hard decisions about Halloween costumes. It was a lazy Saturday morning with the kids watching the cartoon channel and Jeff sleeping in.

As Jan sipped at her third cup of coffee, she flipped through the stack of catalogs she'd collected, put together a list of must-haves for the children, then called and placed an order.

"That'll be five hundred dollars and ninety-four cents, plus forty dollars for ground shipping," the cheery voice on the other end announced.

Jan rubbed the Visa card, wishing a genie would appear to offer her three wishes.

"Ma'am, I'll need your charge card number."

"Yes, of course."

Jan hung up the phone feeling guilty, even though everything she'd purchased was on sale until she thought of Jeff's extravagant spending. No cheap catalog shopping for him. She understood he needed to dress nicely for his job, but the more-for-less store sold brand-name suits that would have done just as well as the pricey ones from Harvey's. It wasn't fair that they could afford to outfit him in style while she clipped coupons and scrimped on necessities.

No sense sucking on the proverbial sour grapes.

It's time to get moving here.

Jan jumped in the shower, dressed, and then got the children going. In the interim, Jeff had risen, grabbed a cup of coffee, and disappeared into the bathroom.

Half an hour later, he strode past her and the children and headed toward the garage.

"Come on kids. Get your coats and shoes on. Daddy's waiting for us."

Collecting her purse and jacket, Jan shooed the children toward the garage entry.

"Jeff. We're ready," she called.

"Wait." Jan stopped when she saw him. "Why are you fiddling with your golf clubs?"

"Oh, didn't I tell you? I'm going to play a few rounds with Mike and Stevie."

Jan drew up her shoulders and crossed her arms tight against her chest. "No, you didn't. You promised Mae and Billy we'd take them to the Mystic Aquarium today. They've been reading books about fish all week."

"Did I?" He made a face. "I forgot about that, but it's tough to get a decent tee time at the club on a Saturday morning." He checked his watch. "In fact, I'm late. You and the kids go ahead to Mystic, though."

"Aw, Daddy." Mae tugged on his shirtsleeve. "It won't be fun without you."

"Yeah," Billy added. "You never take us anywhere anymore." His lower lip stuck out in a pout.

Jeff patted Billy's head. "Sorry, tiger." He stooped to talk to his children on their level. "Tell you what, kids. How about we all go to Boston to see a Patriot's game next week?"

"What's a Patriot, Daddy?" Billy said, looking

confused.

"A football team."

"I don't like football," Mae said. "All the men do is run and tackle each other. It's a stupid game."

"Jeff, the children are really disappointed. Can't you cancel?"

"Too late. Mike and Stevie are waiting. I'm entitled to some fun, aren't I?" He flashed Jan a cheesy grin. "By the way, get a sitter for tonight. Mike and Amy want us to come over for a few drinks later."

When he bent to kiss her goodbye, Jan turned her face so his lips landed on her ear.

Once Jeff left, she flopped down on the settee in the family room and drew Billy onto her lap. Mae crept in beside her.

"I don't want to go to the aquarium anymore," Mae said, chewing on a strand of hair, a habit she had yet to break.

"Well"—Jan picked up the Greenburg Bugle— "let's see what's going on around here." She paged through to the activity section. "How about we go to the apple festival in Matlin? It's only a half hour drive. It says here they have face painting and booths selling all kinds of handmade things."

"Jewelry?" Mae brightened.

"I don't know, but what do you say we find out?"

****

Six o'clock. Where is he? For the umpteenth time, Jan punched in Jeff's cell phone number and left a voice mail. He had yet to call back.

They'd been back from the festival since two. The aroma of Chicken Parmesan permeated the kitchen.

She dialed Amy. "Have you heard anything from

the men?"

"What do you mean? Mike and Stevie are right here. We're having dinner. You and Jeff are coming over at eight, aren't you?"

"Jeff's not home yet."

"Really? The guys played only nine holes. Jeff dropped them off this afternoon, but he didn't come inside. Mike's shaking his head no. He thought Jeff was headed home."

"Obviously not. And he's not answering his cell. Do you think something's happened to him?"

"Gee, I hope not. Let me know."

The oven timer dinged, and a bell went off in Jan's head. *I've been a fool.* He expected she would be out with the children most of the day.

About seven, Jeff finally showed up.

"You were gone a long time." Jan's voice was frosty as she continued dipping her homemade caramels in chocolate and setting them on a cookie sheet to dry.

"Mike and I stopped off at the clubhouse for a few pops afterward."

"Really?" Jan whipped around. She wanted to see his face when he lied to her. "Mike's been home for hours." She squared her shoulders, suppressing the rage that had eaten at her gut for the past hour.

Lifting her chin, she spotted a red mark on his neck that looked suspiciously like a hickey. Her heart dropped into her stomach. "Where were you, Jeff? Tell me. I want to hear your story."

"What are you, a time cop? I knew you were out for the day, and I didn't want to come home to an empty house. I went back to the club and had a few drinks with August. You remember him, from Saint

43

Andrews."

"You said with Mike."

"Did I? I meant August."

"Who is she, Jeff?"

"Why are you so paranoid lately?" He reached out to touch her cheek.

Jan grabbed his left hand and looked at it. "Your wedding ring. Where is it? Did you take it off on purpose?"

"Don't get all crazy on me now. I was going to tell you. I was taking a long shot today and swung so hard that the ring flew off my finger."

"Oh, yeah, right. Tell me another story."

"Really, Jan. It must have been loose. Ask Mike and Stevie. They were there. We scoured the grass for it, but it may have gone in the drink. The Club is on the lookout, so maybe it'll show up." He reached in the cupboard for a glass and filled it with ice.

She wanted to believe him, just as she wanted to believe she hadn't heard him tell another woman he loved her, hadn't seen that hickey—if that's what it was, and that he'd killed time with a church acquaintance at the Ninth Hole Bar. She never used to question Jeff's honesty. Was she becoming a shrew? She twisted the hard gold band on her fourth finger and found it turned easily. If she flipped her hand, it's possible it would fall off.

"Okay, I'll buy the ring thing, but what about that mark on your neck?"

"Mark?" He touched his neck. "Beats me. Maybe when I shaved…"

"Maybe." Jan's mouth tightened. Was she really, as Jeff said, paranoid? "But that ring, it can't be replaced." She bit her lower lip.

"It's a piece of metal, that's all. I don't know why you have to make such a big deal about it."

His cavalier comment stabbed Jan like a knife. Yet, she bit back a retort. To her, a wedding ring *was* a big deal. It symbolized their bond, their love for each other. Why couldn't Jeff understand that? Maybe he doesn't care about the ring anymore because he loves someone else. The woman he likely spent time with this afternoon. Inside her, Jan's heart squeezed into a tight knot. She didn't dare get into accusations, especially when Jeff was pouring himself another cocktail.

"Haven't you had enough to drink with your *friend*?" The snippy words spilled out of her mouth before she could hold them back. He'd hurt her, and she wanted him to know she wasn't as gullible as he believed.

"Let go of it, Jan. I told you, nothing happened!" He stormed off, his hand cradling his drink, leaving her feeling like an idiot.

Packing up the candies, she put them aside for another time and phoned Amy to cancel, dreading the night ahead.

Chapter Six

Sunday morning arrived bright and shining. Leaving Jeff sleeping in bed, Jan hustled the children off to church. Mae was due at Sunday school. She would be making her first communion in the spring. On the way home, she decided it was high time she cleared the air of her doubts about Jeff's fidelity.

Once in the garage, she turned off the engine of her 2005 sedan, bustled the children into the house, and shooed them to their room to change out of their dress clothes.

She found Jeff in his bathrobe at the kitchen table drinking coffee.

"How about some scrambled eggs and bacon, doll?" He looked up from the Sunday papers. "I could eat a cow."

She slammed her purse down on the counter. "How about some answers?"

"What are you talking about? Geez. I only wanted breakfast not an attitude."

"So you forgot about yesterday, then?"

"I told you. I lost the ring playing golf and met up with an old friend. What's your problem?"

"I don't want us to bicker about this. Something's going on with you." Jan pulled back a chair and sat across from him then reached for his hand. "Please, talk to me."

The blue of Jeff's eyes clouded. Tears brimmed, threatening to spill out onto his cheeks. Brushing at his eyes, he turned from her and stood. "Forget breakfast. I'll throw on some clothes and get something out."

"But…" She grabbed at his sleeve. He wouldn't look at her.

"I don't deserve you." His voice cracked.

He left the kitchen, head down, shoulders sagging.

Jan stared after him, not knowing what to make of his odd response. Jeff seldom showed any sentiment. When his parents died in that auto accident, he was stoic. When Lyco fired him, he went into a quiet funk for days. Today, she swore he had tears in his eyes. That scared the bejesus out of her. Something was wrong, very wrong.

Jeff's unusual behavior continued throughout the morning. Around eleven, Jan glanced out the kitchen window, pleased to find him in the backyard raking leaves. Billy and Mae were helping by jumping in and out of the piles he amassed. Normally, Jeff would have shouted for them to get away from the leaves. Today, he didn't seem to care. Since their conversation, he'd been oddly nice to her. He took the garbage to the garage without being asked, and when she went into the bedroom, she found he had made the bed. A first.

Why all of a sudden? Was he trying to prove he really was a good husband and father? She didn't know anymore. She used to be able to predict Jeff's moods, read his thoughts. She'd always admired his ability to meet challenges, to beat the odds. These days it seemed he couldn't care less about succeeding in his job or being a good husband and father.

With a sigh, Jan turned from the window to rustle

up lunch. This afternoon, she'd get the fall bulbs in the ground and dig up the dahlias for winter storage.

She was about to call Jeff and the children inside for soup and sandwiches when Diane phoned. Her neighbor was a snarky but savvy former debutante who earned money on the side creating jewelry—and a bona fide member of their morning coffee klatch. She lived two houses down on their side of the street.

"Funny you should call just now, Di. You were on my mind. How are things going with Ted?"

"Same old," Diane shot back. "At least I've got him washing his own clothes. It's time he helped out around here instead of moping around."

Diane turned down a wealthy Greenwich lawyer to marry a high school gym teacher whose physical education program had been cut from this year's budget. She could be flippant about Ted's jobless situation, but Jan knew deep down it was Diane's way of coping.

"Lucky you. I can't even get Jeff to pick up his dirty clothes from the floor."

"You're too nice, Jan. You need a backbone. Just stop kowtowing to him. You'll see, he'll come around."

"I'm getting there. Old habits are hard to break. So, what's up?"

"Ted and I just spiffed up the living room and rearranged the furniture. I thought we'd show it off. What are you guys doing tonight?"

"The usual. Nothing. We can't afford to go out much these days."

"None of us can. That's why I think it would be fun to have a potluck dinner. I've invited Rana and Larry, Amy and Mike, and Candy said she and Bob would come. Frank and Tina DiGiorno blew me off."

"Too bad. It would have been nice to get to know them better, but it will be good to catch up with everyone else—especially Amy. We were supposed to get together with her and Mike last night, but it didn't work out."

"Jeff problems?"

"Nothing I can't handle, friend. I have a big batch of turkey chili simmering in the crock-pot. I'll bring that over—and oh, how about some apple pie? New crust recipe."

"Perfect. I'm making a big salad, Rana's bringing Chicken Divan, and Candy said she'd bring hotdogs and beans. Leave it to her to weasel by with an easy-peasy meal. Come about six."

"Mae and Billy have school tomorrow. I'll see if Stevie can come over." Amy's fifteen-year-old son was their go-to sitter. He was in and out of their home as if it were his own.

Between baking and planting bulbs, Jan's day flew by. At five thirty, she ladled chili into bowls for Billy and Mae, and then got ready to go to Diane's.

When she heard Jeff running the shower in the bathroom off their bedroom, she brushed her teeth and washed her face in the kid's bath, then sat at the vanity table in their room to pat on moisturizer and apply lip-gloss. She tugged off the elastic from her usual ponytail and brushed out her shoulder length, naturally wavy hair. Most of the women invited to Diane's didn't go out very often so Jan dressed up. She pulled on a pair of black leggings and donned a low-cut, peach colored sweater that added color to her pale skin.

Jan had just shoved her feet into the faux leather

black boots that added three inches to her height when Jeff pushed open the bathroom door, fresh from the shower, with a towel wrapped around his waist. He was clean-shaven and, man, he looked good. Was it odd that he could still turn her on, even though she knew he might love someone else? Someone prettier than her, more fun to be around. Water beads glistened on the fine auburn hair covering a portion of his lean, muscled torso, and disappeared under the towel. He wasn't a hairy man, which was fine with her.

Jan smiled and whirled around. "You like?"

"Oh, yeah." Dropping the towel, he wiggled his finger at her. "Come here."

"Jeff, it's almost time to leave."

"So what if we're a few minutes late?"

Grabbing Jan by the hair, he pulled back her head. "I could eat you up." He ran his tongue from her throat down to her cleavage sending tingles of desire to her breasts and groin. "You make me horny when you dress sexy."

She melted into him, feeling the hardness of him ready to send her flying into that zone of need and want until fireworks went off in her head and they were one. It had been so long since they'd made love that she craved it like a sumptuous piece of chocolate. Her fingers circled his nipples and pinched them into hard nubs.

Releasing her, he locked the door. He turned to her with purpose and pushed her flat on the bed.

Jan pulled off her sweater and undid her bra.

Jeff leaned over her, pinning her arms over her head. With his free hand, he grabbed her leggings at the waist and ripped them down as far as her boot tops, taking her panties along with them.

"Yes, yes," she moaned, moving her hips to welcome him. "Please." Jan pushed up her breasts, wanting him to suckle her, wanting his tongue to travel down her body, wanting his fingers inside her, probing and bringing her to orgasm.

He stuck his tongue down her throat, injecting her with the disgustingly sour taste of whiskey.

Gagging, her stomach turned nauseous.

Jan's body went still.

Jeff didn't seem to notice or care. Without ado, he sought entry and rammed at her insides like a piston until she was sore. She wanted to push him away, end it. Turning her head to the side, her eyes filled. *A sex toy…that's all I am to him.*

"You're dry." Jeff pulled away, his penis deflated.

"Of course I am. Hello. Foreplay would have been nice." Brushing the wetness from her cheeks, Jan rolled away from him to put herself back together.

The thumping at their bedroom door cut blessedly short any further conversation. "Mom, Stevie's here."

"Be there in a minute, Mae."

"Sorry, you weren't ready, babe." Jeff shook his head.

"I'm sorry, too. For a lot of things."

****

Stevie's stammering little boy reticence disappeared whenever he was around Mae and Billy. With his curly blond hair and devilish grin, he must have the teenage girls going wild. Yet, he never let his good looks go to his head.

By the time Jan reached the living room, Billy had tackled Amy's son. The two boys rolled gleefully on the rug. Mae stood by cheering them on.

"Stevie, get Billy bathed and make sure Mae showers. Lights out by eight for Billy. Mae can stay up an extra half an hour. She has reading to do for school." She leaned over her son and tweaked his nose. "Be a good boy for Stevie."

Jeff had followed her into the living room. "Hey, Eagle Boy," he said to Stevie, "that was a great shot at our game yesterday. You're really coming along."

Stevie stood. "Gee, thanks, Mr. Simmons. You really think I'm that good?"

"Why sure. With a little practice at the driving range, you'll be a pro."

Leaving Jeff to kiss Billy and Mae goodnight, Jan headed for the kitchen to grab the crockpot.

"Jeff, don't you want to bring a six-pack? And I could use a hand with the pie."

"Sure, babe." In the kitchen, Jeff took her in his arms. "You know I love you, don't you?"

Inwardly, Jan sighed with relief. Nothing's worse on a man's ego than not being able to perform. Yet, he had come to her, and that's what counted most. She leaned her head against his chest. He wasn't perfect, but he seemed to be trying to make them work.

"I'm sorry for accusing you last night."

"I should have called."

Jan didn't reply.

Ten minutes later they stood on the front porch of the Harper's taupe raised ranch ringing the doorbell. With a big grin, Ted ushered them inside after taking the beer and dessert from Jeff. Daisy and Porky, their two spaniels, circled them with doggy excitement.

Ted Harper was built like a linebacker with his

bulging muscles and tiny waist. He stayed in shape by jogging ten miles a day and working out in the basement gym at their home. Jan wouldn't exactly call him handsome, but his comfortable-looking face and kind manner made people instantly like him. He was especially good with the children. It was common to see him in the *cul de sac* coaching Billy or Mae on proper batting stance or showing them how to pitch a ball. Ted had a calming effect on Diane's energetic quirkiness. As a pair, they balanced each other.

She and Jeff followed Ted to the kitchen, where Jan set down her chili. Ted handed her a glass of Pinot Grigio while Jeff helped himself to a beer.

"You're the last ones here." True to her artsy style, Diane was a vision of fall in high top tan boots and a rust colored suede skirt. The huge sunflower printed on her olive green shirt picked up the colors in the beaded belt she wore around her slim hips.

"You made that belt didn't you," Jan said, admiring the delicate handwork.

"Every single bead. Twelve hours, but who's counting. Tomorrow it goes on sale online. I think I can rake in a couple of hundred for it."

"Too expensive for me. I ran into Loreen from The Sweet Shop at church this morning. She agreed to put out a few of my gluten-free goodies to see if they'll sell."

"Got to start somewhere, girl. Now you and hubby go check out my new décor while I put my magic touch on this harvest salad."

Stunning, was the first word that crossed Jan's mind when they entered the crowded living room. Instead of curtains, long strings of clear crystalline beads draped over a rod across the top of the bay window mirroring the dark clay and rich brown colors of the walls and furniture. It was apparent that she and Jeff were the last to arrive. Rana and Larry, who sat entwined on the oversized lounge chair, waved hello. Diagonally across from them, Candy and her husband, Bob, hogged the sofa.

"Come sit by us," Candy said with a flirty smile directed at Jeff. She patted the empty space that separated her from her husband. The ballsy woman had come on to Jeff ever since they moved in, which made Jan wonder about the health of Candy's marriage. *Jeff, my sink is clogged. Jeff, my precious kitty is stuck up in the tree*. Bob never seemed to be around when Candy needed something done. Candy only spoke to Jan when she needed something. *Could Peaches stay with you while I run to the store?* It wasn't a question. Jan supposed she should be more tolerant. Candy and Bob worked reverse schedules so one of them would always be home with their three-year-old daughter.

Jeff fell for Candy's come hither smile and started toward the couch, which would have left her to sit elsewhere.

The words, *I love you*, popped into Jan's head. No wedding ring and he had gone AWOL for hours yesterday. Hadn't she seen Candy's turquoise car head out yesterday afternoon?

Shooting Candy the evil eye, she linked her arm through Jeff's. "Not there, honey, near Amy and Mike. I don't have much chance to talk to Amy." She dragged him away.

"Hey you two, plop yourselves down." Mike stood and gave Jeff a guy-type smack on the back and her a peck on the cheek. She was stunned all over again by Mike's good looks. His coal black hair and flashing green eyes were a striking contrast to the red polo shirt he wore. Women were attracted to him, and he knew it.

Greeting Amy with a smile, she and Jeff dropped cross-legged onto two vacant pillows Diane had placed on the scratchy straw mat that covered most of the hardwood floor. Amy wore her dark blonde hair close to her head, like a cap. Pearl studs poked through her tiny earlobes. The kindness in her face put Jan instantly at ease.

They were catching up when she and Amy tuned into the men's conversation.

"Looking good, my man," Mike said.

Jeff patted the back of his head. "Yeah, got me a new do at The Men's Club."

"You too? Man, they sure know how to treat a guy there. Old Frank's an okay guy too. Invited me over to the house Thursday night for a game of poker. Said to bring a friend or two. Anyone here in?" Mike glanced at Larry and Ted, then Jeff.

Larry and Ted shook their heads no.

"Sure thing," Jeff said.

Jan tugged at Jeff's sleeve and hissed in his ear. "We're supposed to go to Mae's school Thursday for Parent's Night."

Jeff waved her away. "You don't need me along to talk to a second-grade teacher. She's going to tell us that Mae's doing a good job."

"That's not the only problem, Jeff. You're walking in blind to the DiGiorno house. You don't know how they play. What if they set high stakes?" Jan gave him a meaningful look. He had already lost a hundred dollars to Mike on the series playoffs last week, and who knew how much a poker game could cost them.

"Don't be a wet blanket," Jeff said.

"Hey, Bob," Jeff called. "You working Thursday night?"

Bob nodded. "Count me out."

With a black crew-cut hair, a throwback to his Iraqi War days, Candy's husband still looked and acted the part of a soldier. His words were clipped. While he was always pleasant enough, he seldom socialized. In fact, it surprised Jan he had come tonight.

By seven, everyone had enjoyed a round of cocktails, and the noise level in the living room had risen to a loud chatter.

Diane rang the cowbell she used to call the children in from outdoors. "Food's up. Come on guys, fill a plate and find a seat at the table." She cocked her head toward the dining room.

With Ted in the lead, their group filed into the room and slid onto the benches placed on either side of the pine table. Jan ended up wedged between Jeff and Mike. Jeff, she noticed, had heaped his plate with the dogs and beans Candy had brought. So unhealthy.

The group continued conversations that had begun in the other room, mostly about the kids, jobs, and house projects in the works.

"We're going to convert our garage into an efficiency apartment for Rana's parents." Larry put his arm around Rana and pulled her closer.

"Built in babysitters," Rana chimed in, fluffing her long brunette mane.

"Yeah, but they'll be in your face all the time," Amy reminded her.

"It would be nice if my parents lived close by, but I wouldn't want them in the same house," Jan commented.

"They're fine where they are in Jersey." Jeff's voice was flat.

"Wait." She touched his arm so he would look at her. "I thought you liked my parents."

"Yeah, as long as they keep their noses out of my life I do."

Whoa. Where did that come from? Why, her parents treated him as a son ever since high school. When his parents died in that car crash, he practically moved in with their family. When he was with them, which was less often these days, he acted caring enough.

By the time they finished dinner, Jeff had gone through all the beer he had brought and cajoled Ted into fixing him a vodka on the rocks. His voice was loud, offensively loud.

"These two guys walk into a tittie bar…"

Jan nudged Jeff and said under her breath. "Not here. For God's sake, Diane's kids are around."

Jeff's elbow jabbed her arm hard enough to hurt. "Shut up! You're always trying to tell me what to do."

Jan drew back holding her sore arm and stared at her dinner plate to avoid the sympathetic eyes of her friends.

Ignoring her, Jeff leaned in. "Now where was I? Oh, yeah. These two guys walk into this tittie bar and…hey, Ted, how about fixing me another drink." Jeff held up his empty glass. "This one had a hole in it."

"You've had enough, Jeff," Ted said. "Settle down." His voice was even but as firm as a teacher controlling a disruptive child.

Jeff reached into his back pocket and dug out his wallet. He slammed a one-dollar bill on the table. "Here. I'll pay for it."

The room went silent, except for Mike, who snickered.

A flush of angry heat went through Jan's body. She bolted up and pulled Jeff from his seat. "We're done here."

Jeff shook off her arm. For a moment, his eyes went stony, and then he belched.

Ted rose, but no one else moved. "I'll get your jackets," he muttered.

Jan slunk out of Diane's house with Jeff lurching behind her.

Once outside, she turned on him. "What's gotten into you? You humiliated me in front of our friends."

His mouth formed a silly grin.

She closed her eyes for a second to find her calm. *He's drunk. What's the use?*

Chapter Seven

"I got to get out of here, Tina. I'm going nuts." Frank's feet dug into the plush carpet they'd installed. The stuff that was in here was crap. Back and forth, he paced. "Garden's gone to seed. I got the shop going, but I don't need to spend all day there. Eh." He spread his arms, hands in the air. "It's getting fucking cold. What am I gonna do all winter?"

Tina nestled into the Italian leather lounge they'd dragged here from the old house, turned a page of her book, and then looked at him over her cat-eye glasses. "The yard's a mess, Frankie, leaves all over the place. I miss our gardener. Why don't you get some exercise? Prepare yourself for later."

She lifted her book. One of those cheap romance novels she liked to read. He didn't mind. "Lots of great ideas in here. You should read this one. It's called," she turned the cover toward her, "*Sex on the Beach*." You know, like that fancy cocktail I like. It's about…"

Frank's hand went into the air. "Spare me." Stepping to the bay window, he shoved open the heavy brocade drapes. The squirrels were having a heyday with all the acorns. In the spring, he'd have a hell of a time when they sprouted.

Hauling his oldest overcoat from the closet, he put it on then traded his house slippers for garden shoes. "I'll be outside," he called to Tina.

In the garage, Frank checked out the overloaded rack holding his yard tools. He wasn't sure what he would need, so he bought two of everything figuring Tina might want to help. What was he thinking? A powder puff of a woman wasn't going to turn yard jock and ruin her manicure.

Taking down the V-shaped rake he'd used in June to clear the crap from the place he wanted to plant his garden, he made his way out front, kicking at the leaves. Darn things were killing the sod he'd just put in. *You're dead. Gone.* Attacking them with the rake, he put muscle into the job, thinking of Tina, snuggled in her chair and getting all hot over that sexy book.

Speaking of hot. Here comes that babe across the street with the little blond kid. She's smiling at me.

"Hi, Mr. DiGiorno." She wore her hair pulled back in a tail that wagged when she talked. "It's that time of year."

Frank leaned on the handle of the rake. "Getting cold," he said as a way of conversation. "Time to clean up the place. It's Frank, call me Frank. Who do we have here?" He bent over to talk to the kid. He was so bundled up in his coat and hat that he could barely see the kid's face.

The kid looked down at the ground, not answering. *Shy.*

"Billy, say hello to Mr. DiGiorno." The mother squeezed the kid's hand. *Nice.*

"Hello," the kid mumbled.

He had to learn to talk to kids. Little Frank Junior would be running around the yard in a few.

"I helped Daddy rake our yard," the kid finally said.

"Oh yeah?" He rewarded the kid with a big smile. "Where you headed?" Frank asked the babe.

"Bus stop." She pointed to the top of the street. "Mae's due in any minute."

"I got an extra rake in the garage, Billy is it? How'd you like to show me how many leaves you can help me collect while your mom gets your sister? We'll have a contest. Yeah. Bet I can rake faster than you." He gave the kid a light punch on the arm, coaxing a smile out of him.

"Can I, Mommy?" The kid looked up, and Frank knew he had him.

"Are you sure it's all right?" The babe's forehead made lines, and her lips got tight as a clam. "I'll only be gone about," she checked her watch, a cheapie, "ten minutes or so."

"Why sure. When you stop back, you'll all come inside for coffee. My Tina gets lonely, and she's shy about meeting new people."

"I'll have Mae with me. And she'll…"

Frank held up his hand. "Just half an hour. We got coffee cake."

"All right then. Billy"—she kissed the kid's cheek like she was never gonna see him again—"be a good helper now."

The babe walked away, only turning back twice. Maybe she trusted him.

"I need a rake Mr. Di…Giorn…"

"I'm Poppa Frank, son. Let's find you a tool."

The kid didn't get much done, but Frank let him win the leaf-raking contest anyway. He didn't need to impress this kid, but it was nice to feel like a grandpa.

Like clockwork, the mother was back with a

redheaded kid in tow. Frank ushered them all inside, surprising Tina.

"Frankie, you should have warned me," Tina said in a hushed voice. "I'm not dressed for company." She patted her shiny hair and smoothed the front of the dress she wore around the house. It didn't do her figure justice, and it was ugly as sin, but he knew the lush body underneath, and that's what mattered.

In moments, Tina wore her company face. Her talented lips tipped up in a smile that crinkled the skin in the corners of those dark eyes that could turn black when she was mad at him or to brown velvet when he made her happy.

"Sit. Sit," she said to the babe and kids, as she rushed to get a fresh pot of coffee going and dump the cake from the market onto a dish.

Frank stood back, enjoying his Tina making nice with the neighbor lady and sucking up to the kids. This was a nice change from the old place where their only friends were thugs and whores.

Sliding into his chair at the head of the table, he leaned forward and butted into the conversation. "Tell me about this guy, Bob. What's this action about him sponging off people?"

The babe laughed. The kids giggled. Tina gave him a cock-tingling smile.

Chapter Eight

Jan held Jeff's T-shirt to her cheek, still warm from the dryer. Whenever he wore one, she used to love to nuzzle his chest and feel its softness. Her teddy bear, she called him then. With a sigh, she added it to his stack of clothes, lifted the basket, and headed to their bedroom to put away the clothes.

As she set the shirts on top of the cherry wood dresser, their wedding picture caught her attention. In it, Jeff smiled down at her with such love that her heart filled with emotion. His arm cradled her as she looked up at him, sharing the private moment captured in the shot. Now, he barely made eye contact with her.

With a sigh, Jan opened his top drawer and started to stack the fresh shirts on top of the others, as she usually did, and noticed those underneath were yellowing from not being laundered frequently.

She scooped up the shirts, intending to rotate them to the top of the pile. Her knuckles touched something small, hard, and cold lying on the wooden base of the drawer.

She knew what it was, yet she turned away, squeezing shut her eyes so she wouldn't have to see it. But it was there, his wedding ring, hidden in his drawer underneath his clothes.

Jan rolled it through her fingers then slipped it on.

Staring at her hand, her vision blurred dulling its

gold luster against her skin. She clutched her shirt, digging the ring into her chest until it hurt. *I allowed this. I let him hurt me.*

He'd lied to her—lied about everything.

Jan slumped backward, landing at the edge of the bed. *How could he do this to me, to us?* Her lips trembled, and her eyes filled. She should be angry, throw the ring in his face and yell at him. Yet, a part of her just died.

Numbly, Jan rose, replaced the ring, and left the drawer hanging open. His T-shirts remained stacked on the dresser. Maybe later she'd put them away so he'd never know she found the ring, never caught him in the lie. Then, she could go on pretending the loving husband in the picture hadn't become a lying cheating bastard.

Brushing the wetness from her cheeks, Jan walked from the room.

She got as far as the kitchen when it hit her hard.

He's been playing you. Get back in there, shut the darn drawer, and find out what else he's been up to.

In the bedroom, she flung open the door to their walk-in closet. The scent of Jeff's citrusy aftershave made her cross her arms and hug herself, missing the way it used to be with them—shower, shave, make love.

Shaking herself out of the past, she methodically felt around in every jacket pocket and turned his pants pockets inside out. Her efforts produced one screw, a gum wrapper, and a few coins. *Nothing here.*

His office. Of course.

Turning on her heel, Jan strode down the hall and pushed open his door. *Yuck. It stinks in here.* Doing her best not to inhale, she skirted the stacks of folders littering the floor—you'd think he would have filed them—to reach Jeff's desk, a nightmare of yellow-lined papers bearing Jeff's scratchy script topped with empty glasses and dirty cereal bowls. Telephone and charge account bills and crumbled receipts, which she expected were to be submitted to Klean Kare, lay scattered on the desktop. She squelched the urge to tidy up and organize them.

Jan picked through the mess, unfolding small slips of paper, carefully replacing them as she found them and moving on to search through others. She wasn't sure what she was looking for, but she'd know when she found it.

Aha. Jeff's company charge card bill.

Easing the unfolded pages from their spot, Jan pushed back Jeff's plushy chair and sat down to scan through it. Sure, she'd heard about a new customer here and there, but Jeff hadn't been forthcoming about how he spent his day.

Hmm. Charges for gas, car repairs, but the Siesta Hotel? She knew the place, a no-tell motel along Bunker Turnpike. Jeff's job did not entail overnight stays. A cold shiver raced through her body. She ran her finger back and forth across the black text. It wouldn't disappear. She needed it gone, out of her sight. But there it was, *proof.* Foolish Jeff had put the charge on his business account to hide it from her, she guessed. What would Klean Kare think about this?

Jan's heart clutched at the thought. She flashed back to the day Lyco fired him, and their world crashed down. He'd driven out of the garage in his black company sedan to meet his boss for lunch. An hour later, he was dropped off home. No car. No job.

She wasn't sure which was worse, Jeff sleeping with another woman or him being fired for the second time in a year. How would their family survive another crisis?

A sudden calm washed over her. Squaring her shoulders, she checked her watch. She had time before picking up Billy. She needed to know more. Everything. The worst. Then she'd deal with it.

Tucking the charge card bill back in place, Jan's gaze landed on a telephone bill. He had used his business phone the night she'd heard those awful words. Picking up the bill, she flipped the pages to the call details. His territory covered the northeastern part of Connecticut, so why would he be calling Bridgeton?

Out of curiosity, Jan picked up the phone and dialed.

"Bridgeton Hospital," a bright voice answered. "How may I connect you?"

She hung up, confused. It made sense that Jeff would call a hospital, yet if memory served her, Bridgeton wasn't part of his territory. An answer niggled at her somewhere back in her brain, but she couldn't quite nail it down.

Bang.

The brunt of what she'd found hit her like a sledgehammer. The room closed in on her.

I have to get out of here.

She barely made it to the bathroom before she hurled her breakfast.

After rinsing out her mouth and splashing water on her face, Jan caught her reflection in the mirror. She looked awful, and it was almost time to get Billy.

Wetting a washcloth with cold water from the bathroom sink, she held it against her hot cheeks and swollen eyes to calm the redness, then blew her nose. She wasn't quite put together, but it would have to do.

Jan had just grabbed her purse to leave when someone knocked on the back door.

Oh, no. It's Candy. What does she want now? The woman was pushy as all get out.

"Jeff's not home," she said, opening the door.

Candy held three-year-old Peaches by the hand. The child broke loose and ran into Jan's kitchen. "Billy. I want to play with Billy. Where is he?"

"At school, dear," she replied.

Peaches frowned, plopped down on the floor, opened up a lower cabinet, and set to work emptying it.

"I know Jeff's at work, silly," Candy said, ignoring her child. "It's you I wanted to see."

"What do you want?" Jan struggled to remain calm.

"I'm off work from the hospital today and have a few errands to run. Would you mind watching Peaches for an hour? She ran her fingers through her hair to fluff the blonde tendrils creeping down her neck.

Wow, she's gone blonde. Jeff has a thing for blondes.

"I'm about to leave to pick up Billy. Isn't Bob home?"

"He's sleeping, and I hate to wake him." Candy's husband worked the night shift. Candy was a nurse by day.

Nurse. Hospital.

Jan narrowed her eyes at Candy. "What hospital do you work at?"

"Crappy commute. Takes me over an hour. Bridgeton General," Candy said, with a flick of her manicured hand.

Jan's insides did a backflip and bile filled her throat. *Holy stink. Jeff's screwing Candy!* With effort, she kept her voice controlled and a lid on her temper.

"How interesting. Going through some bills this morning, I saw Jeff's been making several calls to your hospital, which I thought odd because it's not part of his sales territory."

Candy's smile dropped, but she didn't say a word.

"I also found a receipt for the Siesta Hotel. No place I've ever been. Have you?" Jan pushed her face up to Candy's, smelling makeup.

Candy's hand went up in front of her. She took a step backward. "It's not what you think…"

Hands on hips, Jan zeroed in on her. "Just what *should* I think when it's obvious you and Jeff have been sneaking off together?"

"I…well, I." Candy studied her red flats then looked up at her with blazing brown eyes. "He loves me."

"Get out of my house." The words spewed from Jan's mouth like lava from a volcano, startling Peaches who had just started the dishwasher running.

Peaches ran to hug her mother.

Wisely, Candy pushed the child behind her and stepped back just as Jan slammed the door in her face.

"Home wrecker!" Jan pounded on the closed door until her knuckles turned red and sore.

What's the use?

She knew what she had to do.

****

The cheater is home.

Jan had spent the afternoon alternating between crying jags and anger. Now, she seemed to be in the angry mode. She slid the meatloaf from the oven and dumped it upside down on a platter, splashing oily fat on the front of her shirt. Grabbing a large knife, she hacked it into chunks as if it were Jeff's throat.

"Dinner, kids. Mae, Billy. Two-minute warning. Shut off the TV." Jan fixed plates for her and the children and set them on the table with a bang.

"What's going on?" Jeff entered the kitchen, rolling up the sleeves of his dress shirt. He sniffed the air. "Meatloaf, my favorite. Did you make gravy and mashed?" He plunked down at the table in front of Jan's plate of food.

"Get your own, you jerk." She swiped the food away from him.

Jeff's head snapped up. "What's going on here?"

"You're a cheating, lying craphead. That's what's going on." She pointed her finger at him, scowling, but kept her voice low for the children's sake. "It's Candy, isn't it? You call her at work. You sleep with her at a sleazy motel, and like a fool, you put the charges on your business card."

Jeff pushed his chair back from the table. "Where do you come up with this stuff?"

"Oh, no you don't. I'm not falling for that ploy." Jan crossed her arms in front of her chest. "Answer me."

His granite eyes bored into her. "Go screw yourself, bitch."

Her hand went to her mouth at his vulgar words. "How dare you speak to me like that?"

"I'll speak to you any damn way I want to." He leaped from his seat, knocking over his chair, and brushed past her. "I'll pick up something out."

"No denial? No, I'm sorry?" She shouted at his back. "You know, I only married you because my folks wanted me to."

Turning, he stared at her for a steely moment, his blue eyes cold and hard.

She had cut him deep with that last dig. As many times as she'd thought it, she'd never said the words aloud. If only she could take them back.

His shoulders dropped. Lips clamped tight, he set off toward the living room. The front door slammed shut, leaving Jan hollow inside.

She clutched at the counter inhaling large gulps of air. *You can just go to hell, Jeff Simmons. You don't deserve me.*

Jan looked up to find Billy and Mae cowering in the doorway. It was hard to protect them from what was going on. They lived here, too. She didn't try to coddle them. She couldn't pretend even for one minute that everything was fine, that they shouldn't worry.

"Sit down, Billy, Mae. Your dinners are getting cold."

Blessedly, they complied without a word to her about anything they might have witnessed or heard.

With time on her hands, she worked up all sorts of nasty things she should have said to him, but in the end, what difference would it have made? She would only be hurting herself because she doubted Jeff cared.

Jan paced the floor in front of the living room window, edgy and tense. She had to do something or she would go nuts. Finally, she went into the kitchen and took ingredients from the cupboards and the fridge—eggs, milk, butter, sugar, cocoa, and gluten-free flour. She turned her thoughts to making grown-up Whoopee pies to take to Loreen's shop in the morning. The batch of magic bars had sold out, and Loreen was anxious for more.

The hum of the mixer soothed Jan's ragged nerves as it churned the butter and sugar and beat in the dry ingredients.

Once the pies were baked and filled, the ho-hum brown blobs sat on the counter. She wasn't in the mood to be creative, yet she needed to make them appealing so they would sell. Filling her decorator with seasonal orange frosting, she made two dots for the eyes and one for the nose. Her hand shook.

He betrayed me.

She couldn't bring herself to carve the smile.

The chocolate pies with their googly eyes and missing smiles blurred. Jan's head dropped into her arms and, not for the first time today, she wept.

She wept for what was and what wasn't, and what might've been.

An hour later, with the kitchen tidied and the coffee pot set for the morning, Jan dragged her weary body to the bedroom. Jeff wasn't home yet. When he came in, no doubt he would be drunk and nasty. Tonight, she had no energy to deal with him.

She closed the bedroom door, turned the lock, and crawled into bed. For the first time in their marriage, she would sleep alone. Yet, she couldn't help but wonder if Jeff sought refuge at Candy's. Bob would be at work now. Peaches should be asleep. Was he in Candy's bed kissing her, snuggling her, and murmuring sweet nothings in her ear like he used to do with her?

No, no, don't think about it. He doesn't matter anymore.

Jan stirred at the odious sound of the garage door opening. Her stomach clutched with trepidation. What would he do when he found she'd locked him out of the bedroom?

As heavy footsteps approached, she scrunched under the covers, her hands fisted against her chest, afraid to breathe. The doorknob rattled as Jeff turned it back and forth.

"Open this door. Now!"

She didn't answer him. Instead, she put the pillow over her ears to drown out his angry voice. The children would hear him and wake up. What was she thinking? They would be frightened too. They were in Mae's room. She'd moved Billy's bed there weeks ago. They seemed to need each other these days and snuggling in with her wasn't the answer as long as Jeff shared the room. She envisioned them curled in their beds in fetal positions, frightened little lambs. At least she'd had the forethought to shut their door. She didn't dare go to comfort them. In Jeff's drunken mood, she feared for her safety and prayed her children would be smart enough to stay put as well.

Finally, Jeff's voice grew hoarse, and the pounding became thumping, echoing low on the hollow door. If Jeff managed to kick through, Jan hoped he wasn't powerful enough to knock it down.

Once his footsteps retreated, the tension in her body eased. She unfolded her legs and stretched out from her pretzel position, pleased with herself for not giving in to him. Maybe Jeff slept on the couch or holed up in his office. She didn't give a flying fig, as long as he wasn't sleeping next to her, slobbering over her, trying to screw her.

Done.

Done with all that.

Done with *him*.

****

Jeff was scarce for the next day and night. He had left before she rose in the morning, assumedly for work—although she couldn't conceive of him calling on customers without showering and changing his clothes.

"Where's Daddy?" Mae asked.

Jan cupped her chin and looked into her innocent brown eyes. "I'm not sure, honey."

"You made him mad. He was home last night, yelling. Billy woke up and was crying. You didn't come," Mae accused.

"I'm really sorry. Will you forgive me?"

Mae looked away. "Maybe." Then she turned back and narrowed her pale blue eyes at her mother. "Are you and Daddy getting a divorce?"

"No, honey." *But soon.* "We just have some things to figure out."

"Oh. Okay. Can I watch cartoons?"

"Sure."

It's amazing how accepting children could be. If only she could be as complacent about Jeff and his deceitful ways.

****

About five on Tuesday night, Jan was in the kitchen, her haven, when Jeff came home bearing a bouquet of Shasta Daisies, the same flowers she had chosen for their summer wedding. No roses and baby's breath for her. Daisies were simple. Amy, her Matron of Honor, carried flowers in a straw basket. Jan's were clustered into a simple bouquet tied with a white ribbon. Jeff, so handsome in his white tux, wore a single daisy on his lapel.

He was still handsome, her husband, the liar, the cheat, the drunk. Bringing her daisies wasn't going to soften the blow he had given her heart.

Jeff stood before her with his head hung and his face wet with tears.

Was he getting a conscience all of a sudden? Did he think he could buy her back with a few flowers?

"I'm not for sale." Crossing her arms and lifting her nose in the air, she turned and stirred the sauce for the children's mac and cheese.

"Jan, come on. Don't be like that." He pressed a hand on her shoulder.

She flicked it off and whirled around, wielding the dripping wooden spoon as a weapon. "How dare you touch me."

"Please, honey." He knelt on one knee like he had years ago.

"You don't deserve to call me honey." Setting the spoon back in the pot, Jan ran her finger over the half-carat marquis diamond she'd worn since their engagement. It had been Christmas Eve, just before they went to midnight mass when he proposed. That was the last time Jeff had bowed to her. The overhead light shone on Jeff's head making a circle on his crown. This man was no angel. The wedding ring he'd refused to wear was back where it belonged, on his left hand's fourth finger.

"I'm sorry. Sorry for everything. I need you in my life. I'll do anything to make things right."

"I don't think you mean that, Jeff."

"I do. I love you."

"No you love her, helpless Candy, the woman you've been sneaking around with for Lord knows how long right under my nose. You've made a fool of me for the last time. I wonder how many of our friends have already figured out you and Candy are an item? And what about Bob?" She grabbed the phone. "What would he do if he learned what his wife was up to?"

Jeff sighed. "Put down the phone. It's over between Candy and me. She was just a diversion. I needed a perk."

"Perk my ass. If you're smart, you'll shut up while you can, because I have half a mind to sock it to you." She held the dripping spoon in smacking position.

Jeff shot up from his kneeling position and stepped out of reach, his hand in front of him. "Whoa. What's gotten into you? I just told you, it's over. I'm done with her. Forever. Please." He held out the flowers.

"Go away. I don't want your flowers." Stepping back, Jan held back a sob. "What happened to us, Jeff? Tell me. What have I done to deserve being treated like this?"

The daisies fell to the floor. His arms went around her, and his hot tears soaked into her blouse.

She was sobbing, too, wretched messy, sloppy tears that made her nose run. Sniffing, she shook herself free. So much for being tough.

"Jan, I love you. I've always loved you. Candy was just a fling because I was depressed about losing my job. Even with this new job, I'm demoted. I don't know if you can understand this, but I needed to feel like a man again."

Jan's heart hurt as if he had stabbed her there. "I don't make you feel manly? Is that what you're saying?"

"No, honey, please. Stop it. I didn't mean it that way. You are plenty woman for me." He ran his fingers through his cropped hair and shook his head. "I don't know what possessed me to get it on with her. She's not even pretty like you are." He caressed her chin, and she let him. "What can I do to make you believe I love you?"

She had never seen this groveling side of Jeff. *Ever.* Not in all the years they'd been together had he ever apologized for anything he had done. Maybe he truly did love her. She wanted to believe that, but in some ways, she wasn't sure she still wanted his love. Now that she was finally getting some guts, she wasn't going to return to her old doormat ways.

"I don't know what to say. You've been miserable to live with, and I'm not sure you can change. What's to stop you from sneaking around now that I'm on to you?"

His lips closed tight, and his chest swelled as if it would burst open. Jan could tell he wanted to spew some nasty words at her, but he didn't. His shoulders dropped, and he took a ragged breath. "I'll make things right. I promise you." Jeff stooped down to gather the flowers back into a bouquet and held them out.

Against her better judgment, she took them.

Chapter Nine

They made a truce of sorts. Jeff was ultra-polite to her, and from the squeals of joy coming from the family room, he was playing Dragon with the children—a childhood game where he roared and tried to eat them up. Just having the children laughing again was enough to convince Jan she had made the right decision in giving Jeff a second chance.

Tonight, they sat at the dinner table as a family. Jeff was close-mouthed about the chicken dogs and vegetarian beans she served up. She figured if he was so hot on gulping down Candy's fare, he could darn well eat hers. She was sick of going overboard on big meals to suit his tastes when she and the children were satisfied with simpler foods.

"I'll be paying bills after dinner," he said to her with a pointed look. Jeff's hoarding of their finances drove her nuts. She was more frugal than he would ever be, yet, he guarded the chore like a dog with a bone. And she allowed it, even as calls came in from collectors looking for their money. Whenever she broached the subject, Jeff insisted the payment had been handled. Another lie? She hoped not.

"Money shouldn't be a problem this month, right?" Jan nodded her head up and down. She wanted him to agree they were finally caught up.

"I don't know."

Translation—he's going to be in a miserable mood when he attacks the check register. Time to get out of Dodge.

"I promised Amy I'd stop over for coffee tonight. Mike's out, and we haven't visited in ages." Go for broke, she told herself. You've got him by the balls now keep squeezing. "Can you manage the children for an hour or so? They need to bathe and get to bed." The question hung in the air, with the children all ears.

"Oh goodie, Daddy. I'll pick out my books." Billy leaped from the table and ran off.

Jan smiled to herself. Billy would return with an armful of his favorites and want Jeff to read him every single one of them.

"The children have missed spending time with you," she said.

"Sure. Whatever."

Half an hour later, with the dishes done and Jeff somewhat in control of the household, Jan sat at Amy's kitchen table, her hand cupped around a warm mug of decaf herbal tea. Amy Wilkins nee Parry had been her best friend since grammar school. When she found she was pregnant, Jan went with her to break the news to her folks. In the end, Amy quit school, kept the baby, and married Mike, a huge decision when many women sought abortion for out-of-wedlock situations. That week, years ago, sealed their friendship. Even though Jan went on to graduate, they stayed in close touch. Unlike her, who went from high school to marriage and children, Amy took classes at the local college and acquired a teaching degree. She worked at Greenburg Day School with special ed kids, so she was seldom part of their neighborly morning coffee chats.

Here, in her cozy kitchen with its peachy walls and warm oak cabinets, Jan could unburden, yet trust Amy to respect her privacy. Like sisters, they told each other everything. She knew about Stevie's dyslexia, and Amy knew about Jan's brother's death and how it almost split their family.

"Have you laid down the law on Jeff's alcohol problem, yet?" Amy's tone was accusing, and rightly so because they had already discussed the issue. "An Alcoholics Anonymous group," she continued, "meets at Saint Andrews once a week. Jeff should go. It's perfectly confidential. And you"—Amy pointed her finger at her—unpolished, short nails neatly trimmed, not bitten to the quick like hers were—"should join a support group for families of alcoholics. I think it's called Al-Anon."

Jan let out a long breath. "I suppose it wouldn't hurt to talk to someone. I doubt Jeff will go to a meeting or even admit he's become an alcoholic. I can't change him, but maybe it will help me deal with him."

"That's my girl." Amy squeezed Jan's arm affectionately. "You're tougher than you think. If Mike pulled a drunk on me like Jeff did at Diane's last week, I wouldn't stand for it, and neither should you."

"If only Jeff's drinking was all I had to deal with. There's more."

"Candy?"

"How did you…"

"Lucky guess. I saw the way they looked at each other at Diane's. You called him on it. Right?"

"Darn straight, I did. He said he broke it off. That he loves me." Jan shrugged. "Sometimes I wonder what love is anyway."

"So you took him back?"

"On my terms. He's got to earn my trust and respect all over again—and no sex."

"No sex? How's he dealing with it?

"I could care. I'll be darned if I'm going to catch a nasty venereal disease from him. Being Jeff, he refused to get tested."

"Didn't you see any signs? I mean. When did he see her?"

"Hard to tell exactly. Because of his job, he had plenty of time to hook up with her between customer calls, and he always seemed to have errands to do at night. I think I knew all along but didn't want to face it. He's been walking on eggs around me the past day or so, and I kind of like it."

Jan's cell phone chimed. *Jeff. Bills. Stinko.*

She listened to him rant, then clicked off.

Her shoulders dropped. "I have to go home. Jeff's upset."

"Has he been drinking?" Amy put her arm around Jan's shoulder. "Will you be all right? I could go with you."

"No, it's okay. It's still early. I can handle this."

By the time Jan walked home, Jeff had worked himself into a frenzy. She entered the kitchen, where he paced clutching a cluster of papers.

"I'm here. What's up?" She tried to act nonchalant as if she didn't have a clue why he was upset. She had been watching her pennies, so if they had problems, she wasn't to blame. After all, *he* was the big-time money manager.

Jeff pivoted to face her. "See these?" He waved the packet in her face. "We can't pay them because you're spending too much money. Money we don't have." Plucking out one of the papers, he said, "Macy's. Here's a charge in the woman's department. How do you explain that?"

"I bought something for myself for a change. Unlike you, I paid sale price."

"Well then, what about all these other charges? You really did some damage shopping catalogs for kids' clothes. It's got to stop!"

Something inside Jan cracked wide open, and suddenly she was drowning in raw fury.

She stuck her face right up to Jeff's. "I've had it with you. Had it up to here." She chucked her hand under her chin. "You, of all people, have a lot of nerve telling me to watch my spending. I take care of the household expenses. You know, food, clothes, and laundry supplies."

She poked a finger into his chest. "Why don't *you* cut back. Buy your clothes at a cheaper men's shop, and certainly, we can do without all the vodka and gin you bring home in those huge bottles. I never see *those* expenses."

"What I buy and how much is my business. I make the money here."

"I contribute too."

"Yeah? Where's the money? Come on, fork it over."

He was right. What she made at the bakery barely covered the ingredients, but she'd be darned if she would give over the little she earned so he could spend it on himself.

"I'm just getting started."

"Right. And how long will it take to make a

profit?"

"I don't know. I could get a full-time job. Certainly, I'm as capable as you are."

"The money will go out to sitters because *I* have a *real* job."

"And a built-in sitter and maid." Jan took a calming breath. "Jeff, we're bickering like a couple of kids. We have a problem and one-upping each other isn't getting it solved."

The hot steam that Jeff had been spewing fizzled. She saw a hint of defeat in his eyes. "What about these bills? They're due, and we can't pay them." He spoke in a near whisper.

"Give them to me. I'll see what I can do." She held out her hand.

He gripped them to his chest, then stared at her. "You want to take over?"

"Sure. I'll see what we have and set a budget. It will be fine, Jeff. You'll see. Now hand over those bills, and I'll get started."

His hand clutching the bills relaxed and came away from his chest. "Here." He gave her the stack. "*You* worry about money for a change."

****

Over the space of a few days, Jan familiarized herself with their charge card activity and bill paying cycles. Jeff is right, she thought, chewing the eraser on her pencil. His paycheck barely covered their monthly nut. He's treated his income like his very own treasure trove, and now they were deep in debt. Lord knows when he would demand to take back the family accounts. Clearly, they needed a budget—and she needed to earn more money.

She'd stashed profits from her baked good sales in the blue teapot that once belonged to her grandmother. She liked that she could go to her private savings without guilt. So far, she'd saved close to fifty dollars. Adding that little bit to Jeff's pay would make little difference. In the morning, she'd talk to Loreen about a real job.

Returning to the problem at hand, Jan opened the checkbook to tally their out-of-pocket expenses. Flipping back a few months to get an idea of how the money should be split up, she gasped at her latest calculations.

"No, that can't be right." Starting from scratch, she recalculated.

Her head exploded. She hurled her pencil across the room. Shoving back her chair, Jan took off down the hall with the check register and slammed open Jeff's office door.

"Get out here! We need to talk."

Jeff's expression soured. "Can't you see I'm busy?"

"You've been busy all right. Busy spending money in the wrong places. You whined about my spending. Well, it seems I'm not the problem, *you* are. The charge card expenses for your clothes are outrageous, but can't compare to the money you spend at the liquor store."

Jan stuck the checkbook under Jeff's nose. "Look! Look at all these checks you've written to Tie One On Liquors. They total half your take-home pay. Yet, you dare to make me feel guilty for buying clothes for the children when all the while you're squandering money on stuff that goes in one of your ends and out the other. How could you be so selfish?"

Jeff's mouth dropped open.

"What, nothing to say? Well, I'm not through. *You're* the problem, Jeff. Not me. You're drinking us into debt. Get help."

Whirling around, she stomped down the hall toward the kitchen, barely conscious of Jeff's footfalls behind her.

"But, honey, I need an occasional drink to relax. Can't a man relax?"

"Relax?" Jan stopped short, and he nearly rammed into her. "You call inhaling gallons of liquor relaxing? We can't afford for you to relax, as you call it. We have two children to take care of. Taking a deep breath, she worked to calm herself. Yelling at Jeff wasn't solving any problems.

"Look." Her shoulders must've dropped about two inches. She touched Jeff's shoulder. "You need help. Your drinking is out of control. Alcoholics Anonymous meetings are held at our church every Tuesday. I checked. Why don't you go and try it out?"

"Alcoholic? I'm no loser alcoholic." Jeff's face grew red. "How could you even think that? Having a drink now and then doesn't make me a drunk. The only help I need right now is a wife who will cut me some slack."

He grabbed Jan's arm and pulled her face close to his. She smelled gin on his breath, and it sickened her further. The nights with him were bad enough, but with him drinking earlier in the day the children would be more exposed to his bouts of anger, of needless blame. Thankfully, neither Mae nor Billy was indoors right now.

"You know, you've become a real bitch lately," he

said in a low, threatening voice.

"You disgust me." She jerked her arm away, knowing she'd find it bruised, and made a beeline for the liquor cabinet. "Bitch, huh? I'll show you a bitch in action!"

Snatching up the large jug of gin Jeff had left out on the counter; she dumped its contents down the sink, earning a rush from the satisfying gurgling sound it made as the bottle drained.

Pulling open the upper cupboard, where they stored the liquor, she repeated the process.

Whiskey? Gone.

Rum? Gone.

Vodka? Gone.

Jan's body quivered from the exertion. Alcohol fumes emanated from the sink. A battery of empty liquor bottles sat on the counter, ready for the recycle bin.

Throughout, Jeff stood frozen in place, a look of incredulousness masked his face.

"I forgot. The beer." When she opened the refrigerator, Jeff snapped out of his catatonic state.

Seizing her by the shoulder, he twisted her around to face him. "Enough!" he shouted.

His voice dropped to wheedling level. "Calm down, honey. What did you want to do that for? You're the one worried about money, and you just dumped a bunch of it down the drain."

Jan shook off his grip. "Don't patronize me, Jeff. I can't stand the sight of you right now. Get out of my house!"

Once the back door slammed behind him, Jan dropped into her chair at the kitchen table and wrapped her arms around herself in a tight hug. Amy was right. Jeff needed help, and so did she.

The kitchen door inched open and tiny footsteps approached her. The children must have seen their father bolt out of here. Had he spoken to Billy and Mae? Upset them? Poor lambs.

"It's okay, Mommy, don't cry," Billy said, rubbing her back.

"It smells like Daddy in here." Mae sniffed the air. "What are all those bottles doing on the counter?"

"Mae, please get an empty brown bag from the closet. They need to go in the recycle bin."

"Daddy looked mad," Billy said. "Is he coming home for dinner?"

"I don't know, sweetie." *And I don't care.*

"You don't love Daddy anymore," Mae accused.

Jan wasn't sure what to tell Mae. She saw the signs, knew how their life had deteriorated, so she said nothing. Jan pushed the hair from Mae's face and kissed her forehead then opened her arms and gathered the children in a family hug.

Somewhat calmed, she filled a saucepan with water and set up three mugs. Opening the cupboard, she took out two instant hot cocoa packets, the bag of marshmallows, and a chamomile tea bag for herself.

A somber mood never lasts too long with active children. Once Mae and Billy finished their drinks, the kibitzing began. Mae giggled because Billy, who had slipped under the table, was tickling the bottom of her bare foot.

"Make him stop, Mom," she begged.

Jan laughed for the first time in days. "Why would I do that? I think I'll tickle you, too."

With that, she circled the table, lifted Mae from her chair, and kissed her on the cheek. "Come on you guys. Get into your nightclothes, and I'll read you another chapter of Harry Potter."

Later, huddled on Mae's bed and lost in the story, the three of them traveled into a fantasy world. For that short time, they were at peace.

Chapter Ten

"Hey Tina, put out some nuts. I got the guys coming over for a game in a few minutes."

"Now, Frankie," Tina said, putting on her diamond earrings and smoothing her chignon in place. "I don't want to come home to find my house smells like a men's bar. Tell them. No smoking in the house."

Frank kissed his wife on the cheek and patted her on the rump. "You go on and have a good time visiting Lucille and the baby tonight."

Frank turned to Vinnie after Tina left. "Geez. Worry, worry, worry. That's all these women do."

"Yeah. Tell me something I don't know. So who ya got coming over tonight? Some of the old gang?"

"Naw. This is my new leaf you're looking at. See? I'm squeaky clean. Thought I'd get to know a few neighbors. A couple of the guys your age want a little action." He leaned in toward his son-in-law. "Now this is the deal. We ain't gonna rip these guys off. We're gonna play nice and civil."

Vinnie shrugged. "If that's the way you want it, Pops. But if we don't take them for big bucks, why are we even bothering ta play?"

Frank handed Vinnie a cigar and said, "Got to do something at night here in the country. Be a good boy and go open the window over the sink for Tina, so she don't come home and beat me up."

Vinnie pushed up the sash with one hand. Rolling the tip of the cigar in his mouth before lighting it, he said, "Pops, I been wanting to ask ya. Don't ya feel trapped in this dinky little house? No offense, but you could've afforded one of them big places on the hill."

Frank wrapped his arm around his son-in-law's broad shoulders. "I'm only going to tell ya this once, so listen good. It ain't the money. I got plenty of that stashed away. I move into a showy house, and right away, I got the cops on my tail. Here, no one knows who I am. See, nice and low key."

He puffed on his cigar and then slowly blew out the smoke. "Course, it took some doing to get Tina to agree, so we made a deal. We live here and in the spring fly to Italy to visit her family. She misses them. Wants to bring them over, but I don't know." He shook his head. "I worry they will be safe."

"Why wouldn't they be, Pops? You got protection." Vinnie puffed out his chest. "You got me, The Family."

"That's the problem. It's not too hard to for me and Tina to stay under the radar, but having a whole clan could bring attention to us. Then the Camiglios will figure out where we are and bango." He pointed with his finger. "We'll all be dead. You know"—he pressed his hand on Vinnie's shoulder—"I worry about you and Lucille. You got a kid now. I want to see him grow up clean. *Capiche*? Why don't you take a look at that nice house up the street? It's for sale. Just think. You could walk down to see us and save yourselves the drive in from Hartford. You will be safe. The kid can go to a nice school with nice kids. No guns. No killing. I lost my brother, and I don't want to lose you too.

Through the screen, Frank heard footsteps and voices and went to get the door. He clucked approvingly, as Mike and Jeff entered the narrow hallway. "Hair's looking good," he said, shaking hands. "Come on in the kitchen and meet my son-in-law…uh, Greg, yeah, Greg." *Not smart to use real names. Ya never know how it's gonna come back at ya.*

Vinnie gave him a funny look and then seemed to go along with the ruse. *Smart guy, his son-in-law.*

Once introductions were made, Frank took the cellophane off a new deck of cards and threw it down on the kitchen table. "What do ya guys want to drink? Beer? A little Chianti? Something stronger?"

"Just beer for me," Mike said.

"Same," Jeff added.

Frank handed the two men bottles of dark beer, and then poured himself a glass of Chianti. Vinnie fixed himself a whiskey on the rocks.

"Cigar?" Frank offered his box of Cubans. "You guys smoke?"

"Not cigars." Jeff gave his buddy a look.

"What? We got cigarettes, don't we…uh…Greg?"

Vinnie stuck his hand in his breast pocket.

"No, we're good," Mike said. "Just a beer will be fine."

Hah. Pot smokers. I knew it. Frank exchanged looks with his son-in-law. *Just beer and no cigars? Maybe this wasn't such a good idea. They seem like a couple of duds. Now my Vinnie, he's a real man.*

"So youse guys live around here?" Vinnie asked. "Nice street. Pops loves it."

Frank got down to business. Puffing on his cigar, he shuffled the deck, the cards warming to his hands.

"Let's open with a dollar each." He set his cigar to rest in the ashtray.

Vinnie shot Frank a look as first Jeff, then Mike threw dollar bills in the center of the table.

"Good, boys," Frank said encouragingly. "That's the way to play."

With practiced hands, he dealt out the first hand and laid the remainder of the deck face down on the table. These guys were green at this. He could tell by their expressions when they saw their hands. A professional would never hide a smile or wrinkle a forehead. Vinnie held his hand with a blank face. That's the way to do it.

When Jeff won the first game with a full house, Frank shook his head. Maybe he hadn't shuffled the cards enough. Guy's got good luck. Frank watched Jeff scoop up the pot that had grown to twenty dollars. The man was actually gloating!

Vinnie stood to get the men another round of drinks and gave Frank a look that said, *What is it with this guy?*

Mike asked for another beer, but Jeff said, "Greg, how about pouring me a glass of that good stuff you're drinking?" And then he turned to Frank. "Let's up the ante. This isn't even lunch money we're playing for here."

Mike put a hand on Jeff's arm, as his friend tossed a twenty on the table. "Are you sure you want to do that pal? It's a little steep for me."

"What? Are you afraid you might lose?" Jeff asked him.

Frank watched thoughtfully, taking a puff of his cigar. The guy with the reddish hair was really cocky.

He could be trouble. Vinnie was trying to suppress a laugh. Frank could tell by the way his son-in-law kept his lips tight, while his cheeks puffed.

Mike added his share to the pot.

As the night grew old, Frank observed the two men with increased interest. Mike, the dark haired one, had won the last hand, and he saw beads of sweat on Jeff's forehead. He didn't need any trouble here. Maybe getting the neighbors involved in a friendly little game hadn't been a good idea. First, this guy wants to do twenties, and then he ups the ante to fifties. The dude seemed like such a lightweight coming in. Who would've thought he'd have a hustler on his hands. The only problem was the guy couldn't play worth a damn. Now he was into some serious bucks with Vinnie. Not good.

"Time to call it quits for the night." Frank gathered the cards into a neat stack.

"Another hand," Jeff said. "I feel a hot streak coming on."

"Game's over," Frank said with authority. He wasn't used to anyone arguing with him, but Jeff pressed on.

"We can't quit. You've got to give me a chance to win back my money."

"When Pops says the game's over, it's over." Vinnie's dark eyes smoldered. "Now, how you gonna pay me what you owe?"

"I'll have it next week," Jeff replied, scowling. He rocked back in his chair. "Are we doing another game then?"

Vinnie's eyebrow shot up as he looked quizzically at Frank.

When Frank shook his head *no*, Vinnie wrote down the amount owed and a telephone number on a paper napkin and slid it across the table to Jeff. "Call this number tomorrow to work out a payment plan."

It was interesting, Frank noticed, that Jeff appeared relieved. The guy was in for it. Vinnie could be a tough cookie where money was concerned. He had trained him well.

Chapter Eleven

Unlike other area schools, Cardinal Hewing held its Open House for parents at the end of October. Since Jeff chose to play poker at the DiGiorno's, Jan rode over to school with Diane.

The desks in Mae's room were arranged in groups of six. When Jan entered, Mrs. Cowley, a short, plump woman with graying hair about her temples, stood up from her desk, which was catty-corner facing the door. Other parents milled about looking at the artwork covering most of the walls. Some flipped through folders on their children's desks.

Jan introduced herself.

"Would you like to see some of your daughter's work, Mrs. Simmons?" the teacher asked. "This is Mae's desk. It could be a little neater, but you know children."

Jan peeked inside, and sure enough, crumbled papers were stuffed in along with the workbooks. "I can't seem to get her to pick up her things at home either," she confessed.

"She's still young," Mrs. Cowley assured her. "She'll outgrow it. You'll see." Pointing to the back wall, she added, "We asked all the children to draw their families and houses. Mae's are over here."

Jan followed Mrs. Cowley, wondering why she chose to spend extra time with her when other parents waited.

They stopped in front of Mae's pictures. The first one depicted their house. The lawn was green, the sky was blue, and Mae had colored in a bright yellow sun at one corner.

"Why is our house black?" Jan asked.

Mrs. Cowley lifted her shoulders in a small shrug. "The children color in groups and have to share the crayons. Perhaps black was the only color she could get a hold of."

"Maybe, but what about this one?" She pointed to Mae's other piece of art. "If this is supposed to be our family, it's missing one person. And we don't own a cat. Are you sure this is her work?"

"She wrote her name at the bottom. If you don't mind my asking, is Mae's father alive?"

"Why yes," Jan sputtered, "of course he is. I don't understand why Mae didn't include him in her picture."

"Perhaps she ran out of time," Mrs. Cowley reassured. "She's keeping up with her classmates pretty well in her reading, but she's having trouble with math. We're starting subtraction. Maybe you could work with her a little on that at home."

That's odd. Mae was no math whiz, but she'd never had a problem with it. From the pictures Mae had drawn, it was clear Jan's daughter was disturbed with the goings on at home. Now her schoolwork suffered. Jan steadied herself against the tension that threatened to overwhelm her. Mrs. Cowley suspected they had problems. That's why she singled Jan out.

"Certainly," Jan said, not convinced that Mae had actually forgotten to include her father in her family picture. Mae was always the first to run to hug him when he came home from work and constantly prodded him for attention. Lately, she'd been hanging back. Had Mae omitted Jeff from the picture as a way of excluding him from her life?

Mrs. Cowley handed her a workbook. "This will be good practice for Mae," she said with a motherly smile. "I hope everything goes better for you at home."

"Uh…why, thank you, Mrs. Cowley. We're working on it."

****

Jan was reading in bed when Jeff came home from the DiGiorno's. While she had pretty much forgiven him, she had trouble forgetting. He seemed to be drinking less, as far as she could tell, and had shown more interest in the children. Yet he had a long way to go to earn her trust. He would want to know about Mae's drawings, but he would be hurt at learning he'd been omitted from her family picture.

"How was the game tonight?" Jan called out.

Jeff came into the bedroom, running his hand through his hair. She sniffed the air. Cigar smoke and she could smell the whiskey on his breath from ten feet away.

Without acknowledging Jan or her question, Jeff turned his back and stripped off his jeans. She noticed sweat marks under his armpits and between his shoulder blades. Odd. Summer was long gone. Maybe the DiGiornos kept the heat high in their home.

Jan put down her book and sat upright. "I knew it. You lost, didn't you? How much this time?"

"Leave me alone. I'm tired, and I want to crash." Jeff plopped down on his side of the bed, rolled away from her, and pulled the covers up over his ears. "Are ya gonna keep that light blazing all night?" he muttered. "Turn it off for Christ's sake!"

Normally, Jeff would be bragging and flaunting money if he had won, and would be swearing about every play if he had lost. Instead, he had done neither.

Jan lay awake listening to Jeff snore long after she'd shut off the light. Something bad had happened at the DiGiorno's.

Something he wouldn't talk about.

Chapter Twelve

Rubbing his hands together, Frank DiGiorno chuckled with contentment as he surveyed his crowded barbershop. The shop was netting him more money than old Joe, the former owner, had ever dreamed of making.

As a result of his innovations, men lined up outside the door to receive Marilee and Irene's ministrations. It was a brilliant idea, he thought, to add in manicures and massages. Yeah, that really clinched it for the men. The massages weren't advertised, so wives weren't aware of it—and neither were the police. Nevertheless, the word was out to the local male population about Frank's special back-room services.

Vinnie sat in Frank's chair getting a haircut. Brushing the coarse black hairs off his son-in-law's thick neck, Frank said, "What do ya think. I rename the place The Men's Room and Spa."

Vinnie snorted. "Yeah, that'll get all the wives in here for beauty treatments, Pops. What are ya trying to do? Kill the business?"

Frank lifted his eyebrows as an idea crept into his mind. "We could give the women massages, too. Get some young men in here to do the job. I might even help out." Frank chuckled at the thought and then waved his hand in dismissal. "Nah. I don't need that kind of trouble. Tina'd kill me."

Vinnie stood and reached for the suit jacket he'd hung on the coat rack.

Putting a hand on Vinnie's arm, Frank drew him over to the side and said in a hushed voice, "I've been meaning to ask ya; whatever happened between you and that neighbor guy, Jeff? You square now?"

"Got him started in a little business," Vinnie said with a smirk. "What a loser."

"But," Frank pressed on, "You let him down easy, right? No strings leading to me or you?"

Vinnie smiled. "Yeah, Pops. Real easy. I set him up with Wheezy."

"That's my boy." Frank slapped Vinnie on the back. "Hey, you coming over tonight with Lucille and the baby?"

"Got a job, but I'll send the woman over."

Frank nodded, watching the large bulk of manhood that was his son-in-law strut out the door. *There goes a real man. Takes care of business nice and easy, just like I taught him to.*

Chapter Thirteen

Jan was marking time in her marriage, and she knew it. Yet, having control over their finances made her feel less helpless. She now worked part time at Loreen's Sweet Shop baking her newly launched line of gluten-free desserts. She kept to the budget she'd created for their household, and they were meeting their bills.

Nevertheless, something was off.

She no longer saw charges from Tie One On Liquors, and Jeff wouldn't tell her where he got the money to buy the new TV delivered yesterday.

Sipping a second cup of coffee, she checked on the children. Mae was patiently teaching Billy how to play a board game. It was good to see them getting along for a change. Lately, they'd been picking on each other and arguing over the silliest things. Once, when she reprimanded them, Mae replied sassily, "Why should we? You and Daddy are always fighting."

Jan had no answer for her child's question.

Where had all their bitterness come from? Bickering, jealousy? She knew arguing was normal for siblings—Will and she had done their share of it—but with Billy and Mae fighting was constant. It was their fault, Jeff and hers. Their worst fights were at night when liquor flowed into Jeff's glass like water from a tap and the slightest comment on her part set him on a rampage.

Was it any wonder the children mimicked them?

Clearly, she needed to do something about Jeff. She couldn't put it off much longer.

About nine on this Tuesday morning, Jeff came into the kitchen wearing his jeans and a ratty gray sweatshirt instead of his business suit.

"Aren't you working today?" she asked, frowning.

He dropped into one of the kitchen chairs. "I'm always working. I have stuff to do in my office. I don't need to get suited up for that."

Jan held back her disappointment. She doubted Jeff would care. Not dressing and not leaving the house to call on customers was a sure sign he was slipping again. When he behaved this way at in his old job at Lyco, her efforts to goad him into being more serious about his work schedule were ignored.

Her heart sank into the pit of her stomach. *Here we go again.*

Taking a last gulp of coffee, Jeff set the mug on the table. "Important meeting. Got to go." He gave her the perfunctory peck on the cheek.

"Who are you meeting dressed like that? Certainly, not a customer."

Jeff cupped her jaw. "You ask too many questions." Releasing her, he headed to his office, grabbed his briefcase, and went out, leaving Jan wondering and worrying.

All morning, buckets of chilly rain descended from a charcoal sky, leaving huge puddles in the street. As a treat, Jan took the children out for burgers.

Jeff's car wasn't in the garage when they arrived home. They hurried inside, glad to be warm and dry.

"Daddy's phone is ringing," Mae said.

Even with Jeff's office door closed, the jarring *briing* reverberated through much of the house.

"The machine will pick it up, honey."

Going to the office door, Jan listened as the call ended before it rang long enough to click over to the answering machine. A customer would leave a message. The frequency and type of these odd calls bothered her. Always three rings, not one, not two, not four or five, when the answering machine would click over.

An hour later, when Jeff returned, she confronted him. "Your office phone rings but no messages. What's up with that?"

"Probably a wrong number." Jeff dipped his head. As he turned away, she caught a glimmer of guilt in his eyes.

Wrong number her toothache. These odd calls were a daily occurrence. A signal for Jeff of some sort. From Candy no doubt. He was still seeing her and all the while pretending at being a loving husband.

He doesn't love me. He loves himself.

"You can't have it both ways, Mister Cheater." Jan finished her thoughts aloud.

Jeff rolled his eyes. "Not that again. Don't you ever quit? Try to keep the kids quiet. I need to make some important calls." He retreated to his office hugging his briefcase as if it were a precious child.

Jan's mother claimed every marriage had hurdles, but when you were in it for the long haul, everything would turn out all right if you tried hard enough. Jan knew this for a fact. Her parents split after Will died— she was sure of this because all they did was argue about whose fault it was that their son became a drug addict. Jan used to hide in her room until the arguments blew over. When her father moved out, she cried herself to sleep thinking she'd never see him again. But he came back, and her parents seemed to have settled their differences. They've remained together ever since, never once arguing about Will, never once mentioning his name. As far as they were concerned, Will had never existed.

Jan supposed if her folks could patch things up after such a horrible tragedy hit their family, she should be able to deal with something as minor as a cheating husband.

But she'd tried. She'd tried hard, and it wasn't working. Jeff's affair wasn't the only spoiler. She feared one day he would drink so much he'd lose control and take out his anger on Mae and Billy. She needed to end this farce of a marriage, for the children, for herself.

Although the idea of divorcing Jeff had been at the back of Jan's mind for a long time, this morning it came forward. While she wasn't in a position to take action, her resolve was firm and decisive. Walking out with the children wouldn't work unless she had a decent income. To do this, she needed to amp up her job to the point where she could support them without making drastic changes to Mae and Billy's lives. They were happy here at Charming Way. Now that she handled the bills, she knew how much more money she needed to earn. Tomorrow, she'd talk to Loreen about expanding her portion of the baking business.

A wave of relief washed over her. All of a sudden, Jan didn't care about keeping Jeff in tow. Let him sink his own ship, but he wasn't taking her and the children with him. The onus that weighed on her for the past year lifted, and the future looked bright. No longer would she be running in place. She had a goal.

Get money and then dump Jeff.

Leaving Jeff holed up in his office doing whatever he did in there, Jan and the children tromped across the street to Rana's. She joined Diane, who was seated at the oaken table sipping coffee, once Billy and Mae were happily involved in an indoor game with the other children.

Rana's kitchen was white, except for the Picasso style mural she had painted, boldly bright with strokes of red, yellow, green, and black.

"I love what you did with that wall, Rana," Jan said. "You're so talented."

Rana laughed. "So are you. These toffee bars you brought over are sinful." Grabbing one, she stuffed it in her mouth.

"Lately, nothing I make's been coming out right. She picked up a piece of the toffee and snapped it in half. "See? These are too brittle. They're supposed to be tender so they'll melt in your mouth."

"It's not your recipe, Jan. It's your mood." Rana laid her hand over her heart. "It comes from inside."

"You're so right," Diane agreed. "When I'm depressed, I pick drab colors for my beadwork, so now I try not to create new designs unless I'm in a good mood."

"I suppose. Life's so ho-hum now. I go from one day to the next."

"Don't we all. If Ted doesn't get a permanent position soon, I'm going to stuff him in one of those green trash bags and throw it away."

"Nah," Rana said. "You'd never do that. He's too big to fit."

They laughed. It felt good to joke about their troubles. They all had them. Even Rana, who worried how having her parents living with her would affect their everyday lives.

"Anything promising for Ted?" Jan asked Diane.

"Just part-time coaching and private lessons. Keeps him out of my hair for a few hours here and there, but the old trust account is dwindling." She rubbed her fingers together.

"It's a shame you have to cut into that," Rana said.

"Yeah. Worst case, Ted and I won't be able to afford to follow family tradition and send the girls to my father's alma mater.

"I met the DiGiornos's daughter, Lucille, the other day," Rana said. "If you can believe it, Mrs. D. rang my front doorbell and invited me over with the children to join them for afternoon tea. La di dah." Holding up her teacup, she extended her pinky. "Carrie and their grandson, Frankie, are the same age. I think she wants them to become playmates."

Diane drew in toward Rana. "What's she like? Mrs. D. looks so old fashioned."

"She's lovely," Jan said. "Very gracious."

"But what's with the dress and heels every day. Doesn't she own a pair of jeans?"

"They're from Italy," Rana added. "I've heard that's how women must dress there. The daughter is totally different. She's okay, but a little over the top. Wore so much gold jewelry that she jingled every time she moved. You should see the rock on her finger. The baby's cute. He and Carrie sat on a blanket on the floor and gurgled at each other."

"Did you meet the husband?"

"Name's Greg. He stopped by for a minute to drop off something. Big guy, kind of tough looking. Wore a suit and tie, so he must have a decent job."

"Jeff met him the night he and Mike were invited there for poker, but he didn't say much. I've been curious about him. I see his hot, red car parked in their driveway a lot."

"Are they still playing?"

"Not that I know of," Jan said. "Jeff was close-mouthed about the whole thing when he came home that night, and hasn't said anything about playing there since. But I never know where he is most of the time, anyway. He's been out at night a lot lately."

Diane and Rana exchanged glances. They felt sorry for her. How embarrassing. She didn't need pity, just friends. While they may have been suspicious about Jeff's affair with Candy, she'd told them nothing.

"I'm just as happy Larry couldn't play poker that night," Rana said. "I shouldn't say this because the DiGiornos have always been nice to me, but something's not quite right over there. I can't put my finger on it."

"Maybe it's just they have different customs than us. They're also older than most of the people on our street. They could feel out of place."

"Could be." Rana poured everyone refills on the coffee, leaving Jan to wonder if more had gone on that night at the DiGiorno's than friendly card playing.

Chapter Fourteen

Christmas in New Jersey was imminent. Jan practiced her smile. She would need to look happy when she saw her parents. Each time, it was harder to fake it. With his unexplained "errands" and odd work schedule, she found it difficult to accept Jeff's constant assertions that he and Candy were history as fact. Although, she had to admit Jeff made lame attempts at keeping their marriage going.

Always there was the bed, the dreaded bed. They slept together more for convenience and show than for any sort of intimacy. He knew her feelings but still reached out to her at night. Occasionally, she'd submit thinking maybe having sex would change her mind about him. Bring back the loving thoughts she once had about her husband. Yet, knowing whatever Jeff was doing to her he could be doing to Candy made her skin crawl. The night he made the mistake of calling Jan Candy—talk about sexus-interruptous—ended sex with Jeff for good.

Tonight at nine, with the children in bed, Jan worked on packing up the gifts. Her hand knitted treasures lay folded and stacked on the kitchen table. She worked for hours, putting her offerings into the correct size boxes, and then wrapping them in colorful paper.

Finally, she picked up the last box, the one she

saved for her younger brother, Will, every year since his death at fifteen. Her parents didn't acknowledge him anymore, but she thought about him all the time. Resentment stabbed at her heart. It bothered her that her parents chose to replace Will's presence in their family with Jeff's. It was kind of her parents to take Jeff in, but why did they have to go so far as to discard Will's things, even his school pictures, and let Jeff take over her brother's room. It might be their way of coping with Will's loss and of saving their marriage, but it wasn't hers. If she screwed up, would her parents obliterate her from their life, as they had Will?

Settling a sheet of white tissue inside the thin cardboard, Jan folded it carefully so it would lay flat. She picked up the snoopy bear he carried around as a child. After his death, she found it tucked under his pillow and hid it in her room. As she laid it in the box, like a child in its bed, her wet tears fell like rain, marring the white of the tissue with jagged dark dots. She shouldn't be crying. Christmas is supposed to be a happy time. It used to be. Would it ever be again?

Putting the lid on Will's present, Jan wrapped it, labeled it, and set it atop the rest. His gift would sit under their tree. When the children were asleep, she would open it for him, hug snoopy bear to her chest, and then tuck him back under her mattress until next year. Wherever Will is now—and she hoped he was in heaven—he'll know he is loved and remembered.

****

At Jan's parent's home in Hillsdale, New Jersey, on the morning of December twenty-fifth, their family gathered in the living room to open gifts. The huge fir tree her mom and dad had put up stood adorned with colorful blinking lights and topped with the cardboard angel she had made in third grade. Her father, wearing a Santa hat, sat in an armchair near the tree reading off names on the gifts, which Mae delivered. Soon, each of them had a stack of cheerfully wrapped presents to open.

They took turns to allow time to stop and admire each gift.

Among her gifts, Jan spotted a small package from Jeff, awkwardly wrapped in birthday paper. She'd saved it for last, hesitant to find out what it might be. She turned the three by five-inch gift in her hands and rattled it. "Is it jewelry? You know we can't afford such an expense," she whispered so only Jeff would hear.

"Open it, Jan," Jeff said. "You'll love it. You deserve it."

She should have been smiling, that's what her parents would expect her to do. Yet, it bothered her that Jeff thought what she deserved came in a box.

Jan easily plucked off the stick-on yellow bow and slid her fingers under the tape holding the end of the wrapping.

"Come on, Jan. I can't wait to see the expression on your face," Jeff urged.

"This is not like you, Janice. You always loved to rip into a present." Her mother's gaze was on her, studying her face. "Are you feeling all right? You look worried."

Jan gave her a happy smile. "I'm fine, Mom." She drew out a white cardboard box that enclosed another box.

"Hurry, Mom. I want to see what Daddy bought you," Mae said.

109

Billy scooted next to her on the couch, sucking his thumb.

Opening the end of the thin cardboard outer carton, she drew out a blue velvet clamshell box that screamed big bucks.

Inside was a circular necklace encrusted with diamonds. Its clear stones twinkled with the reflection of the tree lights—greens, yellows, reds, blues.

Jan's mouth went dry. She turned to Jeff, stunned.

Taking her by the shoulders, Jeff kissed her hard on the lips. "I knew you'd love it. Here, turn around. Let me put it on you."

"I…uh…" Moving like a robotic department store dummy, she turned and lifted her hair to allow Jeff to clasp on the gems. Her heart sank to her stomach as the cold metal of the necklace touched her skin. Thousands, this had to cost thousands. Money they could have used to pay the mortgage or to pay down the bills. Where did he get this kind of money anyway?

"Wow," her mother said. "Jeff, you must be doing well at your new job."

Jeff puffed his chest. "I'm top salesman in my region now. Big bonus."

No way. He's lying to them, and if I had the guts to spoil Christmas for my parents and make a scene, I would call him on it here and now.

Dad gave him thumbs up. "Way to go on the promotion, son."

Son? Jeff's not his son. Will was.

"Well?" Jeff said to her.

"It's…lovely." She ran her fingers against the bumpy ring of tiny stones that lay cold and hard against her throat.

Strangling her.

Jan's throat closed. She gasped, trying to catch her breath. Bolting up from her seat, she ran from the living room.

"She okay?" her dad asked. "She seems overwhelmed."

"You know women," she heard Jeff reply. "They're so emotional."

"Aren't you going to go after her?"

No. Don't come after me. Jan slipped into the bathroom, locked the door behind her, and leaned against the vanity for support. Her breath came in short pants.

Inhale, now blow it out.

Steady.

Her stomach tightened, and then a huge sob crawled up and wrenched from her throat.

She grabbed at the necklace.

She couldn't get at the clasp at the back.

She wanted it off.

Finally, Jan wedged her fingers between its hard stones and her neck for relief.

What was wrong with her? Every other woman in the world would be thrilled to be given such an expensive gift. She didn't know much about jewelry, but cheap diamonds wouldn't sparkle like this, or have as much clarity. In the mirror, her wretched, tear-stained face, red eyes, and runny nose were a pathetic match to the stunning beauty at her throat.

I can't keep it.

But if she didn't wear it today, Jeff would make a big deal about it, and she'd be trapped into explaining why to her parents. She had to go back and face everyone, without letting on how she really felt, and spoil the holiday.

Giving her nose a blow, she splashed water on her face knowing a third party had entered her marriage.

Something cold, hard, and beautiful.

****

After a huge turkey dinner, Jan and Jeff packed the two cars they had taken with the luggage and gifts. The kids would ride with her, and Jeff had the loot.

"It's a shame you have to leave," her mother said, both children held against her. "Don't the children have this week off from school?"

"Mom, can we stay?" Mae asked.

"Yay, we're staying at Grandma's." Billy broke loose and raced a circle around his grandmother, clapping.

In one way, it would give the children a break from all the crap going on with Jeff, but leaving them here meant driving down next weekend to pick them up, or her parents coming up and staying the weekend.

"I'm sorry, kids. Grandma has a wonderful idea, but leaving you here would be complicated. Kiss Grandpa and then get in the car."

With lots of grumbling, Mae and Billy complied.

Her mother stared her down. "It's a shame you had to disappoint the children like that."

"Never mind your mother. Another time." Her dad squeezed her shoulder. "By the way"—he nodded toward Jeff—"you must be really proud of your husband's success."

It took all the willpower Jan could muster not to blurt out the truth about Jeff to him—that she was living with a verbally abusive alcoholic who had cheated on her and lied to them. Those things never happened to their family. They happened to other people. When Will became addicted, they sent him away to detox and told people he was at boarding school. Her situation, they would sweep under the rug, as well. Besides, once they knew, it wouldn't be long before they figured out that she hadn't been truthful with them by covering up for Jeff. She wasn't sure she could handle their accusing looks, the hurt, and disappointment.

When her mother reached out to hug her goodbye, Jan couldn't look her in the eye.

****

As the chill of winter set in, hers and Jeff's relationship cooled further until they barely spoke to one another without getting into some sort of disagreement. Jeff blamed others for his faults, which was hardly new. His parents had doted on him, and Jeff was used to having things his way. If the car ran out of gas because he'd neglected to fill the tank, Jeff called the car a piece of crap. When Jeff's boss at Klean Kare began to grill him about his work schedule, Jeff called him a slave driver.

Mae was doing so poorly at school that Mrs. Cowley suggested she stay back a year to catch up with her classmates, and Billy's pre-school teacher said he was picking fights with the other children.

To make things worse, Jan sensed Jeff was about to be fired. Although he made noises about working hard, she saw the reality. He slept late, didn't leave on sales calls until nearly noon, and arrived home tipsy.

Like clockwork, after receiving one of those hang-up calls, Jeff would fly out the door. Even so, he consistently denied having revived his trysts with that one next door—she couldn't bear to say her name anymore. Jan was spitting mad every time she saw the woman, her car, even her little daughter, who was caught in the middle of this mess like Billy and Mae. She was sick of policing Jeff, and although she remained firm on going through with divorcing him, it wasn't quite time to make her move.

But she would, once she had a steady income and enough money saved to support the children and herself. Even if Jeff admitted he needed help and got it, she doubted she could forgive him for all the nights of drunken abuse ripping apart their family. Someday she might come to terms with his cheating. But love? She didn't feel it for him anymore. Her heart had gone numb.

Picking up the laundry basket, Jan lugged it into their bedroom, sorted their clean clothes into piles on the bed, and then started to stash them in the dressers. In her lingerie drawer, she set her bras next to the blue velvet box holding the diamond necklace.

Sunlight streaming through the blinds cast her shadow on the deceivingly soft hairs of the velvet. She stroked the box, feeling the hardness of its shell. The necklace inside waited to be worn, to be held, to be admired. She lifted the lid. The diamonds winked at her in a weird come-hither way, almost as if they were living, breathing entities trying to tell her, *he stole us*.

Jan clamped shut the lid. The stones lied like a man hitting on a beautiful woman at a singles bar.

Jeff *couldn't* have stolen them.

She picked up the box and examined it for the fifteenth time, searching for some indication of where the necklace had been purchased—the name of a jewelry store, a tag on the necklace, anything to identify where it might have come from. She would take it back, get a refund, then use the money to pay the mortgage, the car lease, the groceries, and buy new shoes for Billy and Mae.

Nothing.

The source of money for the diamond necklace was an enigma. Their bank statements revealed no evidence of a substantial withdrawal. Jeff continued to insist he had received a substantial bonus, which she didn't believe based on his obvious lack of performance. She had considered calling Jeff's boss to verify his statement, but it would have been a waste of time and call unwanted attention to Jeff's expenses. Yet, such large amounts of money Jeff seemed to have to spend must have come from somewhere.

Not able to help herself, she drew out the necklace and held it up to the light. The stones glittered like a fancy fishing lure. Did Jeff think that by putting a chain around her neck he could control her again? That thought surprised her.

Suddenly Jan understood exactly why wearing the necklace felt wrong.

Where would she ever wear such a thing, anyway? To the grocery store? The Sweet Shop? Why, she didn't even own a pair of cheap earrings. The only jewelry she'd ever felt right wearing were her wedding rings. She held up her bare fingers and examined the pale indentation on the fourth finger. She had been retaining water. It had taken grease to get the rings off.

The swelling was down, yet she couldn't bring herself to put the rings back on.

Chapter Fifteen

Jan waited until morning, when everyone was out of the house, to take another crack at Jeff's office. He was up to something, and it involved money—and likely a certain woman. It was time to find out what he was hiding from her.

She hadn't been in Jeff's office for a while. When she opened the door and found it neat, you could've knocked her over with a pogo stick. The room smelled stale, with a hint of booze and an undertone of something sweet. She only hoped neither of the children ever went into this toxic place.

Fanning the door a few times didn't do much, so Jan pushed up the window, allowing the chill outdoors to air the foul space so she could get to work. She skirted around the boxes of samples, which had remained in the same spot since their arrival. The pile had dwindled some, which could be a good thing as far as Jeff's job went. Other than needing an old-fashioned vacuuming, the carpet lacked its usual scattering of papers.

Odd. No bills on his desk. Maybe because she handled them now. She noted only a neat stack of work papers and an empty glass reeking of gin.

Paging through his documents, Jan came across no huge orders that might've resulted in a substantial commission. Yet, Jeff's source of big bucks had to be coming from somewhere.

The desk, purchased from an upscale furniture store, was traditional with a kneehole between two rows of drawers and one spanning its midsection. Plopping into Jeff's chair, she leaned back against the soft leather and opened the center drawer, which contained pencils, pens, paper clips, elastic bands, and a few copper pennies. Basically, junk.

When she tugged open the top drawer, it was jammed with papers. She pulled out one bearing the Lyco letterhead. Garbage. He should have disposed of these months and months ago. Not her problem. The bottom two drawers held bottles of gin and whiskey. Another time, she might've dumped the contents down the drain. What good would it do? Until Jeff got help, he'd continue self-destructing. Nothing she could say or do could stop him. She didn't care anymore.

Three drawers down, three to go.

When Jan pulled out the right drawer, the odor hit her in the face like a green haze. Covering her nose against the hallucinogenic smell, she scanned the contents—a small plastic bag, roll-up papers, and a cigarette lighter. Horrified that Jeff would bring drugs into their home, she ripped out the whole set-up and stuffed it in the trash for takeout to the back yard can.

How dare he, after Will!

All her life tragedy had been associated with drugs. Unlike her, Jeff thought smoking pot with his college buddies was a cool thing to do. In fact, he reeked of weed the day he got the phone call at work that changed his life, and hers.

"Mr. Simmons, your parents have been in a fatal car crash."

117

No strangers to grief, Jan and her parents rushed to Jeff's side.

At the news, Jeff closed up on her. His face like stone.

He came home with them that day and never really left.

Jan shut the drawer, closing off the memory of the event that made Jeff a member of their family.

Remembering why she was here in his hellhole of an office, Jan pulled open the last drawer and found it held a hanging file system. Cream-colored folders poked up from faded green holders tabbed with the bold letters of the alphabet.

Her last chance.

There must be something here. She pulled open the heavy drawer as far as it would go. Behind the files, Jeff had stuffed a white bag printed with a familiar orange and yellow design of the local fast-food restaurant.

Oh, Lord. The remains of his lunch. How long has this been here? She sniffed at the air over the drawer. Odd, no spoiled food smell.

Grabbing the bag by its crunched-down top, Jan plucked it from its spot. The paper was crinkly as if Jeff had balled it up to toss it out then smoothed it out to reuse it. Surprisingly, the bag felt too heavy and solid for lunch remains.

Bad vibes wafted from the bag like steam from a cauldron.

Jan held it away. She should put it back, pretend she never saw it.

Okay. Maybe a peek.

Green. Gray. The coppery scent of money.

Oh, God. Big bills.

Shoving her hand inside, she clasped it around one of the banded stacks of hundred-dollar bills. She'd never seen this much cash in one place before. Was it even real? The muscles in her chest clenched so tight she thought they would burst.

This is not good. This is no bonus money. And certainly, much more than his paycheck would ever bring in.

Jan's hand flew to her mouth. *Oh, no! He's robbed a bank.*

Jeff would lie, deny everything and she could be in trouble for having discovered it.

What if the children found out?

She shoved the money back in the bag, rolled it closed, and replaced it in the back section of the drawer exactly the way she found it. Like the diamond necklace, the money needed to remain in place until Jan figured out where it came from and what to do about it.

When Amy stopped by after school, Jan set two cups of mint tea on the kitchen table and a plate of almond cookies. They sat down to chat.

"Has Mike mentioned anything to you about Jeff lately?" Jan began. "I mean, are they still friends?"

Amy paused as if her mind was churning. "I guess. Jeff drops by a lot, but most of the time he's come to take Stevie to the range to hit a few golf balls. Usually after school, before Mike gets home from work."

"That's when Jeff is supposed to be selling cleaning products. He's doing it again, Amy. Slacking off. I know he's about to be fired. I feel it right here." Jan pressed her fisted hand to her gut. "In one way, it's good to know some of Jeff's errands involve helping

Stevie perfect his golf swing. Yet, he seems to have so little time to spare for Mae and Billy. Nothing personal." She touched Amy's hand. "You know I love Stevie, and I'm glad Jeff is helping him. It's just that I don't know what to think anymore. I'm so disconnected from Jeff. Most of the time I don't know what he's doing and who he's doing it with."

"I'm really pissed off at your husband for the way he's treated you and the kids. What's going on with Candy Cane down the street?"

"Don't know. Don't care. She's the least of my worries. Do you know if they restarted those poker games at the DiGiorno's?"

Amy shook her head. "I think our men only went over that one night. Mike won a little money, but he didn't mention anything about Jeff. Maybe Jeff lost." Amy wrapped the string around her teabag and squeezed, then set it on the saucer.

"That's what I thought at first, but Jeff seems to have a lot of money. Did I tell you? He gave me a diamond necklace."

"Oh my gawd." Amy clutched her throat. "Where is it? If I had one I'd be wearing it, sleeping in it even. Showing it off to the world."

"It's stashed in my bureau drawer," Jan admitted.

"Why would you do that?"

She chewed at her lower lip. How would Amy react if she told her about the money she'd found?

"Jan, talk to me. What's really going on?"

"I don't know. It's not like Jeff to give me jewelry. He knows darn well I rarely wear it. I wanted to return the necklace—we could use the money for something more practical, but he wouldn't hear of it. Then I realized I had no idea where he bought it." She leaned in. "Amy, there were no markings from any store on the box. I looked all over. The necklace came in a standard blue velvet box padded with puffy sateen. That's it. That's all I know." Her hands flew up.

"Family heirloom, maybe?" Amy sipped her tea thoughtfully. "Was it his mother's?"

"I went through his mom's things with him when we cleaned out their house. If he found something as valuable as this, I would have known. I can't picture Jeff sitting on a piece of jewelry worth thousands when we've been hurting for money."

"What if he pawned it and then bought it back? That could explain it."

"Maybe, but given Jeff drops money like a bee drops honey, I doubt if he would bother using it to buy me a necklace." Jan chewed her lip. "There's…uh… more."

"Okay." Amy made a come on gesture with her hand. "Spill it. Tell me everything. You know you can trust me not to gossip."

"I do." Jan grabbed her hand. "Thank you for being such a great friend. I couldn't have made it through this past year without knowing you were here and ready to listen." She sniffed back a sob. "Amy, I'm scared. This morning I went through Jeff's office again."

"Go on." Amy's blue gaze drilled into her. "Cough it up, kiddo."

"Cash." Jan sucked in a breath. "The green stuff. I found his stash. Big packs of hundreds. In his desk."

Amy leaned forward, stunned. "Stay calm. Let's think this through before jumping to conclusions. Has Jeff been honest with you about how much money he really makes? Saved up commission checks? Held out on you so he could buy something he wanted without you knowing? Maybe a rich uncle died and left him an inheritance, and he forgot to tell you. Either way, I'd be really pissed off at him if I were you. He lays on the guilt every time you buy something. What's with that?"

"I don't know anymore. I want it all over. I'm so done with living in Jeff hell." Brushing the wetness from her cheeks, Jan leaned forward. "I handle his paycheck and believe me, that's not where that much money has come from."

"Hmm." Amy slid a cookie from the plate and took a bite. "Does he buy lottery tickets? No"—she shook her head—"if he won big, it would be all over the news. I know." She raised a finger. "He and Mike are always betting on games. Friendly kind, not for big stakes, though." Amy shot Jan a look. "Do you think Stevie is betting?"

Jan touched Amy's shoulder. She was upsetting her, now. "Where would Stevie get the money?"

"You're right. We don't pay our son much allowance. Next year he'll be old enough to work after school. Maybe I'll start to worry then. But gambling, do you think that could be it?" Amy raised her eyebrows, her forehead furrowed.

The answer struck Jan like a double barrel shotgun aimed right at her. "I'm such a dummy." She slapped at the side of her head with the flat of her hand. "Two huge casinos are less than an hour's drive from our house. Why didn't I think about that sooner?"

"Jeff must have had a big win and used it to keep going."

"Mike's not going with him, is he?"

Amy smiled. "When would he have time? Are you going to confront Jeff about the money you found?"

"What's the point? He'll make up some story like he always does."

"You know," Amy said, "gambling's an addiction, like alcoholism."

"I hadn't thought of that."

Amy rose to draw her into a hug. "I'm so sorry you have to go through all this, honey."

Jan drew back from her. "I'm going to win this battle, and one day you are going to hear me roar like the biggest, fattest mama lion you ever imagined."

"And I'll be on the sidelines cheering for you, my friend."

Once Amy left, Jan stood at the kitchen window watching her children, bundled in their winter clothing, laughing as they pushed each other on swings. Oh, to be that carefree. Talking to Amy hadn't resolved any problems, but it helped her think things through. Jeff's problems were stacking up like a pile of cheap novels—alcoholism, adultery, and deceit.

She hadn't mentioned finding the pot to Amy. That in combination with the large sum of money could mean he's involved with drugs. No, he wouldn't dare, especially when he knew drugs killed Will. Besides, she'd found only a small packet, enough for a smoke or two. If he were dealing, she would have found much more.

Maybe Amy was right about the gambling. Drinking and gambling. It's a wonder Jeff hasn't had a car accident. Odd. It never occurred to her to suspect he was going to one of the casinos. She never wanted to go. When the children were older, it would be nice to see some of the performances, but betting on stupid cards or the roll of dice on a spinning wheel seemed a sad way to spend a paycheck.

The odds were against winning. Yet, Jeff had to have hit it big to have that kind of money. He should be jumping up and down with glee, flashing the money around. Yet, he hid it in his desk. Why would he do that?

The answer zinged back at her.

Because he doesn't want to share.

Maybe he planned to take off with his honey next door and go on a fancy vacation. Maybe he was going to ask for a divorce before she laid that on him and beat her to the proverbial punch.

"Divorce."

There. She said it out loud.

Chapter Sixteen

That evening, when Jeff came blustering in from wherever, Jan ignored him and continued ladling out bowls of homemade chicken soup and tucking boiled chicken dogs into buns for the children. She couldn't help but notice he wore jeans, which told her he hadn't spent the day calling on customers. How long would it be before Klean Kare gave him the ax? She planned to confront him about the money—and his gambling, but not here in front of Billy and Mae. It would keep. Would he even admit to it?

"Junk for dinner?" Jeff wrinkled his nose.

"Nice try, Jeff," she replied, trying to be civil. "The guilt trip doesn't work on me anymore. You should know I'm taking on a full-time position at the Sweet Shop."

"Making cookies? That's no position. It's kitchen work, hardly worth the cost of a sitter."

Jan grimaced. *Typical Jeff put down. Let it go.* "It's helping pay the bills."

Jeff held up a hand, palm out. "I've got no time for your nonsense. Do whatever you want. I'm expecting a call."

I'll bet you are. Jan waited until she heard the click of Jeff's office door closing before following him. Standing outside, she cocked her ear to the door fighting off a spell of *Deja vu. I love you.* Those awful words that started this whole sordid mess.

"Mom, what're you doing?" Mae tugged at her sleeve.

"Shush." Jan put a finger to her lips. "Go finish your dinner, honey."

Sure enough, Jeff's phone rang three times. Instead of the usual hang up, his voice filtered through the door. "Yeah, what's the deal?" He paused. Then she heard him say. "Okay, meet you there." His words were clear, not muffled, making her feel more the fool for having fallen for his lie last fall. The door was thin, and her hearing was perfectly fine.

From the bold tone of his voice, Jan doubted he spoke to a lover. *So it's not Candy.* She chewed her lip. She guessed the call had nothing to do with gambling, either. So what then?

She had to find out.

Jan rushed back into the kitchen.

"Kids, we're going to take a ride." She hated to involve Billy and Mae, but if she didn't move fast, she'd never find out for sure what Jeff was into.

"But I'm not done with my hot dog." Billy dumped enough catsup on his plate to drown his last bite.

Jan took the bottle from him. "You're done, sweetie."

Hearing the door slam, then the sound of the garage door opening, she hustled the children into their coats. "Let's see who can get into Mommy's car the fastest."

Mae won, likely because her legs were longer.

"Seatbelt, Mae," she said as she clipped Billy into his car seat.

Sliding into the driver's seat, Jan clipped her own

belt, and then backed down the drive, straining to keep an eye on Jeff's taillights. His car was already at the top of Charming Way. *Right turn. Got it. He's headed toward town.*

"Where are we going, Mom?" Mae asked.

Just for a ride," she said over her shoulder. "Mommy has to pay attention to the road. If you both are good, we'll stop for ice cream."

"Yay. Ice cream. I want gummy bears and sprinkles on mine," Mae said.

"Me too." In the rearview mirror, Billy licked his lips. "And chocolate chips. Can I have chocolate chips too, Mommy?"

"Of course."

Jan screeched around the corner onto Devil's Hill, called so because of its many switchbacks that curved in a downward spiral toward Main Street. She swerved right and left—done this so many times the car was in auto-drive. *Drat. Where's Jeff's car?* She didn't dare speed up with the children in the car and risk careening off the road and over the side.

The traffic light flashed red at the intersection of Devil's Hill and Main. Jan stopped, drumming her fingers on the wheel. She'd lost him.

Across the road, the lights of the 24-hour pharmacy and the supermarket glowed against the night sky. Goose-necked streetlamps made a path of beacons on either side of the wide road lined with a variety of shops and buildings. The smaller shops had closed their doors for the evening. If Jeff were going to one of the casinos, he would not have turned toward town. Here, any betting going on might be at O'Brien's Pub.

"That's it." Her finger shot up in the air.

Finally, the light turned. Jan took a left and crawled down the street. No traffic problem tonight, but man, trying to navigate Main Street at lunchtime was a feat for a racecar driver.

"Why are you going so slow, Mom? And this is the wrong way to the ice cream shop," Mae said.

She was being a rotten mother right now, hauling the kids on a wild goose chase after Jeff this late in the day. But she had to know what was going on, and she could think of no other way to find out, except to hire a private detective—which of course they couldn't afford.

"I know. I just have to check something out first," Jan replied to Mae. "Do you guys want to help me?"

The children perked up.

"Watch out your window. The first one to spot Daddy's car gets a double scoop of ice cream." Actually, they both would get the same, but she needed to keep them occupied while she scanned the area for Jeff's car.

Billy clapped, wiggling in his car seat. He loved games.

"Why?" Mae asked.

"Because your father forgot…his cell phone." Jan hated lying to the children, but they couldn't know she suspected their father of gambling for high stakes.

The three of them checked every single one of the cars parked along the road. They passed Loreen's Sweet Shop and The Men's Room, the barbershop owned by the DiGiornos. With happy hour over, she easily found a parking space in front of O'Brien's, welcoming with its flashing red neon sign emblazoned with an elf in a green hat tipping up his glass.

"This isn't Funky's," Mae said. "You said we were getting ice cream."

"We are, honey."

What was she thinking? It wouldn't do to expose the children to a bar scene, and what if Jeff were inside? What would she do? The vision of her, fueled with the strength of an ox, dumping over a card table to the astonishment of a bunch of drunks made her smile. Maybe it's not cards, though. O'Brien's had a pool table.

Frustrated, Jan backed out of the space and drove through the side street that led to the municipal parking lot, which gave access to the back entrances of the stores and restaurants along Main.

"Mom, I don't like it here. It's dark."

"Can we get ice cream now?" Billy whined.

Poor baby was tired. "In a few minutes. Are you looking for Daddy's car? He really needs his phone."

The lot was not well lit, so it was hard to determine the color of a vehicle. Jeff's car was Klean Kare-issued olive green, which shouldn't be hard to spot. Jan inched past a possibility, causing the couple necking inside to start their engine and drive off.

"I guess he's not here," she told Billy and Mae.

It didn't set right with her that the money in Jeff's desk came from winning a bet at a bar, anyway. The bills had been bound and looked crisp and new.

"Do we still get extra ice cream?" Mae asked.

"I want ice cream." Billy's voice trembled. Lord, he was going to cry on her.

"Right now. And yes."

Leaving the lot, Jan headed up the street past Devil's Hill Road. It was only seven, but it seemed later because it was dark and cold. A half-mile down on the right, Funky Sundae was gloriously glowing. *Thank goodness it's still open.* At this stage, she doubted a slice of the carrot cake sitting at home would substitute for the promised treat.

Half an hour later, when she and the children returned home from the proverbial wild goose chase. Jeff's car wasn't in the garage.

Jan sent the children off to put on their pajamas and then zipped into Jeff's office shutting the door behind her. Jeff's desk appeared much the same as it had this morning, which meant he hadn't done much job-related work.

With a sigh, she moved behind the desk and pulled open the lower file drawer.

The fast-food bag was gone.

Chapter Seventeen

It had been nice waking up alone this morning. Idly she wondered where Jeff had spent the night. There went her big plans to grill him about the money. The problem niggled at her like an itch that needed scratching. Obviously, Jeff took the money somewhere. Did he know she followed him up the street? He might've seen her headlights in his rearview mirror and turned toward town to throw her off track while he took the long way to Route 2 and the casinos.

Dummy. Candy. He must still be seeing her again—maybe he never stopped. Did they have a little rendezvous at some expensive resort? That didn't make sense either. What would she have done with her little girl with Bob working the night shift? To her knowledge, Candy had no family in the area, and certainly, she wouldn't have hired a sitter without Bob wanting to know where she was going.

Jan didn't know why she should even care what Jeff did anymore, as long as it didn't hurt the children. Jeff knew she planned to divorce him. She'd told him so many times in the past month. He'd just looked at her and then shrugged as if he figured she was joking. Well, today the joke was going to be on him. *It's over, Jeffie boy. You can screw anyone you want to without feeling guilty because you blew it with me, with us.*

Mae ran ahead, linking up with Kelly and Tara. Jan

held Billy back from joining them. "Stay with Mommy, honey."

At the corner of Charming Way and Devil's Hill, she waved hello, then sat beside Diane on the large flat rock under the aged oak tree, while Billy busied himself collecting acorns. Mae and Kelly had their heads together, no doubt cooking up after-school plans.

Diane pulled her wool hat down, hiding most of her kinky curls. "Brrr. I hate winter. But things are looking up for my sweetie. The coach he's been filling in for at Charleston High just handed in his resignation. Ted's been asked to stay on."

"Wonderful."

"Yeah. I suppose. I'm sort of used to having him around. The important thing is my Ted's flying high now." She shook her head. "You don't know how great it is to see him get dressed to go to work every day. Maybe you do." She grinned. "How's the bakery job going?"

"Can you keep a secret?"

"Me?" She jerked back her head. "Who am I going to tell?"

"Loreen and I are working out a partnership deal. We're meeting with a lawyer to sign contracts this morning. I've been bursting to tell someone. Sweat equity. Eventually, I'll own half the business. We've decided to package gluten-free dessert mixes and sell them online, as well."

"Whoa, kick back, girl!" Diane whacked her on the back. "Sweet deal!"

"Why, thanks." A bubble of happiness welled inside her, and Jan found she was grinning. "I owe a lot to Loreen. She's given me free rein of the kitchen. It's so much fun doing something I love and being paid for it, too. I'll be working more hours, though. Know any good sitters?"

"Hello? This is me, Diane, your good buddy. I can get Mae to and from the bus, and she can stay at our place until you get home. I'd take Billy too, but I do my jewelry work when the girls are in school."

"Thank you." Jan hugged her. "Rana probably can give me a few sitters to call. It'll be easier next fall when Billy starts kindergarten."

"Car coming, kids, stand back from the street." She wrapped her arm around Billy's waist. The girls knew enough to get out of the way.

With a putt-putt, Candy's turquoise car chugged up the road and slowed at the intersection. She looked straight ahead, unsmiling.

Diane leaned in. "Peaches was bragging to my girls about all the presents she was going to get because her father's moving out."

"Really? What do you think it means?"

"That's easy. Unless they sell their house and she moves away, Candy'll be after our husbands."

"Let her have them, Di." Surprisingly, she was relieved Jeff might have someone to go to after the divorce, another issue on today's agenda. "If the men are stupid enough to fall for her games, they deserve her."

Once Jan brought Billy to school, she drove into town and parked in the lot behind the two-story brick building housing the law offices of Jones, Quigley, and McDuff. After her meeting with the divorce lawyer, Loreen would meet her here to see Quigley.

At the entrance, Jan checked the directory for the

correct floor and suite and took the elevator up four flights.

This was it.

Taking a deep breath, she squared her shoulders before pushing open the frosted glass door.

The receptionist, a dignified gray-haired woman, sat behind a computer at a mahogany desk. When Jan gave her name, she pushed a button on her phone.

"Your client's here, Mr. McDuff." She turned to Jan. "He'll be with you shortly, Mrs. Simmons." She looked up at her over the glasses perched at the tip of her nose. "And you are scheduled for Mr. Quigley at ten?"

"Yes. That's correct."

"May I get you a cup of coffee?"

"Why, yes," Jan replied, sitting on the blue tufted sofa. Picking up a magazine from the mahogany coffee table, she thumbed through it for something to do with her hands. Her insides were a jumble of nerves. Today, she would take two major steps to improve her life, Billy's life, and Mae's.

The coffee came in a delicate porcelain cup and saucer, which made Jan wonder if this firm's rates would be too steep for her. She became even more concerned about cost once she stepped onto the rich beige and burgundy Oriental rug in Attorney McDuff's office and found him seated at a large desk with heavy brass fixtures.

"Please sit, Mrs. Simmons." Mr. McDuff indicated one of two antique type chairs facing his desk. Reaching into his vest pocket, he pulled out a gold pocket watch and made a note, assumedly of the start time for their meeting, then asked, "How may I help you?"

Crossing her legs in an effort to get comfortable, Jan leaned forward in the straight back chair. "I want a divorce. Tell me, what do I need to do?"

"The State of Connecticut has no fault divorce." He leaned back in his chair, folding his hands over his rather large belly. "They really call it a dissolution of marriage. Once a petition is filed, there's a cooling off period of ninety days before the actual divorce hearing. Either you or your husband will be required to appear in court as the plaintiff to testify."

She stared at the man, absorbing his words.

"Is your husband still living at home?"

"Yes, but not for long."

"Good. Make certain you do not move out of the house. Once you do, he can claim you left him, and you lose rights to the house. I recommend you go to the bank today and withdraw all the money in your joint bank accounts."

"I don't feel right about doing that."

"It's done all the time," Mrs. Simmons. "You have young children?"

Jan nodded. "Two."

"You'll need that money more than he will, then."

"About your services, Mr. McDuff. How much will they cost me?"

Jack McDuff rubbed his clean-shaven jaw, assessing her as if considering how much money she could afford to pay. "To take your case I'll need a retainer of course, plus expenses. And there are certain filing and delivery fees for the petition. I'll also receive a percentage of the court settlement but don't worry about that. At the hearing, we'll petition to have my fee paid by your husband."

"That's fine," she replied. "Whatever it takes."

After answering a series of questions needed to complete the petition, Jan wrote a check, using the new account she'd opened with her bakery money, and handed it to her lawyer as a retainer. "Let's get things going."

She should have been relieved as she returned to the waiting room to meet Loreen, but she might've been a hunk of stone. Not a twinge of sorrow, even. *Jeff is history. Billy and Mae are what's important.* She'd let them down by not catching on to Jeff's activities sooner.

Once the bakery contract was sealed, she and Loreen took the elevator down and walked together to the parking lot.

"Glad to have you, partner." Loreen drew her into a friendly embrace.

"Partner. I like the sound of that."

"You'll like the profit we're going to make more. I'm not getting any younger." She patted her permed silver hair. "I'd like to spend more time spoiling the grandkids." Loreen cocked her ears at the sound of a siren passing by. "Something's going on. An accident maybe?" She sniffed the air. "Do you smell smoke?"

Jan inhaled. "It's coming from over there." She pointed to a dark gray cloud rising from a bunch of buildings.

"Oh my God! I've got to go."

"I'll follow you."

Revving the engine, Jan punched in the number for Billy's school. "I'll be a few minutes late, there's a jam up in town."

"We'll wait with Billy, then."

Keeping an eye on Loreen's white car, she headed in the direction of the smoke. A few turns and they were on Main Street. Traffic was backed up two blocks and lined up to the right. Fire engines yelled by, followed by police cars, and an ambulance. Whatever is happening must be serious. *Please, please, God, don't let anyone be hurt or dead.*

Jan's cell jingled.

Loreen.

"I can't wait. I'm going to pull the car over and walk."

She should be headed for Fun for Tots. Billy was more important than rubbernecking. Yet, she had to know the bakery was okay. Just a look, then she'd be out of here, Jan promised herself.

Loreen was out of her car taking long strides, almost running, weaving through sidewalk traffic thickened with onlookers.

It's not a sideshow, Jan wanted to say. Someone might be hurt.

By the time she found a space to park, Loreen was out of sight. Jan exited her car, coughing, her nostrils filling with the odors of burning wood, spiked with an electrical smell.

Phone call.

Loreen.

"The whole block is smoking. My shop and the ones near it. They're putting someone in an ambulance. Don't come down here. They won't let you through. The area's cordoned off. Go get your son. I'll keep you posted. There's nothing you can do now anyway." Her voice shook.

No, no. This can't be happening. Jan held back a sob. *Get Billy. Get home.*

In the car, she tuned the radio to the local station.

"Breaking news. Firemen are working to control a blaze they think started in one of the shops along Main Street. Stay posted for updates. We are getting a man on the scene."

Jan drove the back way to Fun for Tots, arriving only a few minutes late. She found Billy just inside the door, his coat on, holding his teacher's hand. It seemed everyone in the morning class had been picked up, except her son.

"I thought you forgot me, Mommy." His lip trembled.

She stooped to pick him up. "How could I forget my favorite boy?" Jan carried him out to the car and buckled him into his car seat.

Her phone rang.

Loreen.

"It's our shop," she said, her voice high and wobbly. "They don't know how the fire started yet, but they say it's under control. I can't get inside. Everything we've worked for must be ruined."

"Don't say that. You...uh, have insurance, don't you?"

Chapter Eighteen

Frank settled the fedora on his head and hauled on his overcoat. "I'm going to the shop for a couple of hours. Be back by supper."

On the kitchen counter, his phone buzzed. Only a few select people knew his number.

"Yeah, Louie?"

"Turn on the news. There's a big fire in town, same block as your shop."

"Who told them guys?"

"No one, boss."

"Then how did they know?"

"I told you, the Camiglios don't know you own The Men's Room."

He'd been smart to change his name before he moved to Greenburg, although it took some doing to get new IDs for him and Tina.

"Somebody ratted on me. Find out who."

Frank clicked off, tossing the phone across the room. "Shit follows me everywhere."

"Tina," he yelled, "start packing."

"But, Frankie, I like it here. It's cozy, and the ladies are so nice to me."

"No one will be nice to you once you're dead."

"But what about Lucille and Vinnie and our grandson? We can't leave them here and just go." She took off his hat and smoothed her fingers through his hair. "Calm down a minute. What did Louie tell you that's got you scared?"

"I'm not scared. I just want us to live without worrying about someone coming after us."

"I know, love, but we can only do so much."

"Someone set a fire."

Tina's hand went to her mouth. "Your shop?"

"Naw, but on the same street."

"Frankie, you're jumping the gun. If that fire was meant to hurt us, why would it start somewhere else?"

"Yeah. You're making good sense. It's just that I can't get out from under it all. I try to keep you safe, but the threat is always hanging over our heads like some black cloud. I worry about Lucille and the baby, our grandson. I don't want him growing up part of this."

"Yet, you handed the business down to our son-in-law. What were you thinking, Frankie?"

"You're right, as always." He kissed her cheek. "Sorry to get you all alarmed. I'm gonna go check things out. Make sure everything's okay. Call Lucille. We got room. See if they'll come and stay here for a while. Their apartment in downtown Hartford ain't safe. Our house is wired against invasion and hardly anybody knows where we live."

"Thank you, Frankie." Tina stood on tiptoe and kissed him on the lips, slipping her tongue into his mouth.

He squeezed her ass. "Maybe I should stay home so you can really thank me."

"Go on"—Tina smacked at his butt—"get out of here."

Chapter Nineteen

Once Jan arrived home with Billy, the stress of the Sweet Shop fire caused her to collapse in the kitchen chair. She couldn't count on Jeff to support them anymore. Her potential for financial independence might have gone up in flames. Just like that. She snapped her fingers or tried to anyway. She was never good at it.

Taking the Sweet Shop contract from her purse, she reviewed it. Loreen didn't own the building, just the right to operate her business there. Depending on what they were able to salvage, they'd be free to reopen in a new spot and, with the insurance money, buy new equipment. Fortunately, insurance would cover most of the damage.

In the meantime, Jan could continue assembling the prepackaged desserts. She surveyed her kitchen. Not here, unless she paid big bucks to renovate the area into a commercial kitchen. But she'd find a place to rent or use and help Loreen get back their storefront. Heck. If she could deal with an abusive drunk day in and day out, certainly she could handle this upset.

A little past three, Jan and Billy headed for the bus stop to get Mae, not that her daughter wasn't capable of coming down the hill by herself. With so little street traffic, she'd be safe. The air was fresh and clean, and the walk helped clear her head.

"There's Poppa Frank," Billy said. "Can I go play with him?"

Jan waved to Frank Di Giorno, who was near his car in the driveway.

"He looks like he's leaving, honey. Maybe another time."

"Aw, gee." Billy hung his head. "Momma Tina always gives me candy."

"Well, young man"—Jan pulled his wool hat down over his ears—"you certainly don't need any more sweets." Grabbing his hand, they walked on to get Mae.

Twenty minutes later, Jan hung up their coats and had just settled Mae at the kitchen table with a snack and a glass of milk when the doorbell chimed. Other than the occasional repairmen or someone selling something, people she knew just knocked on the back door. It's not smart to open the door to just anyone these days.

"Mommy, company's here." Billy tugged at her sleeve.

Leaving Mae working on her homework, Jan went to the living room window and pulled back the drapes enough to see if she should answer.

"Who is it, Mommy?" Billy, who followed her, peered outside also.

"I don't recognize the car, and I can't see who's outside from here."

The bell rang again, followed by a loud knock. "Open up, police."

Jan's hand flew to her mouth so hard it hurt.

Something's happened.

With her insides quivering with dread, she unlocked the door to a tall, dark-haired man in a suit and a uniformed officer with a gun pointed at her chest.

Her knees went weak. She shoved Billy behind her. "Go stay with your sister."

Jan's hands flew up. "I didn't do anything. Please put down that gun. Don't shoot me. I have two children." Her mouth went dry as cotton. She swallowed hard.

The plainclothes man flashed his badge and then nudged the officer. "Put that thing away. You've scared this nice lady half to death."

With a warning look at her, the officer holstered the gun.

Jan dropped her hands to her sides and released a ragged breath.

"Sorry about that, ma'am." The dark haired man flashed his badge. "I'm Detective Hoskins, and this is Officer Welch. Is Jeff Simmons home?"

"Why no. I haven't seen him since last night. Is he all right?" Sure, she wanted Jeff out of their lives, but he was Billy and Mae's father, and she didn't wish him harm.

"When do you expect him? You *are* Mrs. Simmons, I assume," the detective said.

"Yes. Jeff is my husband. He's supposed to be working. He's a salesman for Klean Kare, you know, the cleaning supply company."

She wasn't sure why she volunteered that information, but her mouth kept moving. If the police were looking for Jeff, they weren't here about an accident. Whatever he did must be more serious than a parking ticket. Jan didn't know much about police procedure, but it seemed odd that a higher up would accompany a police officer for a routine charge.

"Please, step inside. It's cold with the door open." She allowed the pair into the foyer. "Now, what's this about?"

The detective pulled a long, folded paper from his inside pocket and handed it to her. "This is a search warrant, ma'am. We have reason to believe your husband is involved in illegal activities. We were told there may be evidence in your home."

"E…evidence?" Jan's mind flashed to the small bag of marijuana she had removed from Jeff's drawer and wondered if Jeff had replaced it. Or, maybe they were looking for the necklace or know about the missing money.

What if they think I'm involved?

Jan's hand went to her throat. "Oh my God, what has he done?" Mae and Billy came beside her. Mae took her hand, and Billy hugged her leg.

"It's all right, darlings. They're just looking for Daddy."

Billy pointed to the officer's holstered gun. "Are you gonna shoot my daddy?"

"Shush." Her finger went to her lips. "No one's shooting anyone."

"Can't say right now." Detective Hoskins responded to her question. "I'm sorry to upset you and your children, but we'll need full access to the premise. Our warrant also covers Mr. Simmons's vehicle, which we assume is not here at the moment.

"No, uh, Jeff drives a company car."

"We understand Mr. Simmons works out of his home. If you'll show us to his office, we'd appreciate it. We'll start there."

She didn't know how she could protect Billy and

Mae from this invasion. They clung to her, and she didn't have the heart to send them off by themselves to worry and wonder what was going on. They were part of this too, and as young as they were, they were entitled to the truth.

"This way." Jan turned. Taking her entourage along with her, they led the detective and the officer into the family room. She flipped open the office door. "In here."

Watching the A team rifle through Jeff's papers and open every drawer was painful. Jan squeezed Mae's hand and kept her other hand on Billy's shoulder, waiting for one of the men to hold up a bag of pot and shout, "Victory."

Detective Hoskins spotted them hovering outside the door. "This procedure will take a while. You certainly have the right to stay, but it might be easier if you and the children left your home for a while."

"You mean *get out*, don't you?"

"No need to take offense, Mrs. Simmons. I see you aren't comfortable. And the children—you understand we'll be going through your entire home?"

"I see." Maybe they had better leave. If it bothered her to watch them ransack Jeff's office, how would she feel seeing strangers go through their bedrooms, their cabinets, and everything else they owned? If the police had a search warrant, they must have presented a valid reason to the court for disrupting their privacy. Besides, subjecting Mae and Billy to this outrage was just plain wrong.

"I understand. You're just doing your job, Detective. Billy, Mae, let's get our coats. We'll walk down to visit Amy. She should be home by now."

Shutting the front door behind them, Jan took the children's hands, and they set off down the driveway. Her mind rumbled with concerns. Leave it to Jeff to bring the police into their home. Because of him, two men were going through her dresser drawers, fingering her bras and panties, picking through her makeup. They were sure to find the necklace, the only item of value other than the wedding and engagement rings she'd stashed away.

Jan pictured the men snooping in her cupboards, checking out the refrigerator, and sneaking pieces of her homemade toffee from the plastic container on the kitchen counter. When they found the blue teapot filled with her just-in-case money, would they think it was stolen?

"Are those men going to play with my dolls?" Mae asked.

"Oh no." Billy's face scrunched. "I left Bob on my bed. Are they going to hurt him? I couldn't bear if they hurt Bob."

Jan knelt down and cupped their chins. "Those men are just looking, my honey buns. They won't take your favorite things."

"What do they want?" Mae asked.

"I'm not sure, sweetie. We'll have to wait until they are through to find out."

"Daddy's going to be mad when he finds out those big men messed up his office."

"Yeah," Billy said, "he's going to yell at them. Mommy, I have to go to the bathroom."

"Can you hold it one more minute?"

"I think so. I'll try."

Arriving at Amy's was like going to heaven. Her

home was always warm and welcoming. Jan knocked on the back door, then opened it, and called out. Her car was in the drive, so she knew her friend was home.

"Come on in." Amy shouted from another room. "I'll be right there." Amy came into the kitchen drying her hands. "That toilet was plugged up again, but I finally got it flushing."

"And just in time too," Jan told her. "Can this young man be the first to make sure it's working?"

"Go ahead, honey. You know where it is."

"Is Mike home yet?" Amy's husband checked usage meters for Greenburg Utilities.

"He's due any time. Stevie should have been here by now, though. I wonder what's keeping him?" She grabbed Jan by the shoulders and searched her face. "What's the matter? You're pale and shaking like a leaf."

"Daddy's in trouble," Mae ventured.

Jan's heart cried when her daughter's voice wobbled. Her poor little girl understood more of this than Billy did. She put her arm around Mae's shoulders, drawing her close. Her daughter was smart enough to know whatever was going on could change their lives for good.

"Mae," Amy said, "why don't you go into the living room and turn on the TV. Find a program you and Billy like."

Mae's frightened gaze flashed to Jan for approval.

"Yes, go ahead, dear. We'll be here a while. Grown-up talk."

Mae set off, looking back at her once or twice.

Go, she motioned with her hand.

Once Mae was out of hearing range, and Billy had

joined her in front of the TV, Amy pushed Jan into a chair at the kitchen table. "Sit. Jan." Settling across from her, Amy leaned in. "Spill it."

"The police are looking for Jeff," Jan said in a hushed voice that grated against her ears like a saw against wood. "They're searching our home for something. They wouldn't tell me what."

Amy drew back. "Oh my God," she whispered. "Do you think it's got something to do with the necklace or that money you found?"

"I don't know anymore. I just don't know." Determined not to cry, Jan blinked back the tears threatening to spill down her cheeks. Her petty worries about Jeff and Candy, or even about him gambling, seemed like cotton fluff compared to the enormity of what could happen next.

"The money's gone, Amy. Jeff went off with it last night, and I haven't seen him since."

"Not good, Jan. What can I do to help?"

"Watch Billy and Mae for half an hour while I head home to find out what's going on."

Jan no sooner finished the sentence when Mae appeared in the doorway. Billy was right behind her. "You're leaving us?" A tear rolled down her cheek.

"Oh, sweetie. Just for a little bit." She drew them both into her arms. "I promise I will be back to bring you home as quick as I can."

"Come on, Mae." Amy took Jan's little girl's hand, "You and Billy can play with Stevie's pinball machine while you wait for your mom."

Billy's eyes lit with anticipation, but Mae appeared wary. "Will you be okay without us, Mom?"

Tears filled Jan's eyes. "I'm never okay without

you. I love you."

Amy touched her shoulder. "Go."

Stepping outdoors, cold, raw air slapped at her face. She cut across Amy's backyard, which was layered with crusty brown grass, to reach the intersection of Pleasant Street and Charming Way. The air weighed heavy with humidity, the sky whitened by its promise of an early snowfall.

The roar of an engine drew her gaze to the top of the hill.

Jeff's car.

It would serve him right to walk into the police net being cast, but, being worrywart Jan, she ran to wave him down. Her feet scrambled for traction on a shiny patch on the road.

Smack.

Right on her butt.

Jeff's coupe slowed. For a minute, she thought he planned to get out and help her up. They hadn't talked, so he didn't know she'd just filed for divorce…yet.

No car door opened.

No amber-haired man strode toward her.

Instead, with a squeal, his car switched gears as he put it in reverse, backed into the nearest driveway, and zoomed off.

Jan blew out a disgusted breath. *That's right run away.* She rubbed at her sore bottom. *How like you to evade responsibility for your actions.* Maybe it was for the best that Jeff turned tail. Now she wouldn't have to watch him be arrested, especially if the police found whatever they came after.

Stepping around the dark sedan parked in her driveway, Jan went inside through the front door, which she had left unlocked. Who would steal anything in a house crawling with police anyway?

Please let them be finished. I want my home back; I want my life back.

In the front hall, she caught a glimpse of her face in the mirror. Her eyes were bloodshot, and her face had as much color as the builder white walls. She looked away, not liking what she saw. Why had she allowed Jeff to put her and the children through the wringer for so long? She should have found a way out of this mess before it came to this.

Jan's head dropped into her hands.

Footsteps.

She straightened up, mopped her face with the hem of her shirt, and sniffed. Where was a darn tissue when she needed it?

Detective Hoskins led the way, with the officer a step behind him. "I see you're back. Good." He had a kind face, despite his professional demeanor.

She looked a mess, but she didn't give a flying crap. Her gaze leaped to the living room floor. End table drawers hung open, sofa cushions lay about on the carpet like dead bodies.

My knitting!

Upended from its bag, the blue sport yarn trailed in a stringy heap across the floor.

"Didn't your mothers teach you anything? Look at this mess." She pointed at the living room. Drawing back her shoulders, she shoved down the rage. "Since when did the word search mean destroy?"

She picked up her knitting needles and held them up. Lost loops slopped over the side and stretched into holes. "It will take me hours to repair the damage you've done here. I can just imagine how the rest of the house must look."

"Ma'am, calm down."

"Well." Jan held up the knitting. "I'm not the criminal here. Why am I being punished? My children are frightened little rabbits. You men need to learn manners."

The officer studied the floor like a chastised little boy. He held his hat in front of him, sliding his fingers around its base, but said nothing.

The detective opened his arms and spread his hands. "You understand this is routine procedure for a drug bust."

"Drug bust? You're kidding." Had Jeff brought in another stash? He hadn't mentioned finding his missing.

The officer straightened his shoulders and thrust out his chest. "We haven't uncovered the marijuana we were told was in Mr. Simmons possession, but we still need to search his vehicle. He checked his watch. "It's after five. Isn't Mr. Simmons due home from work soon?"

"I don't expect him." *Ever.*

"I see." Detective Hoskins handed her his business card. "Please call me when he shows."

"Sure." It'll be a dark day in hell when she called him. Let them pick Jeff up somewhere else.

Stuffing the detective's card in her pocket, Jan opened the front door to allow the officers to leave amid the first flakes of the promised snow. As they made their way to their cars lugging some boxes, she almost felt sorry for them. It had to be hard to destroy lives of innocent people like her, Mae, and Billy in the name of justice.

She needed to get her children home before the snow piled up. First, Jan did a quick scan. As she suspected, no room was left untouched. She stuck her head into Jeff's office, noting his computer had been seized, as well as the boxes that had littered the floor. Her guess was if she checked Jeff's drawers she would find them empty.

Before Jan left, she took a few minutes to tidy up the children's rooms.

In Billy's room, Bob lay on the floor, his spindly legs flopped up and over his oversized body. Picking up the stuffed toy, she hugged his soft body to her chest, understanding the comfort and warmth such a small inanimate thing could provide a little boy. Billy needs him now, and Mae would want the tattered pink blanket she hid under her pillow so her mother wouldn't wash away its special scent. That too lay on the floor.

Outside, snow flurries brushed at Jan's cheeks and clean, fresh air cleansed her nostrils. Night had fallen, leaving the street black with wetness and brown lawns dappled with diamonds. Such beauty made it almost possible to pretend that her home and family were one again—happy, looking forward to life. But she was done with that naïve foolishness. She couldn't undo the damage Jeff had done, but she could keep her children close, let them know how much she loved them, and protect them as best she could.

With Billy and Mae's favorite things tucked inside her parka, Jan took the road, staying to the side, where she could dig her shoes into the lawn and avoid the icy slick. On either side of her, happy homes glowing with outdoor lights welcomed husbands home. Rana would be making Carrie and Derrick's dinner. Ted's car just pulled into Diane's driveway. Even *her* problems were mended now. When was it going to be Jan's turn?

Her feet moved ahead, yet her mind stood still, absorbing the horror of the detective's words. Drugs. Jan's heart stopped. For the police to get a search warrant, Jeff had to be a heavy hitter. How dare he, knowing drugs killed Will?

At the corner, Jan made her way up her best friend's driveway. She owed Amy the details, and she wasn't sure how Amy would react. But this was Amy, and she'd understand like she always has. She'd listen and worry about her and make her a cup of tea.

Jan hurried toward the glow from inside Amy's home, a beacon of hope and love.

Through the paned glass on the back door, she spotted Amy in the kitchen, the phone cradled between her ear and shoulder. She knocked once, let herself inside, and kicked off her wet shoes on the mat.

Her back was to Jan, but from the hunch of her slim shoulders and the hushed tone of Amy's voice, her stomach instinctively clutched.

Setting the phone on the counter with a decided smack, Amy whipped around to face Jan. Her nostrils flared, and her chest moved in quick heaves. "That was Mike. He just spoke with our Stevie." Amy's eyes were as cold as steel, and her words were stilted. "He was arrested at school this morning for being a drug courier. They questioned him for hours and wouldn't let him even make a phone call until just now."

"Amy, I…"

Amy's hand went out in front of her, stopping her from speaking.

Jan froze in place, her heart pounding.

"Your husband got him involved."

"In drugs?" Jan's voice rose, and her body went numb with understanding.

"Mike's on his way down to the station to try and bail him out. Please take your children home, Jan. I don't want them here." She turned away, arms crossed tight in front of her, and leaned over the sink. A guttural sob wrenched from her. Jan wanted to go to Amy and comfort her like she had done so many times for Jan, but she didn't dare.

"I'm so sorry," she whispered.

Without a word, Jan found Billy and Mae, pushed Bob and Blankie into their arms, and hustled them out of Amy's home.

Outdoors, the gentle snow that kissed her face earlier had turned to biting ice pellets. Jan's feet were wet and so numb they might have been wooden. The children wore boots, but she had run out in sneakers. She deserved to be punished. She allowed this to happen.

Stevie, Amy's life, had been turned into a criminal by the man Jan married.

Besides Stevie, how many other children had Jeff turned into addicts? The horror of it bore down on her like a steamroller. Yet, as unthinkable as it was she needed to brush aside her personal feelings and make this wretched situation as transparent as possible for Billy and Mae. She'd pretended everything was going to turn out all right for a long time. For their sake, she needed to pretend a little longer.

"Look, Mom"—Mae's gloved hand pointed toward their house—"the car's gone."

"Yes, but the police made a big mess inside our house."

"Did you make them stand in the corner, then pick it up, Mommy?" Billy said.

"No, honey, I'm afraid we have to clean it up. But it will be fun. We'll make a game of it."

"Oh goodie, I like games."

Jan's ruse worked until they stepped inside.

It hadn't been easy getting the children settled after having had a gun aimed at them by the police and being shunted off to Amy's while their things were pawed at. Now, tucked in their beds and finally asleep, Jan tended to her own needs. After such a harrowing day, her nerves were stretched to the limit. Wanting nothing more than to lick her wounds and fall into bed, she entered her bedroom.

The bed had been stripped naked, exposing the semen stains on the king-size mattress. The mattress where Jeff had repeatedly drilled into her before falling asleep. With a surge of adrenaline, Jan went at the thing, tugging, and pulling at it until she managed to get it far enough off the box spring to bend it. She pushed and shoved, but it was too heavy for one person to turn. It flopped back in place, smacking her on the head. *Darn it, mattress, you're not going to win this battle.* She tried again, and this time, she got it off balance enough to flop over to the clean side.

Jan sat on its edge, panting from the exertion. Around her, everything was in disarray. Dresser drawers were left open, their neatly folded contents left in scrunched cloth balls. The closet door was ajar, revealing hangers with clothes strewn on the floor.

I can't sleep in this room. And I don't want to face

it tomorrow.

She rose, squaring her shoulders to tackle the task of putting her life back together. The pieces would never fit the way they had before, but maybe the finished product would be more bearable.

Working steadily, she set her dresser back in order, only stopping to strip off her clothes and don her favorite pajamas. She hadn't washed up, but she wasn't ready to face the mess in the master bath yet. Closing the last drawer, she turned. Her gaze landed on Jeff's dresser. The vest she'd knitted him for Christmas that he'd yet to wear hung over the bottom drawer like a drooling tongue. Laughing at her, as if to prove how foolish she'd been thinking making Jeff a vest would heal their relationship.

With a lunge, Jan grabbed at the vest with the fury of King Kong. She stretched and pulled at it, then bit at it with her teeth until stitches ripped and unraveled like their marriage had.

Holding the damaged vest in both her hands, she sobbed into it, soaking it with her tears and her runny nose. The darn thing didn't even smell of him. Holding the shreds of yarn away from her with two fingers, she stuffed the mess into a green trash bag, along with the garbage of her life.

"Mom, are you okay?" Mae stood in the doorway, Blankie held to her nose. Mae ran to her, hugged her, and then took her hand. "Come on, you can sleep in my bed with me."

Jan followed her little girl into her room, where Billy slept also, and nestled in with her, trying not to disturb her children any more than she already had.

Tomorrow is another day.

Chapter Twenty

Routine would be better for them. Mae and Billy would attend school, as usual, today. Besides, she promised to help Loreen assess the damage to the Sweet Shop for insurance purposes. With the children at the kitchen table spooning in oatmeal and dressed to go out, she could pretend nothing had happened the previous day; that the visit from the officers had been an illusion; and that Amy hadn't hung up on her when she called. Yet, the protective veneer of pretense wouldn't help her deal with the reality of her life today.

Attired in her oldest jeans and the old denim shirt she'd grabbed, Jan headed out the door with the children. Once inside the garage, Mae's gaze went to Jeff's things, stacked along the wall on his side.

Uh, oh.

Jan had nearly forgotten what she had done the past night. Not being able to sleep, she'd tiptoed from the children's room and quietly set to work packing up every single clothing item that belonged to Jeff, hauled it into the garage, and then dropped off to sleep on the living room sofa.

Letting her backpack slip to the floor, Mae ran over and dragged one of the suitcases away. "He's not moving out. Daddy lives here."

Jan didn't know what to do. Mae loved her father. "Billy, get in the car while I deal with your sister."

Her shoulders dropped, and she sighed. She put her arm around her little girl's shoulders and kissed the top of her head. "I know this is hard, Mae, but it's best for all of us."

"You mean for you, don't you?" she spit out, her gray eyes stormy.

Jan ran her hand along the length of Mae's long, strawberry-colored ponytail. "For you too, sweetheart. Daddy has some problems he has to deal with. It will be easier on you and Billy if he works on resolving them somewhere else."

"But where will he go? Where will he sleep?"

"A hotel maybe, or at a friend's house. He's a grown man, he can take care of himself for a while, don't you think?"

"I suppose," Mae said. Her little face had that beaten look she got when she ended up with the old maid in cards.

Dropping the suitcase, she kicked it and then got inside the car.

Jan's cell phone sang out. She picked up the call from Rana.

"What were the police doing at your house yesterday?" she asked.

Thank goodness her neighbor had the sense to hold off calling yesterday. Jan wasn't quite ready, to tell the truth. She had misjudged Amy's friendship, not that she blamed her, and she couldn't afford to lose another friend right now.

"They were looking for Jeff. He's in some sort of trouble. I haven't seen him since yesterday morning, so I really can't talk to you about it yet."

"I get ya," Rana said. "Let me know if I can do

anything."

"Right." Jan clicked off, clipped Billy into his car seat, and made sure Mae's seat belt was buckled.

Stink. The phone again. She checked the ID. Not Jeff. Diane.

"What'd ya do, rob a bank or something?" she said. "The neighborhood's going wacko."

"No, Di, it's nothing I did. Hey, Jeff's tied up today, and I need a backup in case I don't make it home in time for Mae's bus. You heard about the fire in town?"

"Yeah, the bakery. Hey, don't you work there?"

"Yes. Bummer. Just contracted to partner with Loreen yesterday morning." How long ago it seemed. "The shop survived. Loreen's hired a company to clean up the mess so we can reopen. I'm headed over to help her assess the damage. I'm not sure how long I'll be. We need to see what we can salvage from our supplies and likely will end up doing some reorganizing. I can get Billy after preschool and bring him with me, but I may not—"

"Jan, you don't need to explain. I'm here for the girls anyway. Just call me. Did you see the realtor car in Candy and Bob's driveway yesterday? They must be selling the house."

Jan loved her neighbors, but she wished they weren't quite as nosy. Yet, she hadn't seen Bob's car lately and couldn't help but wonder if Jeff was hiding out at Candy's. His car might be parked on Bob's side of their garage. What if Candy is in on the drug dealing? She's in the medical field. *Oh my God, Peaches.* That poor child has been through as much hell as her children.

"Um, I didn't notice," Jan replied to Diane.

****

After a spending the morning hauling out boxes of supplies and cooking utensils that seemed to have survived the fire, Jan drove home with Billy in time to meet Mae's bus.

"Mommy, you stink," Billy said from the back seat of the Ford.

Black dust filled her nostrils, and her clothes bore a thin film of greasy soot. "I know, dear. Mommy's going to take a shower as soon as we get Mae at the bus stop and go home."

She parked at the side of the road, near the stop.

Unrolling the window, Jan waved to Diane. "I'm home, but thanks for the offer."

"No problem. Anytime. Gawd, you look a mess."

"I know, but the good news is most of the baking supplies in the cabinets are useable, and the insurance company is going to pay for the cleaning and restoration we'll need. In the meantime, the church is letting us use their kitchen to blend our dry mixes for our internet orders. Here come the kids. Can I give you a ride down the hill?"

Diane wrinkled her nose. "I'll walk thanks."

Mae exited the bus, her purple backpack slung over one shoulder, along with Kelly and Tara.

"There's your mom," Jan heard Kelly say.

Mae glanced at Jan's car—she knew her daughter saw her wave. She didn't smile and didn't come over and get into the car. Instead, she started down the hill with Diane's tribe. *Stink. She's got a 'tude on.* She must have been worrying about hers and Jeff's separation all day at school.

"See you at home, Mae," Jan shouted out the window as she drove down the hill. She pulled into the garage, leaving the door open for her daughter. "Billy, it's cold out here. Go on inside. I'll be right there with your sister."

Mae trudged up the drive giving Jan a steely glare.

Meeting her part way, Jan put her arm around Mae's slim shoulders.

She shook it off. "I hate you, Mom."

Jan dropped her arm and continued walking beside her little girl. "I'm sorry you have to go through this, honey. Let's go inside where it's warm. I'll make hot chocolate, and we'll talk about it."

Mae didn't say anything but slipped her hand into hers.

In the kitchen, Jan heated milk, and then added sugar and cocoa, letting Mae stir the mixture as it warmed. Helping seemed to calm her. Mae's initial anger seemed to have passed. Now, she seemed deflated.

Billy kicked at the underside of the table and hummed to himself.

To go with the cocoa, Jan put a bag of jumbo marshmallows, toothpicks, and her kitchen shears on the table, along with their mugs.

"It's done, Mom." Mae lifted the wooden spoon, allowing the chocolate milk to dribble back into the pan.

Once Jan filled their cups, they settled around the table.

Billy reached for the bag of marshmallows.

She touched his hand, so small under her own. "Not yet, sweetie. First, we have to make marshmallow men."

Billy sat up in his chair, his face brighter.

The children watched with interest as Jan snipped a marshmallow into chunks, then used them to fashion a head, arms, and legs. A few toothpicks attached the bits to another marshmallow, creating a marshmallow person.

"See?" She danced the little guy toward Mae's cup, and her daughter rewarded her with a smile.

"Me now," Billy said, as she created another marshmallow man.

Mae floated her marshmallow man on top of her cocoa. "You're going to tell us that you and Daddy are getting a divorce, aren't you?"

Reaching over, Jan ran her hand down the braid that hung over one shoulder, then tucked her hand under Billy's chin. "You both know Daddy has some problems that haven't gone away."

"He drinks that stinky stuff all the time that makes him yell at us." Billy held his nose.

"And he never plays with us anymore," Mae added, picking off marshmallow man's appendages and popping them into her mouth.

"I want a wheelie." Billy's face scrunched as if he were about to cry.

"Daddy doesn't have to live in our house to give you a wheelie, Billy."

"Don't cry." Mae stood to hug her little brother. "Daddy will come to see us, won't he, Mom?'

"Of course. He loves you both."

"Maybe he'll bring us toys," Billy added with a teary smile.

"If Daddy's moving out, can we get a kitten?" The

last of marshmallow man disappeared into Mae's mouth.

"We'll see." Jan tweaked her braid.

The children laughed. There was freeness to the house they hadn't felt in a long time as if the air was cleaner, newer.

The garage door groaned.

They lifted their heads, listening.

"Daddy's home," Mae said. "What should we do, Mom?"

"Nothing, honey. Finish your cocoa. He'll come to see us soon enough."

"I want to see Daddy." Billy bolted from the table and raced to the door.

Mae and Jan stood, but didn't move.

Billy tackled his father as soon as he came through the door from the garage. "Daddy, Daddy. I missed you." Jan's son hugged Jeff's legs in a hold that would do a sumo wrestler proud.

Jeff stopped short. Dark circles lay under his eyes. His shirttails hung out from under his parka, and his slacks were wrinkled, making Jan suspect he'd slept in his clothes.

"I missed you too, sport," he said to Billy." Picking up his son, he swung him around in a poor excuse for a wheelie.

Billy giggled. "Your face tickles, Daddy."

Jan gave Jeff a cold stare. "I've been trying to get a hold of you. I'm surprised you took the risk of coming here. I hope you didn't run over your things pulling the car in because they're on your side of the garage."

"I saw them." Jeff set Billy down. His face was hard. She saw no sign of remorse for what he had done.

"The police came here looking for you. They searched our house and upset the children. I saw your car come down the road and then leave yesterday. You ran away like the chickenshit you are and left me to deal with the fallout."

"Mommy, you said a bad word." Billy tugged at the hem of her sweater.

She rested her hand on his little curly head.

The doorbell buzzed, followed by banging on the door.

"Open up. Police."

Jeff froze, his eyes wide. "I'm not here. Tell them." Whirling around like a dervish in heat, he bolted for the back door.

Billy began to bawl.

Mae hugged her brother, wet tears streaming down her face.

Jan stooped to their level. "Let Mommy handle this. Mae, take Billy into your room and close the door. Find a game you can play. And don't come out until I say so."

For once, her children followed orders without argument.

The pounding continued until Jan opened the door to yesterday's team, Mutt and Jeff, both holding out badges.

"What? No guns today?"

"We're armed, but I hope we won't have to use violence to capture Mr. Simmons. We followed his car here. Stand aside, ma'am."

Detective Hoskins removed his gun from under his jacket and dropped his arm to the side, gun nose down. If the dratted thing went off, she'd have a nasty hole in

164

her floor. He glanced over her shoulder, eyes flicking from side to side around her, giving him a view of their vacant living room and the doorway into the kitchen.

It was too late to save Jeff, and she didn't need these officers rampaging through her home for another search and capture, terrorizing Mae and Billy further. "He just went out the back door." Jan pointed toward the kitchen.

"Take the door and check the perimeter," Detective Hoskins said to Officer Welch. "I'll do a quick check of the house and meet you outside."

Okay, don't believe me, she thought. "I'll be waiting in my daughter's room with the children. I assure you, he's not there."

Jan walked away, realizing he followed her.

"Ma'am, just a quick look. Sorry." He poked his head in the door of Mae's room.

Mae and Billy cowered on her bed, Billy hugging Bob and Mae with the ragged remnants of her baby blanket held to her nose. They started at seeing the detective.

"How are you kids doing today?" he said with a friendly smile. "Is it okay if I look under your bed and inside your closet, Mae?"

He remembered her daughter's name. Surprising.

"He's not here," Mae told him. "He's outside."

"Yes, your mom told me, but I have to check around anyway in case he snuck back in."

"Daddy's playing hide and seek, isn't he, Mommy?"

"Yes, dear." Jan wedged herself between the children on the bed and held them close. At this point, she could do little to assure them everything would be all right when she didn't know herself.

Oh Lord, sirens.

Jan's first instinct was to shield the children further. Close the blinds and wait. But Mae and Billy had already bolted to their bedroom window, which viewed the front of the house.

"Mom, look at all the cars."

Standard squad cars and a few regular cars parked in the *cul de sac* and at the bottom of their driveway. Uniformed and plain clothes men piled out of them in pairs, weapons at the ready.

Did they really think Jeff was that dangerous? To her knowledge, he'd never handled a gun. He had to be scared. Although the horrendous crime he committed warranted his arrest, did they really have to go after him with hit men?

"Mom, why are they all carrying guns? They're going to hurt Daddy, aren't they? I shouldn't have told the big man where he went. It'll be my fault if they hurt Daddy."

"Mae, that's nonsense. The detective already knew Daddy went outside."

"Because you told him first." Mae pointed an accusing finger at her.

Billy bawled. "I don't want them to hurt Daddy."

"Calm down children. The police have guns because they think he might have a gun too, and they don't want him to shoot them. We know he would never do that. They don't know Daddy like we do. If they find him, and he holds up his hands like this"—she raised her arms—"the police will see he won't hurt them, but they will take him into custody."

"You mean jail. Daddy's going to go to jail."

Mae's lips stretched tight.

Gratefully, Jan heard the front door shut—behind Detective Hoskins, she assumed. They were free to move about the house. She held off dealing with Mae's concern.

In the hall, the sound of the garage door opening indicated someone had entered or was planning to leave. Had Jeff snuck into his car with a scheme to zoom away?

No, he couldn't have. Not with the driveway blocked with cars.

Jan put her ear to the door leading to the garage. Voices, several of them. None sounded like Jeff.

A male voice boomed loud enough for the door to vibrate against her ear. "Hey, Stan. This must be his car. It's plate number HOV 233-31 we've got the search warrant for. He can't have gone very far on foot. I'll check it out. You radio the others to check the neighbors' houses and that patch of woods out back."

Jan and the children raced from window to window to see what was going on. Their yard crawled with armed men, who split off. Some headed for the woods at the end of the *cul de sac*. Others went across the street to Rana's and over to Diane's. Another pair crossed their property line toward Candy's house. Had Jeff gone there to escape the police? She couldn't help but worry about the little girl. Where was Peaches during all this commotion?

Jan's cell phone vibrated in her jeans pocket. Not a good time to talk to anyone. She snuck a peek at the caller ID, and her stomach dropped into her lap a bit further.

Her mother.

She didn't dare answer it, even though she owed her parents the truth. They wouldn't be happy.

The sounds of opening doors and voices from the garage kept Jan in place. Were they looking for Jeff or...

"Pay dirt. We've got this guy nailed!"

At the words, her knees turned to rubber. No going back now. She could only guess, but they must have found the evidence they needed to convict Jeff. Drugs. The horror of it all had her sliding to the floor with her head in her hands. "I can't go through this again."

"Mom, don't cry. It's going to be all right. You said so, remember?"

Jan mopped her eyes with the tail of her shirt, still reeking of smoke from the Sweet Shop fire.

Mae held out her hand to help Jan up from the floor. "Billy and I will take care of you, don't worry."

Her babies. When had they grown up on her?

Jan and the children maintained a post at the window, watching the commotion as if it were a TV program—NCIS, Miami Vice, or something like that. Yet here it was, a crime scene in their front yard. After the find, a few cars departed, back to base she assumed, but now a team of men headed for Candy's front porch, guns drawn.

Her heart thumped double time. *They've found him.* She couldn't see much from the window, but she had to know.

"Billy, Mae, keep an eye out for Daddy. I'll be on our porch. Don't come outside."

"Be careful, Mommy," Billy said.

Putting on her coat, Jan stepped out onto the porch to see what was going on.

Men surrounded Candy's house, guns aimed to shoot.

A voice boomed from a bullhorn mounted on the squad car parked in Candy's driveway. "Come out with your hands up, and no one will get hurt."

Candy's door remained shut.

The voice boomed again. "Mr. Simmons. We know you're in there. The house is surrounded. You don't want us to come in after you."

Jan held her breath.

Candy's front door creaked open.

A shoe, then the man.

Jeff took in the scene then backed against the door, hands up. "Don't shoot. I'm unarmed." His face was as white as the paint on the door.

Jan wished she could say she wanted to go to him, comfort him, but she couldn't. Any feelings she once had for Jeff had turned numb. So she just watched. Jan knew he saw her because he glanced over and tried to catch her eye. She wouldn't look at him.

"Stand down," Detective Hoskins told the team. They dropped their weapons to their sides.

The detective kept his pistol drawn as he approached Jeff. Jan couldn't hear what he said, and she didn't dare move closer, but Jeff dropped to his knees, hands behind his back. Once he was handcuffed, the detective pulled him to standing and motioned with his gun for Jeff to go ahead of him.

Behind her, the front door opened. Mae and Billy slipped out and came beside her. She took their hands.

"Where are they taking Daddy?" Billy shrieked, as the detective pushed Jeff down into the police cruiser, and then got into the front seat. The rest of the team scattered toward their cars.

Then, just like that, it was over, leaving Candy standing on her front porch holding Peaches by the hand. She must have just come home from work because she wore her nurse's uniform.

Impulsively, Jan started toward Candy, motioning Mae and Billy back into the house. They had come out without their coats, and the air was cold.

Candy sent Peaches inside also and started toward her. Jan wasn't sure what there was to talk about, but she met the woman part way

"I called the police, Jan. On my cell when Jeff wasn't looking. I knew he was fooling with marijuana but didn't realize how serious things were until today. He spilled it out to me, expecting me to feel sorry for him. I didn't know what to do, so I pretended I was okay with what he had done. To kids, can you imagine?" Candy held up her cell phone. "I have the police on speed. Not sure why, but it came in handy today."

"I'm glad you called. The police would have found him anyway, but at least he wasn't harmed."

"But you were, and it's my fault. I never meant to hurt you, Jan," Candy said in a small voice. "I was lonely, and Jeff was nice to me. I'm so sorry."

It was hard to forgive a woman who had slept with her husband and even dyed her hair to please him. Yet, she looked pathetic with her shoulders dropped and eyes brimming with tears. Jan realized Candy had also been Jeff's victim. He had taken advantage of Candy's weaknesses, as he had so many other people in his life—her, Billy, Mae, and her mom and dad.

Jan narrowed her eyes at Candy, noticing her

brown roots but no longer giving a hoot. "You had a husband of your own. Why would you go after mine?"

Candy's gaze steadied on the icy brown lawn. "I was married to Bob, but he never was a real husband, you know, in bed. He likes men."

How demoralizing to be married to a man who preferred his own sex. No wonder Candy had gone so far to prove her womanhood.

At Jan's expense.

Candy's hand pressed onto Jan's shoulder. "Why am I telling you my problems? You must be in pain after all that has just happened."

"Listen, Candy." Jan steadied her gaze on the woman. "I'm divorcing Jeff. He's no prize, and I imagine he'll be doing jail time, but I'm sure he could use a friend."

When Jan returned to their home, Detective Hoskins waited on the porch.

"We're done here, Mrs. Simmons. Do you still have my card?"

"Somewhere."

He half smiled, revealing a dimple on one side of his face. "In case you can't locate it, here's another. At your husband's arraignment tomorrow, the judge will decide if bail is appropriate to his case. You'll want to contact your lawyer and advise him or her of the situation so he or she can be present."

Jan wrung her hands. "I…" *Maybe the McDuff group. No, they handle divorce. He'll need a criminal lawyer.* "Can you recommend one?" How on earth was she going to handle this? Hiring a lawyer would be expensive. The detective mentioned bail money. No way was she putting up even one dollar to pay for the defense of a man who would harm children or to set him free.

"I can arrange to have a court-appointed attorney assigned to him."

"Yes, please." Jan lowered her eyes so the officer wouldn't see her tears. She studied a patch of ice on the porch. She should salt it before someone slipped and sued them.

At the thought, her insides quivered like a bunch of flowers in a stiff wind. She was going to lose her cool and become a crying heap if the man didn't leave right this minute.

He touched her arm "Feel free to call me for updates. You go inside, now. Your children need you." He glanced toward the window, where two wide-eyed, pale little faces looked back at her.

Hold it together, Jan. For them.

Chapter Twenty-One

Frank woke from his nap with a start. "Sirens. What the fuck?"

Leaping from his lazy boy, he ran to the window and pulled back the heavy drapery. "Shit, Tina. Come look at this. The fuzz are swarming all over the Simmons's house."

Tina came up behind him and peered over his shoulder. "That poor lady and those sweet children. Wait a minute." She grabbed his shoulder and whipped him around to face her, no small task for a person half his size. "What do you know about this?"

His hand flew in the air. "Nothing, Lovie."

"Nothing, huh?" She pinched his cheek as if she were chastising a bad little boy.

"Ouch. Let go." Man, he was in trouble. Maybe later she'd spank him. His lips curled into a smile at the thought.

"Tell me. You know something." Tina's beautiful brown eyes turned dark as night, and her face flushed like it always did when she was good and pissed off at him. She twisted her fingers, digging her long nails into his cheek.

"Okay, okay. Come on. You're hurting me."

Thank the baby Jesus, she finally let go. He touched the sore spot on his cheek. "Did ya draw blood, my love?"

Tina laughed, and he relaxed a little. Amazing how such a petite person could bring a big guy like him to heel like a lovesick puppy dog.

"Looks like a hickey." Her talented pink tongue licked at her finger as if it were a tasty lollipop, and then gently rubbed the sore spot. "Better?"

"Yeah, how 'bout…"

"Not so fast, Romeo. Explain."

Frank drew in a breath. "It's nothing I did, you understand."

"Sure. You're as pure as the Virgin Mary." Tina's hands were on her hips, and her gaze cut through him like a knife. "Go on."

He raised his hand. "The truth. The guy lost big at poker and ended owing Vinnie a bundle."

"Poker? Here? You mean that one time you had the neighbor guys over you set him up?"

"No. Honest. I didn't. Vinnie and I played it cool. Small stakes. But that asshole across the street started raising the antes. So what was I gonna do? Finally, I shut down the game."

"So he paid Vinnie back. Right?"

"Well, in a matter of speaking…"

"Cough it up."

"Louie, the guy's pimping for Louie. Well, actually, Wheezy."

"That little worm?" Tina smacked her forehead. "*Madonna mia*. How *could* you?"

Frank shrugged. "Nothing I can do about it now."

Tina's finger drilled into his chest. "Figure out a way to help that nice lady. That's what you can do. *Capiche?*"

Dropping her hand, she turned her curvy back to

him. As her head moved, he got a side view of her pert nose. "And you're sleeping on the couch tonight."

****

Seven a.m. and already the day had turned sour.

Slamming the Hartford Crier to the floor, Jan kicked it until all the pages flew up and over the kitchen. "Stink! Stink! Stink! How could you! To our kids!"

Greenburg Man Nabbed Selling Pot to Kids

Jeff made the front page, the big time. With his unshaven face, he appeared more a convict than a husband and father. He'd always wanted to be a big shot. Now he'd done it, but not for a good reason. The front page landed face up. She kicked it again and then flopped into a kitchen chair.

Grabbing her cell phone, she scrolled through new messages and missed calls. Nothing from Rana, nothing from Diane or Amy; only a voice mail from her mother berating her for not calling back. Normally, she didn't care what people thought, but she wondered if Rana and Diane would shun her because of Jeff's actions. Maybe they wondered if she was party to them.

Jan straightened her shoulders and lifted her chin. *If that's what they think of me, I don't need them. I know I am a good person. That's what matters.*

"Mommy, you made a big mess in here." Billy rubbed his eyes, looking even younger than his four years in his fuzzy, footed pajamas.

"You slept later than usual today, young man."

"I kept waking up. I thought I saw a man in my room with a big gun. He was this tall." His hand went up to show her, and then he stretched higher on tiptoe. "Bigger than this, even."

175

"But Mommy saved you from the man, didn't she?" Jan picked him up like a baby and held him in her arms. "Our house is locked up tight. No one can come in unless we let them in. You're safe as can be, sweetie."

"Can I get down now?"

She allowed Billy to slip out of her arms. Immediately, he knelt and pointed at one of the sheets of paper. "There's Daddy's picture. He looks mean. But he isn't mean is he, Mommy?"

"No, sweetie. He's just not smiling."

"Can I watch TV? I know how to turn it on. Mae showed me. Can I, Mommy?"

"Don't you want some oatmeal first?"

"I'm not hungry."

"Go, then."

Wading through the newspapers, Billy set off.

She should go check on Mae, although, with it being Saturday, her daughter had no reason to be up early. Maybe she's awake, but not willing to come out and face the day. Not that Jan could blame her. She didn't want her to see the article on Jeff and freak out. With a sigh, Jan bent to the task of collecting all the papers and putting them in order.

Only then did she sit down to read exactly what her soon-to-be-ex-husband had done. Photos of schoolchildren and quotes from mothers included in the article made Jan's stomach churn with nausea. A shiver ran through her body from head to toe. She'd shared a life with a man capable of corrupting and endangering children. Well, he was locked away now, and that alone was a relief.

Grabbing hold of the offensive front page, Jan

crumbled it into a ball, tossed it into the sink, and set a match to it. She stared at the growing flames as the edges caught fire and curled into a powdery gray ash.

Her symbolic act of destruction helped defray some of the inner rage that had been eating at her gut, but it hardly made the problem of Jeff being in prison go away. Even though he was a stinking rat, because of the children she felt a certain obligation to his wellbeing. With no other family, who else would help him?

The house phone rang. Without much thought as to who it might be, Jan picked up the call.

"Honey, you have to help me." Jeff sounded anxious, upset. "I'm stuck in a cell along with a bunch of drunks they threw in here last night. I need fresh clothes and my toiletry kit right away. I'm supposed to get a lawyer, but no one has shown up. Can you get down here and bail me out?"

"When hell freezes over." Jan punched the disconnect button hard enough to jam her forefinger.

She waited for him to call back, but he didn't. Then, she recalled police shows. He likely was allowed one phone call. And he wasted it on her. Too bad.

Jan dropped into a kitchen chair. She didn't like the hardened person she'd become. The old Jan would've sympathized with Jeff and helped him out with what little money was in their savings account. Hers now, and she would need it to keep them living in this house and eating regularly. Surely, Jeff could help himself. He'd been Mr. Moneybags, treating himself to any toy that he fancied. He must have a secret stash of cash somewhere. Maybe a separate bank account even. Drat, she'd never thought to check for that. No matter. The point was she couldn't afford to give him money. He was on his own.

A pang of guilt struck like an arrow, straight through her heart. She should at least check in with the detective. The children would want to know what was about to happen to their father. She'd left Detective Hoskins's business card on one of the end tables in the living room. Picking it up, she carried it into the kitchen and called the station.

He was at his desk.

"Jan Simmons, here. I spoke with my husband a short time ago. His court-appointed attorney hasn't shown up yet, and he seems frantic."

"I'll check on that for you. How are you and the children holding up today?"

Jan sighed. "Barely. You and your crew gave us quite a fright yesterday." She wanted to be angry with the detective, but she couldn't be. He actually seemed to care.

"I know, and I'm sorry. Mr. Simmons's arraignment was supposed to be this afternoon, but he'll need time to update his lawyer. It's possible the court will put it off until the next session, which is Monday.

"Arraignment?"

"Yes, that's when he will be asked to plead guilty or not guilty. Bail will be set or denied. If it *is* denied, or you choose not to pay it, the judge will recommend he be sent to a detention facility pending the trial or plea bargain."

"How much do you think bail will be?"

"It depends on the judge and the crime. If your judge decides bail is appropriate, and it's more than Mr. Simmons can afford to pay, he can opt for a surety bond."

"You'll have to excuse my ignorance, Detective, but I'm not familiar with that."

"Of course, I understand. With a surety bond, you only need to put up a small portion of the bail demanded along with some collateral to ensure your husband will appear in court on the slated date. The money is non-refundable, and they can go after you for the rest of the money or whatever you've put up for collateral, the deed to your house for example."

"No way. I don't want any part of that. Jeff will have to handle that on his own," Hard Hearted Hanna replied. "What are the charges?" she asked, softening her voice.

"Drug trafficking, plus several counts involving minors."

"So it's serious." Jan knew that already, yet hearing the words from an authority made it all too real. She eased into a nearby chair.

"Yes, as compared to the minor routine arrests our local department deals with."

She sucked in a breath, recalling the evidence found against Jeff and the fact that Stevie ratted on him. The court would find him guilty, for sure.

"My husband asked for clean clothing and, if possible, I'd like to speak with him directly."

Jan didn't really want to see Jeff, but she hadn't talked to him about what he did. She needed to see for herself whether he was repentant in any way or just a plain old rotten apple. Facing him would be tough, but it might give her closure.

"Visitations aren't routine. Our cells are just places to hold folks for a short period until they go home on bail or are sent to a larger facility. He has been asking to see you so I suppose I could give you a few minutes to talk to him when you drop off the clothes. Have the officer at the front desk page me when you stop by. I expect to be here until two."

By ten, the children were up, dressed, and arguing over who was cheating at cards, while Jan's phone hardly stopped ringing. In a way, she was glad to learn she still had friends. Diane called, and so did Rana. She also received a call from Jeff's boss, who heard the news and informed her Jeff was officially fired from his position.

Finally, Jan shut off the power on her cell phone and stuffed the kitchen cordless in the dishtowel drawer. It preyed on her that she had yet to deal with her folks. *Later, not now*.

Jan bundled the children in warm clothes and boots and sent them out to play in the yard with Diane's girls. To calm her nerves, she began making an experimental recipe for caramel nut brownies.

Jan had barely put the ingredients in the mixing bowl when Mae hammered at the back door to come inside. Billy was with her. Their cheeks and noses were red from the cold, but Mae's mouth was tight, and it was obvious Billy had been crying.

"Mom, Kelly and Tara said Daddy is a jailbird. What's a jailbird?" Mae demanded.

Diane's girls had likely heard the talk. Everyone in the neighborhood would have seen the morning paper by now, or maybe Jeff's arrest had been on the radio. It was a front-page headline. She hadn't figured on everyone in town knowing about Jeff—bakery customers, the children's teachers, and other parents. Her children would *not* be shunned because of Jeff.

"Just what it sounds like, a person who has been put in jail."

Wiping the tears from Billy's eyes, Jan unbuttoned his coat and laid it over a kitchen chair. Mae kicked off her boots.

"My dears." She knelt to face them. "When Daddy was arrested by the police yesterday, they took him to the station and are holding him there. I'll be going to see him after lunch, and then I'll be able to tell you how he's doing."

"We want to see Daddy," Mae whined. "Can we come, Mom? We'll be good."

They missed their dad already. As difficult as it had been here, the house held a hollow expectation.

"I can't take you along. You won't be allowed in to see him. Like when Grandpa was in the hospital that time he had an operation, you had to stay with Grandma in the waiting room when I visited him. Besides, the detective who was here yesterday is only letting me in as a favor."

Billy's face scrunched up as if he were about to wail, and Mae's lower lip trembled. Jan lifted her chin. "I'll see if you can stay with Diane or Rana. Won't that be fun?"

Both nodded solemnly, seeming to agree, until later, when Jan prodded them to start toward Diane's so she could leave.

"Mom," Mae said defiantly, with Billy standing behind her, "we are going with you. You *need* us."

Stink. Her children inherited her stubbornness. They must be frightened, yet they were willing to overcome their fears to keep her company while she saw their father. Their eyes held sorrow and sensitivity.

Jan's eyes watered, and a warm tear dripped down her cheek. "I'm sorry, but…"

"We can wait in the car. You're scared too, Mom." Mae hugged her.

Jan enfolded Billy in their hug and then held her children away so she could face them. "This is the deal. If I take you with me, you'll have to wait in the lobby."

Maybe it was wrong to expose Billy and Mae to a dreary jail environment, but wasn't it better for them to face the reality and to learn doing something bad has consequences? Besides, jail is only a building, and they won't see their father behind bars. Knowing their father is safe and warm and being taken care of will comfort them.

With the children in tow, Jan parked her car in a visitor spot in the side lot of the Greenberg Police Department. With its cozy red brick facing and its sprawling lawn, the building was less than intimidating.

"Remember, now, this is a place of business, like the library. I'm counting on you two to behave."

Inside the front door, they climbed a staircase into a vacant waiting room—a hallway really, with several doors and an elevator, all sealed shut with coded locks. The area was no larger than their dining room at home with pale green walls and two plastic chairs that looked as if they belonged in a school cafeteria. Certainly, it had been a mistake to give in to the children's demand to come along.

A uniformed, stout woman with a butch haircut monitored a switchboard behind a metal grid. She didn't look up when they entered.

Jan approached, cleared her throat, and spoke. "We're here to see Detective Hoskins."

"Do you have an appointment?"

"He's expecting me."

Her eyebrows went up. "You brought children?"

"If it's all right, they'll wait for me out here."

She waved her hand in the air. "I can't be responsible for them."

"I'll make sure my brother behaves, ma'am," Mae said, sounding more grown up than her nine years.

"I shouldn't be too long, and I certainly can't leave them in the car."

"Very well then." The woman put the handset to her ear and spoke into the mouthpiece, paging the detective.

While waiting for a response, Jan settled in on one of the chairs and took Billy on her lap. Mae squeezed in close on the second chair.

A few minutes later, one of the doors opened, and Detective Hoskins appeared. He'd shucked his jacket, removed his tie, and had opened the collar of his white dress shirt and rolled up its sleeves.

Setting Billy down, Jan stood with Mae beside her.

"Mrs. Simmons, sorry to keep you waiting. Well" —his gray eyes twinkled as he stooped to the children's level—"I see you came to help Mom."

"She needs us," Mae offered.

"I'm sure you're a great help. You're Mae and you"—he gently poked at Billy's stomach, making him giggle—"are…"

"Billy. I'm Billy. And this is Bob." He held up his stuffed toy in front of him.

"Hello, Bob." The detective picked up Bob's arm and shook its floppy hand. "Pleased to meet you."

"Detective," Jan said, "Mae and Billy insisted on

coming with me, so I'm sorry for the inconvenience. Is there somewhere more pleasant where they can wait?"

Detective Hoskins merely smiled, and when he did, his right eyebrow dipped, making him appear younger than she had first thought. "Come on in, all of you." He punched a code in a door, opened it, and then waved them inside.

Jan and the children followed him to his office, a cubicle, really, with a gray metal desk holding a laptop and stacked with manila folders.

"Sit down, Mrs. Simmons." He indicated the matching metal chair beside his desk and then poked his head around the nearest cubicle.

"Emma, take a break from whatever you're doing and meet Mae and Billy. I have a feeling they would enjoy a snack and something to drink from the vending machine. Would you mind taking care of that for me?"

An officer with cropped blonde hair and a broad smile appeared. "Sure thing, boss. Come on kids, what'll it be? Candy or chips? We've got all kinds of soda, too."

"I'd like a cup of coffee, please," Mae said in her new grown up voice.

Emma looked at Jan for approval.

"She can have decaf."

Once the children were off, Detective Hoskins sat behind his desk and tented his hands. "Mrs. Simmons, I apologize again for frightening you and your children yesterday. You understand we didn't know what sort of situation we'd find inside the house. We needed to be thorough, to protect ourselves. Policemen have families too, you know."

The tightness in Jan's shoulders eased a bit. He had

children; that explained his kindness toward Billy and Mae.

"This is how it went down," he continued. "A high school boy who was caught smoking marijuana confessed he and several of his friends were buying it from a fellow student. The rest was simple. We put a tail on the young man he identified and caught him in the act. When we took him in for questioning, he named your husband as his supplier and provided us whatever information he had about the process. Based on that, we were able to obtain a search warrant, but until yesterday, when we found the stash of marijuana in your husband's car, we had no physical proof."

"I had no idea all this was going on, Detective, or I would have certainly done something about it. Jeff's never done anything illegal before, not that I know of, anyway, so I never dreamed he'd gotten into drugs. My husband and I…well, we haven't been on the best of terms for a long time."

Detective Hoskins raised his eyebrows, causing a few lines to appear on his forehead. "Unfortunately, that sort of thing happens to nice people like you all the time. A guy isn't making enough to support his family, so he looks to other opportunities. The FBI has been trying for years to bust a drug cartel operating out of Hartford. They sell small amounts via local networks— maybe a few pounds of marijuana or cocaine at a time. These operators latch onto people like your husband who want to make quick money."

Drug cartel! Wasn't that Mafia stuff? How on earth had Jeff become involved with such low life? "But where would Jeff get the money to buy it? We are barely making ends meet at home."

"Your husband would've only needed a cash outlay for the first buy. He may have even purchased it on credit. Once he sold the drugs at a profit, it would have been easy to set up a regular schedule to buy more."

Detective Hoskins paused, giving Jan time to digest the information, but it was too much to absorb at once. Why, of all things, had Jeff chosen to be involved in something as serious as drug trafficking, especially since he knew how she would feel about it? If they were that desperate for money, they could have taken out a loan against the house, or even asked for help from her parents.

Although, she knew only too well that Jeff would have been too proud to let anyone, even his wife, know he needed or wanted money that badly. Why, since he turned over their household finances to her, he hadn't spoken about it—as if her being in charge of something so vital were an embarrassment.

"Your husband is small potatoes, Mrs. Simmons," the detective continued. "But he can lead us to the big guys. While smoking marijuana isn't habit forming, kids like the thrill they get from it and are tempted to go on to try addictive substances, like heroin and coke. We can't protect every kid from getting hooked on drugs, but we can try to save the ones in our district."

"If Jeff cooperates and names his source, will you go easy on him?"

"We can't be sure what's going to happen until all the facts are in." Detective Hoskins stood. "If you leave that duffle for your husband, we'll get it to him as soon as we've checked thru it."

"Nothing but clothes and toiletries."

"Razor blades?"

"I see your point. Thank you, then."

As if on cue, Emma returned with the children, who were happily munching on Cheetos and candy bars.

"Emma can take you to the visiting area," he told her, "and I'll take these energetic youngsters out on the side yard to see if they can beat me at a game of horseshoes. Emma will wait for you while you speak with your husband and then show you where to find us when you're through."

"I don't know how to play horseshoes," Billy said.

"It's like tossing beanbags." Mae shot a how-dumb-can-you-be look at her brother.

The detective laid a hand on the back of Billy's neck. "Let's go, then. Come on, Mae. I'll bet you can't beat me. I hold the championship here."

"Well, I beat my friend Kelly at beanbags, so maybe I'll beat you, too." Mae held up her fist and grinned.

The children seemed to trust Detective Hoskins enough to go with him, despite the fright they had when he'd entered their home gunning for their father. Jan watched the three of them leave, one tall dark-haired man with her two babies trotting along beside him. When had she last seen her children smile?

"Are you ready to visit with your husband, Mrs. Simmons?"

Jan took a deep breath, unsure of how she'd find Jeff. Would he be blustering and angry about having been caught or pull his poor-me shtick?

"As ready as I'll ever be."

She followed Emma down several corridors, all painted the same sickly green. Maybe the paint was on sale. Each door they passed through needed to be unlocked with a code, even the elevator to the lower floor. Unlike the top floor, the cinderblock walls were a sunshiny yellow, a color that seemed to masquerade happiness. Yet, the stone was impenetrable. She sniffed the air. That disinfectant smell. Familiar. The same Klean Kare product she used to clean the bathrooms at home. This facility must be one of Jeff's accounts. How ironic.

"The visiting area's through here." Emma punched in a code to allow Jan inside a barren room with a wooden table and two chairs. "I have to stay in the room, so just pretend I'm not here." She remained at the door.

Wearing his street clothes and reeking of body odor, Jeff was escorted in by a prison guard. Maybe it was a good sign that he hadn't been issued prison garb. His wrinkled dress shirt hung outside his slacks and was unbuttoned halfway down, exposing his T-shirt. He had an all-over shaky appearance. Sweat poured off him, darkening his amber hair, and separating it into spiky strings. A hot shower and deodorant would help.

He looked so pathetic that Jan couldn't stop herself from touching the rough day old stubble on his face. "Why, Jeff? Why did you do it? We would have made it without you breaking the law."

"I'm sorry." He wouldn't look her in the eye. "I don't know what got into me. It seemed like a big shot thing to do, to be making all that money. To have money in my pocket I didn't have to share. Not with you, not with anyone, but I guess that was wrong."

Jan's body went stiff. "You guess? What you did was illegal and harmed schoolchildren. Your selfishness brought men and guns into our home yesterday and scared us all half to death. How could you, Jeff? You knew Will overdosed on drugs when he was only fifteen. It was someone like you who got him started."

She caught her breath, wanting to beat on Jeff's chest, only holding back because the guard watched with concern. "Doesn't that bother you, Jeff? You're a father. What if someone gave drugs to *our* children? How would you feel about the person who did this?"

Jan stopped short and gulped back the rage. "Forget it. All you ever think about is yourself, your needs. I'm through with you. I've filed for a divorce. Did you get my message?"

"No, my cell phone battery kicked out on me." Jeff blew out a breath. "Whew, you move fast."

"I hired a lawyer last week, before all this, and I'm glad I did."

Jeff's foot moved in tiny circles, making scraping sounds on the cement floor.

"I've been a real creep."

"Yes. You. Have.

"I'd like nothing more than to forget you ever existed, but as Billy and Mae still care about you, I feel a certain responsibility. I'll be at your hearing once it's scheduled; but unless you have a stash of money somewhere to hire a fancy criminal lawyer, I'm afraid you'll have to rely on a court-appointed attorney."

Jeff spread his hands. "If that little son-of-a-whore hadn't blabbed to the police, I wouldn't be here, and I would have netted a bundle. How much is left of our savings, Madame Treasurer—or have you spent it all on stupid stuff?"

"So this is who you really are. All those years I fooled myself into believing you loved our children and me and were doing your best. If I have any say about it, you'll never be left alone with Billy and Mae again." Jan jammed her thumb against her chest. "They're *my* children now."

Whirling away from him, she strode to the door. "Emma. I'm done here."

Chapter Twenty-Two

Frank paced the house, holding baby Frank against his chest, patting the kid's back, and jiggling him the way Lucille had taught him.

"Come on, kid, calm down."

Niente. The kid wouldn't stop screaming. He'd plugged the nipple in the kid's mouth and watched him glug down a full six ounces as if it were manna from heaven, changed a disgusting shitty diaper, and still, he screamed like murder.

His gaze went to the clock over the door. Christ the stinking little black hand didn't want to move. An hour Tina and Lucille had been gone, and it seemed like days. He peered out the front window, watching for Lucille's baby blue SUV. Hell, they were only going to the supermarket. How long could that take?

The screaming stopped, thank the Lord, and then baby Frank let out a macho belch. Right on his shoulder. Shit, his silk shirt, wet with drool or something worse. Whatever it was didn't smell too good. He hoped to hell the dry cleaners could do something. The fucking shirt cost two-hundred clams.

He held the boy away from him. "What did you just do to *Nonno* you little dickens?"

Frankie squirmed between his hands and smiled and cooed.

"That's better, all better now. How about a little

nap? *Nonno* needs one too."

As if the kid understood him, his lower lip stuck out in a pout and then his face reddened, and he let out a wail.

"Oh, look," he held baby Frank up to the window, "*Nonna* and *Mamma* are home." Thank God.

The back door opened, and the two women bustled in carrying bunches of lumpy plastic bags. Since Vinnie and family moved in, they'd gone through food like truck drivers.

Tina spotted him standing in the doorway. "Oh, Frankie, I missed you, you adorable thing."

Frank smiled and moved toward her.

"Come to *Nonna,* sweetie. You're such a good boy. Yes, you are." She smiled at the kid and then cuddled him against her breasts.

Like she used to do with him.

He sighed, almost feeling the soft skin of Tina's plump breast against his cheek. The past week had been hell. All Tina thought about was the baby. The baby needs this, the baby needs that. He's hungry, poor thing. Aw, look how sleepy he is.

Well, what about him, Frank, her beloved husband? The one who painted her toenails, gave her massages—all over—and made her scream with ecstasy, had she forgotten about that?

Bah. "I'm gonna take a nap," Frank said turning away.

"Not so fast, Grandpa. Here." Tina handed him the baby. "Put him in his crib for a nap while I get these things unpacked."

"Lucille, you help your mother."

"Can't, Pop. I've got to meet Vinnie. We got a date

with a realtor, and guess what?" She smiled that smile that always zinged to his heart. No matter how grown up she got, she'd always be his little girl.

"What, baby?"

"One of the listings is that blue colonial on the corner of Pleasant and Charming. Wouldn't it be great to be neighbors?"

Frank kissed his daughter's cheek. "I hope it works out. It's nice having you around." *Except I miss my privacy and my wife.*

Once Lucille left, Frank put the baby in his crib and gave the musical mobile over the kid's head a spin. That thing went around, jingling so fast that the kid would either fall asleep or get dizzy watching it.

He pressed a hand into the small of his aching back and then flopped on the bed. It was soft, and the comforter curled around him. All he needed now was his Tina massaging his back and cooing sweet words into his ear, and he'd be a happy man. But that wasn't going to happen. From the kitchen, cabinet doors slammed shut, and drawers opened.

And baby Frank was fussing again.

He'd pretend he was asleep, and Tina would handle it, he thought, shutting his eyes and rolling onto his side, away from the door.

Bzzz. Bzzz.

Frank bolted to sitting. "Fuck. What's that noise?" Damn cell phone in his pocket. He should let it ring and call them back later.

Bzzz. Bzzz.

Oh hell. He dug the phone out of his pocket and scanned his finger over its face to take the call. Louie never called unless there was a problem.

"Yeah? What the fuck do ya want?"

"Boss. We took a hit."

"A hit? Who? Where?"

"Car explosion." Louie hesitated. "It's Vinnie. I couldn't get close enough to see his condition, but the ambulance took him away on a stretcher. Lots of blood."

Frank held the phone away from his ear. *I didn't hear that.*

"Louie. You're joking, right? And if you are I'm gonna kill you. I mean it."

"No joke, boss. It's true. Downtown Hartford by the hospital. Jeez, I just saw him, too. We were having lunch at Pastrami's, and he left to meet his wife. Stepped in his car, fired the engine, and *boom*. He went flying from the car, landed on top of the awning of the hardware store, then rolled off onto some old guy walking along the sidewalk."

"And you're fine?"

"I was inside the restaurant finishing up my meal. I saw it all through the window. Cracked the glass in front of my eyes. Yeah. I'm okay."

The phone dropped from Frank's hand.

"Tina," he yelled.

Baby Frank began squalling again. He didn't blame the kid.

Tina raced into the room and picked up the baby. "What's the matter with you? You woke him up."

"Tina"—he patted the bed—"sit. I gotta tell—"

"Oh no, what happened. Frank, you're white as a ghost. It's bad. Who?"

"Our son-in-law." His eyes closed, and his chest tightened like a screwdriver. Shit happens in this

194

business, he knew that. People died. People who deserved to die. Not people like Vinnie who were indestructible. "Car explosion."

"Is he…"

"Don't know. An ambulance took him away, though, so maybe he made it."

Tina collapsed in a heap against his chest, with baby Frank squashed between them. He wrapped his arms around his wife and held her close. "Where was Lucille going?"

"Let me think. The houses they were supposed to see are offered by Brownstone Realty."

"Main Street. I know the place. I'll go find her, and we'll go see what's going on with Vinnie."

Madonna mia. This has to end. Frank backed out of the garage and raced up the street, not caring if he got nailed for speeding. Lucille would be a mess when she heard. He had to calm down so he could be strong for her.

He slammed his fist down on the steering wheel. *Somebody's gonna die for this.*

Chapter Twenty-Three

Mae and Billy wanted to know the details about her session with their father, so Jan painted the rosiest picture she could without lying. They all needed a cooling off period, so she swung into the parking lot behind the Sweet Shop. The cleaning company had done a bang-up job of ridding the place of grime and odor, and Loreen had reopened the shop at some point while she had dealt with Jeff's arrest.

"Where we going, Mom?" Mae asked from the back seat of the car.

"To get something yummy to eat."

The back door to the shop opened into the kitchen, where Loreen's matronly figure bent over the counter transferring warm cookies to a display tray. Her hands and arms moved mechanically from the repetitious chore.

"Mmm. It smells so good in here," Mae said.

Billy rubbed his tummy.

Loreen turned to Jan, her raised eyebrows creating furrows in her pale skin. Flecks of confectioner's sugar lay like snowflakes on her wiry, silver hair. "Oh, hi, I didn't expect you to come in today." Her gloved hands dropped to the side. "I heard."

Her words hung in the air, waiting for an explanation of some sort.

Does she think I was involved in Jeff's mess? That

my cookies were selling because I laced them with…oh, no. She wouldn't. I wouldn't.

Her hand went up in front of her. "I swear, Loreen. I never knew about this."

"Daddy was bad, Miss Loreen," Billy said. "Mommy's good."

"Of course she is." Loreen's stance relaxed, causing her face to soften to the sweet, caring woman Jan knew. Snatching two cookies from the tray she'd prepared, she looked at Jan. "These aren't gluten-free. Is it all right for the children?

Jan nodded, her face hot and eyes filling. "Oh, Loreen. It was so horrible. We just came from the police department."

Billy and Mae looked up, listening, cookies poised in their hands.

Jan sniffed back a sob. "I need to bake. To do something useful."

"Good." She handed her a chef's apron. "We are sold out of your brownies right now. Let's see"—she put a finger to her forehead—"I also could use cranberry scones and more sugar cookies. Those go fast."

"Can we help?" Mae asked. "I help my mom cook at home all the time."

Loreen ruffled Billy's hair and smiled at Mae. "Of course, just be careful around the ovens and don't eat all the cookies."

Jan breathed in and out, allowing the tension in her neck to ease, then set to work mixing the grains and flours needed.

The afternoon passed quickly.

When they returned home to the scene of

yesterday's horror, Jeff's car was missing from the garage. The police impounded it, but his things remained stacked to the side, where she had left them. When she went into the house, the lingering smells of Jeff's presence tainted the air. The house would need a thorough going through to get rid of the scent of his aftershave, the dirty glasses left in his man cave and office, and the extra bedding in the family room, where he had been sleeping since she had ousted him from the bedroom.

The children must have felt it too—the loss, the emptiness. Jan knew she should be happy he was gone, but she didn't feel proud of herself. She allowed him to continue being a spoiled individual instead of forcing him to man up to life. She had always given, and he had taken. Now, he's taken everything she ever wanted. Her needs were simple—a happy home.

And she darn well was going to have it.

She'd hidden from the reality of the world long enough.

Slipping her cell phone from her pocket, she powered it up. Before making the call to her parents, she settled Billy and Mae in front of the TV watching a new DVD they'd picked out on the way home. With the children out of earshot, Jan dialed the New Jersey area code, hesitated, then punched in the remaining numbers.

As always, her parents were at home.

"Something's wrong, Jan," her mother said. "I can tell from your voice."

"Everything's wrong." Jan steadied the tremble in her voice. Telling the truth about her situation was harder than she thought it would be. "Jeff was arrested yesterday. He's in jail right now."

"Oh, no! There must be some mistake. What is he supposed to have done?"

Her jaw went tight. As usual, her mother was ready to deny whatever she was going to tell her. Jeff never did anything wrong, as far as her folks were concerned.

"Selling marijuana to high school kids, using Amy's son as a go-between," she blurted, without the usual sugar coating. Jan regretted the bluntness of her words as soon as they were out of her mouth. She didn't want her parents to hurt as much as she was hurting. Jeff's actions would stab at their hearts twice as hard because of Will.

Dead silence.

"Mom? Are you still there?"

"I don't believe it. How could he do such a horrible thing?" Her voice was thin and wobbly. "Your dad and I will be up first thing in the morning."

Oh, stink. "It's all right. You don't need to come up. There's nothing you can do right now."

"Don't be ridiculous," she said indignantly. "We're your parents. You need us with you. Pack your things. You and the children are coming back to Hillsdale with us for a while."

"No, Mom. Jeff's arraignment is Monday, and I have a job."

"Then we'll take the children home with us. They don't need to be exposed to all of that."

She was right, except it was too late to protect Billy and Mae. Jan didn't have the energy to argue with her. When it was time, she would stand her ground. "We'll talk about that when you get here, Ma."

****

Just before noon on Sunday, Rana knocked on the back door, her cheeks flushed from the cold, and a jaunty wool cap pulled over her ears. Her gloved hands held up a bundle wrapped in a towel. "I know your folks are coming up, so I made you Shepherd's pie. It's still hot. Just came out of the oven."

"How kind of you. It's my dad's favorite. What a relief not to have to worry about what to serve for dinner tonight." Taking the dish, Jan set it on the stove. "Come on in. I'll make coffee."

"Love to, but I can't stay." Rana looked her up and down. "You look like crap."

"Thanks, I needed to hear that." Jan ran a hand through the tangles in her hair. "Guess I'd better spiff up before the parents arrive."

Rana drew her into a hug. "You've got to be going through hell right now."

"Jeff's bail hearing is Monday, and then we'll go from there. The odd thing is that I didn't expect it to be lonely here without him. Last night I found myself listening for the garage door to open and his car to drive in. Isn't that weird?"

"Did you know?"

Jan shook her head. "I'm such a dummy."

"Love is blind. It's true, you know. We see what we want to; believe what we want to. I know you have your own problems, but I just found out those stomach cramps Dad's been complaining about are caused by cancer. He's known for a while but didn't tell any of us." Rana's eyes filled. "I've got to go. I'm taking him to the doctor this morning."

"I'm so sorry. Makes you feel betrayed, doesn't it?"

"Yeah. He kept telling me he was constipated. Colon cancer. If he and Mom hadn't moved in with us, I still might not know."

"All this and you're worried about me? You even brought me dinner? I know you have your hands full, and so do I, but I miss our talks. Let's squeeze out an hour next week for coffee."

"I miss you too, friend. You know what they say; a friend in need is a friend indeed. My mother's a mess about this. She knew, but Dad wouldn't let her tell anyone. What if they hadn't moved here? What if they were still in Maine? I might've never known until—"

Jan grabbed her by the shoulders and held her gaze. "Don't think about that. They're with you now. You're helping them through this. And Rana, I will help you however I can."

"Thanks, I need all the support I can get. Good luck with the folks."

How lucky I am to have such caring friends, she thought as Rana turned to leave. Earlier, she'd had a wonderful conversation with Diane, who encouraged her to stand tough. And yesterday afternoon, Tina DiGiorno brought them a huge pot of chicken soup.

As the back door closed after Rana, Mae burst into the kitchen. Her face glowed as if she'd just opened a gift.

"Mom. They're here."

With a pang of resignation, Jan plodded to the foyer. Dealing with her parents wouldn't be pleasant. She flung open the door, just as her mom and dad were getting out of their white sedan, the biggest model they could find. Dad wasn't the best of drivers, so it was comforting to know that tank of a car might protect them. They looked tired, older than they had at Christmas.

Her mother looked up and spotted her. "Janice." She moved toward her, arms wide apart.

Despite the cold, Jan ran down the porch steps in her slippered feet and fell into her mother's arms. "Oh, Mom. It's been awful." She sobbed into her mom's shoulder, the rough wool of her good coat dampening under her cheek. "I didn't want to tell you because there was nothing you could do to help. I wanted you to think everything was fine." Jan's words came out in huge gulps.

"There, there, honey." Her father's hand was warm on Jan's back, his familiar scent of spice and cigars zinged to her heart. He couldn't protect her from what was going on, but having him here sure helped.

Sniffing, Jan pulled back. "Come on. Let's go inside, it's freezing out here." With her arms cradled around their shoulders, they made their way up the steps where the children waited to be hugged.

"You didn't bring in our luggage from the car." Her mother gave her father the same stern look she gave Jan whenever she failed to complete a task.

"It'll keep," her dad said, helping his wife off with her coat.

"I hope we don't have to sleep on that awful pull out couch. Last time, my back ached for months afterward." Jan's mother straightened the hem of the silky flowered blouse she wore over her slacks.

"I'm putting you and Dad in my room. You'll have a private bath and everything."

Her mother's eyebrows went up. "That's right, Jeff isn't here now. It's odd not to have him greeting us at the door. What ever happened to that poor man?"

Not ready to get into things while standing in the hall, Jan ignored her comment. "Are you hungry? I have chicken salad."

"Oh, no. We stopped and ate on the way up. We didn't want to be a bother."

"Coffee then." Jan turned. "We can sit in the kitchen."

"I could use a shot of something stronger," her dad said.

"Sorry, my house is now an alcohol-free zone."

"I see. Well, coffee then. Mmm. You've been baking again. It smells good in here."

"Calories you don't need, Bill." Jan's mother pulled out a chair and sat, taking Billy onto her lap. Mae scooted in next to her grandfather.

Jan hadn't planned for the children to be part of this conversation, yet she didn't have the heart to send them off to their rooms when their grandparents had barely arrived. She kept her explanations simple, omitting Jeff's affair with Candy for the sake of the children—they didn't know, and now the situation was moot.

Jan's parents sat stone-faced across from her until she finished.

Finally, her mother spoke. "How could you have let this happen, Janice? You mean to tell me Jeff did all this right under your nose?" She hugged Billy closer. "You poor child."

"Now, now, Mona. Don't be so hard on her." Jan's father shook his head. "I can't believe Jeff would do such awful things. He sure had me fooled."

Jan caught Mae staring at her with a confused look

203

on her little face. Up to now, Mae had been her ally. How would seeing her mother through her grandmother's critical eyes change things between them? Clearly, she'd dropped off her pedestal as a good mother.

Jan's head fell in her hands. "You're right, Mom. I've been chastising myself about all the should-have-dones, should-have-knowns, and should-have-guessed. But all that doesn't matter now, does it?" She looked her mother square in the eye. "This is my family. Billy and Mae. We are going to get through this."

In a show of solidarity, Mae came over and put her arms around her and Billy, who had crawled off his grandmother's lap at her first critical words to settle on Jan's lap.

"I've taken off my rose-colored glasses, as you both need to do, and faced reality. I'm a single mother with two wonderful children. Together, we are going to have the normal happy life we deserve."

"Without a man?" Her mother said, eyebrows raised.

"I don't need a man. Not now, not ever, maybe. I am through being controlled, put down, and made to feel like nothing. I've learned from this, Mom, Dad. I am a capable woman and a good mother. I will do whatever needs to be done to make things right."

"Pah. All talk you are." Jan's mother glanced around the kitchen. "You'll have to sell this house, get a small apartment. Something you can afford. Jeff won't be supporting you anymore. Dad and I have room. You can move in with us until you get back on your feet. Wouldn't you and Billy like to come live at Grandma's?" she said to Mae.

Blessedly, the children didn't reply. They snuggled closer to Jan. They loved their grandmother, but at times had been the brunt of her sharp tongue. A visit was fine, but 24/7 wouldn't work.

Jan bit the inside of her cheek, tasting blood. With the children listening, she wasn't going to get into this with her parents. They didn't know about Jeff's earlier job loss, because she had covered it up, and she saw no reason to tell them now. They'd managed because she had made it so by clipping coupons, shopping sales, and making do whenever she could, all the while with Jeff spending dirty money on himself.

Who's the jerk now?

Why hadn't she seen it, pushed him about the source of extra money?

Spilled milk.

"It's not going to be easy," Jan responded, "but I'm used to managing our money. Between our savings account," *the one she had recently drained and put in her name*, "and my bakery business, we'll do all right."

"But what about Jeff? You can't just forget about him and leave him stuck in jail."

"His arraignment is scheduled tomorrow to give his attorney time to review his case, and then we'll see." Jan omitted the fact that Jeff had to use a court-appointed lawyer because she wouldn't spend money on a criminal lawyer. Her parents would want to foot the bill, and she didn't want them dipping into what little retirement money they had socked away for the likes of Jeff.

"I don't know what the bail is going to be, but unless he's got money stashed away somewhere, he'll have to stew in lock up until his case is heard."

"It's a shame about that boy." Her father ran a hand over the few hairs barely covering his head. "He seemed like such a good guy. How did he go wrong?"

"I wish I knew. There's a side of Jeff none of us knew because he hid it from us." *And I hid it from you all these years.*

"So you'll live here in this house for a while then?" Jan's mother's haughty demeanor eased, her shoulders dropped as if losing a battle. "But the children. They don't need to be exposed to all that court stuff about their father." She smiled. "Mae, Billy, wouldn't you like to come and stay with Grandma and Grandpa for a few weeks? We'll go shopping at the toy store and eat pizza, and we'll take you to the new aquarium. We'll have such fun."

"I'm staying with my mom." Mae snuggled closer.

"Me too." Billy wiggled off Jan's lap. "Can I go play with my trucks, Mommy?"

"It's a shame," her father said. "You're going through with the divorce, I gather."

"In progress."

"Yes. It's best. You're doing the right thing. I see it now, don't you, Mona?"

Her mother sniffed. "I suppose. You'll be excommunicated from the church, you know."

"Yes." Jan had heard this all before. "It doesn't mean God doesn't love me."

"You can get it annulled then the Catholic Church will take you back."

"Right. For money and a lie. Annulled, as if my marriage never happened? Give me a break."

Her mom inhaled and exhaled, clearly disgusted.

Jan let it slide. She was done falling for her

mother's guilt trips. If she wasn't happy with Jan's decisions about her family, her mother could go pound sand. Her parents had pooh-poohed her when she first confessed Jeff's drinking problems. She didn't need their advice now.

After warming up the Shepherd's pie and putting together a salad, they sat down to an early dinner. Hardly anyone spoke. Jan's mother picked at her food. Her dad took seconds. She looked across the table at their sullen faces. Jan accepted they were upset because she waited until things were bad before sharing the extent of her troubles with them, and even more so that Jan and the children would remain in Greenburg. Let them be.

Leaving her parents loading the dishwasher and storing the leftovers from dinner, Jan bathed the children and put them in their nightclothes. It was nice having her parents here, even though they'd had some words, it was clear they cared.

Some time later, when the children were asleep, Jan settled in on the pullout couch Jeff had used to read before she went to sleep. A romance, something sweet and easy that would relax her.

Wails of anguish emanated from the children's bathroom.

She dropped her book and ran to find out what was going on. She knocked on the bathroom door. "Mom? Open up. It's me."

The knob turned from the inside, and her mother fell into her arms. "He's dead. Our Will is gone. It's my fault. I should have sent him to a private boarding school when I saw the low-life kids he was hanging around with. They did it to him. Got him involved with drugs. And now my son is gone forever."

Jan held her mother while she cried, realizing she was sobbing along with her. "How could you know what would happen? You did what you could. You sent him to detox. Will did it to himself."

"But he was so young, my baby boy. Now we've lost Jeff, too."

Pulling away, Jan gripped her mother's shoulders so she would face her. "You were kind to Jeff, but he was never your son."

"Don't you think your father and I know that? Jeff was homeless. We took him in because you cared about him. We did it for you."

And I married him to please you. How could she *not* marry him after they'd taken him in as a family member? They expected it of her. "But you gave him Will's room."

"Where else could we have put him? Certainly not in your room. Why, you two weren't even engaged yet." Her mother cupped her chin, her nose red and eyes streaming with tears. "I'm so proud of you, my perfect girl."

Jan knew she was far from perfect, but she didn't correct her mother.

A large hand rested on Jan's shoulder. "Me too, honey," her father said.

Jan made tea, and in the quiet of the evening, she and her parents sat at the kitchen table and talked as they never had before. They shared memories of Will, the good ones, and cried over his loss. She told them her plans for the future and found they were behind her one hundred percent.

For the first time since Will died, Jan was at peace

with her emotions and actually slept through the night.

The next morning, Jan's parents drove off after one last attempt at taking Billy and Mae with them to Hillsdale. She promised to drive to Jersey with the children the following weekend.

Shortly afterward, Jan was wiping the counters and clearing the remains of the hearty breakfast of bacon and eggs she had served when she noticed a pale blue square of paper with writing on it poking out from underneath the toaster. Pulling it out, she drew in a breath—a check from her father for five thousand dollars.

Her parents lived well, but frugally. Her mother taught school, and her father worked in retail. Between them, they managed fine. For them, this represented a lot of money. On one hand, she could use the boost; on the other, no way could she accept it.

Chapter Twenty-Four

That night, Jan had energy to burn. Her nerves were on edge, and she couldn't seem to settle down. She'd paced through the entire house, checked the children, who slept like little lambs, and now considered the furniture arrangement in the family room.

Since she'd kicked Jeff out, Jan had enjoyed the comfort of his chair, positioned perfectly to view the TV. During the day, light coming through the window made it hard to see the screen, not to mention sitting in that spot brought memories she intended to forget.

I could fix that, she thought, surveying the room.

Jan didn't dare try to lift the weighty chair, so she pushed at it until she got it positioned on the adjacent wall, then dragged over the hassock and the end table.

"Whew." How odd to be sweating inside when it was twenty degrees outdoors. She turned down the thermostat, then flopped in the armchair, surprised at the lift she felt from making such a minor change.

Picking up the remote, Jan flipped on the TV, preset to a sports channel, and scrolled to catch a sitcom she couldn't watch when the children were around. Raunchy, but funny enough to make her laugh, to bring her out of her troubles and put her in a different world for a short time.

Leaning back, she sipped on her water, nearly

choking on it when the phone in Jeff's office rang.

She listened to it ring, and ring, and ring until the caller finally gave up. With the answering machine confiscated by the police, the caller had no way to leave a message. She didn't know who it could possibly be. Certainly not Candy or one of Jeff's co-workers, who surely must know he'd been fired. His drug dealer must know he was in jail.

Briing. Briing.

Jan sat upright in her chair. Now, she was annoyed. It was late for anyone to call.

Rising, she opened the door to Jeff's office. It still smelled of him. His chair was pushed back, but except for the presence of the hard-wired phone, the desk was bare, and the floor had been cleared of its clutter of boxes—thanks to the efficiency of the police, who confiscated Jeff's papers and electronics as potential evidence.

She stared at the phone. "You got me out of a comfortable chair, now ring, darn it."

Nothing.

"Okay, whoever you were. Maybe you've got the message. Jeff isn't here." Jan took the phone off the hook, flopped back into the cushy chair, put her feet up on the matching hassock, and raised the volume on the TV.

She'd just begun to relax again when the house phone rang. They had a cordless system, with extensions in the kitchen, master bedroom, and in the family room right next to Jeff's chair. Her chair now.

Jan didn't feel like talking to anyone, so she let the call go to the house answering machine in the kitchen. While she would have to get up to hear the actual words, she could tell if someone left a message.

She cocked her ears. Nothing. Likely, a marketing call.

Briing. Briing.

Persistent jerk.

Jan grabbed the phone on the first ring and pressed "Answer."

"Stop calling. Take me off your call list or I'll report you to the FCC."

At first, she heard a wheezing sound, and then a raspy voice. "Tell him he owes us ten grand."

"Who *is* this? How did you get this number?"

The phone went dead.

Tell him he owes us ten grand? Jan's hand went to her face. Of course. For the stash the police confiscated. She'd bet Jeff was supposed to deliver it, get paid, and share his cut with this character. Who were these people, and how far would they go to get their money?

Wrapping her arms around her body, she tried to shake off the cold fear that she and the children could be in danger. How had that sinister sounding man gotten their home number? Did he know where they lived? She shut her eyes briefly.

Would she ever be rid of the fear?

Jan had to do something, but she wasn't sure what. She ran to the living room and grabbed Detective Hoskins's card from the end table. As she turned, she caught the glint of headlights in her peripheral vision. It was past ten when few cars had reason to come down their street.

Jan edged over to the window, staying to the side where the drapery would hide her, and peered out. She sucked in a breath. A dark sedan had parked on the street in front of their house. If it hadn't been for the outdoor lights she'd left blazing, the car might've blended into the night. How odd. The car's headlights were off, yet a tiny glow from the interior indicated the vehicle was occupied.

As she stood watching, the car sped away. Once it cleared her driveway, the headlights clicked on leaving behind a dark shadow. She might've thought nothing of it if she hadn't received a threatening call moments before the car appeared.

Shuddering, Jan checked the locks on all the doors and windows and then picked up the phone to call 911.

What did she have to report except that a car parked in front of her house and then left? It could have been a group of teens fooling around or someone who'd made a wrong turn and was resetting a GPS.

Still, Jan couldn't shake the feeling the call and the car were somehow connected and that her family was in danger.

Taking the card from her pocket, she noted it listed Detective Hoskins's home number, as well as his office at the police station. At this hour, she couldn't disturb him at home, but at least she could alert him to the situation. He would understand her fears weren't groundless. Punching out the department number, she left word for him to call her when he came in in the morning.

Although emotionally and physically exhausted, Jan was afraid to turn off the lights and go to bed. The house echoed with silence. She strained to listen for odd sounds—a door creaking, a grunt, the smash of a windowpane. All she knew was she didn't have the money they wanted.

But how could she be sure?

Jeff had told her nothing. At least he could have warned her. Didn't he care that his actions had put her and the children in jeopardy?

Leaving the porch lights and every lamp in the living room switched on, Jan made a sorry attempt at watching TV, a comedy. Yet, her fear overshadowed every funny line. When was all this going to end? She wiped at her eyes.

She wouldn't cry; she wouldn't.

With her elbow on the armrest and her fist held to her mouth, Jan stared at the moving figures on the TV in a funky haze.

She must have nodded off. When the phone had the gall to ring again, she wasn't sure how much time had passed.

Stink. What now? Jan snatched up the phone, squashing the temptation to let it go to the answering machine.

"Leave me alone, you thug—and while you're at it, you can go to—"

"Mrs. Simmons? Detective Hoskins here. You called tonight? What's the trouble?"

"Oh, Detective, I'm so sorry. I thought it was that awful man calling again. It's so late. I didn't expect to hear from you tonight."

"Yeah, I know. The job doesn't stop when I leave the office. I try to stay on top of open cases."

"I think Jeff's in danger; I got a threatening call, and then this car—"

"I'll be right over to interview you unless you'd rather I wait until morning."

"Now? You want to come here? Sure. Yes. Thank

you. I've been so frightened." Jan bit her tongue.

She wasn't sure why she cared, but entertaining a man in her nightgown would send the wrong message to the kind detective. After splashing water on her face and brushing her hair, she tossed on her jeans and a sweatshirt.

Within half an hour, Detective Hoskins arrived, appearing weary, but concerned.

"Would you like some coffee?" Jan offered. That was the least she could do. The poor man had gone out of his way to help her.

"That would sure be nice, Mrs. Simmons."

"My name is Jan."

Detective Hoskins nodded. "Andy. That's what my friends call me."

While the coffee perked, Andy called the station and asked to have Jan's house put on regular patrol. Meanwhile, Jan put a few pumpkin muffins, leftover from breakfast, on a plate and set it on the kitchen table, along with two mugs and a container of cream cheese.

"Milk and sugar?" She set the pair on the table.

"By all means," he said with a boyish grin. A past-five o'clock shadow covered his normally clean-shaven jaw, giving him a scruffy look.

Once he fixed his coffee—three sugars and enough milk to turn it a sickly tan, Andy began asking questions.

"Did you get the license plate of the car that drove away?

"Did you notice the color or make of the vehicle?

"Could you make out how many people were inside and if they were male or female?

"Was a man driving?"

"No, no, no, no, and no." Jan shook her head negatively, feeling like a doofus. Had she presence of mind, she could have grabbed the camera and used its zoom lens to take photos and at least have some sort of proof that she hadn't been delusional.

"Okay, then. What about the phone call? Can you recall anything distinctive about the voice?"

"Why, yes." Jan bolted upright in her chair. "How could I forget it? Male and scratchy."

"Anything else? Think."

"Hmmm." She pursed her lips. "There was this sound, like whoever it was had trouble breathing,"

Andy nodded. "Probably asthmatic."

"Do you know who it might be?"

"No, but every identifying feature helps us narrow down the suspects, Mrs. Simmons…Jan."

His cheeks flushed. Maybe he's not so tough.

"I'm going to put in a court order to have wiretaps placed on both your husband's office phone and your home phone, if that's agreeable to you," Andy said, all business. "If we can trace the call, we may be able to locate the kingpin behind this drug ring. We can get the taps in tomorrow afternoon. Will you be home?"

"I'm supposed to work, but if your men call my cell phone," she ticked off the number to him, "I'll run home to meet them."

"Sure, that'll work." Andy closed the notepad and took a sip of his coffee, which had to be cold, and eyed the muffins. "Those look homemade."

"Yes, I'm part owner of the Sweet Shop in town. I make all their gluten-free pastries."

Picking up a muffin, he broke it in half and then slathered it with cream cheese. His hands were big and

216

strong, making her king-size muffin appear small. His fingernails were bitten to the quick. She supposed tension came with his job. He took a bite. "Gluten free, huh? I'd never guess."

Jan sat straighter in her chair, trying to repress the pride she felt at carrying off the taste and texture of traditional food. As she looked across the table at this nice man, a sense of comfort made her relax her shoulders and smile. It sure felt good to know Andy was there for her, doing his darndest to keep their shrunken family safe.

Jan hid her feelings by taking a sip of her own coffee, which remained hot. She never could tolerate cold coffee—and couldn't figure out why anyone would add ice to it.

"Do you have a family?" she asked, to make conversation. Jan had to admit it felt awkward sitting across the table from this man and conversing as if they were an old married couple.

"I have a son, Oliver. I call him Ollie. He's about Billy's age. He lives with my mother because of my odd work schedule," Andy answered, brushing a hand through his dark chocolate curls. "I spend as much time with him as I can, but it's not the same as having him live with me. Oh, the woes of being a single parent."

"I guess I'm in the same boat, except I'm lucky to have my children with me. Do you find it hard to go home to an empty house at the end of a day?"

"It's not so bad. Nellie, she's my cat, greets me at the door, and follows me around like an old fishwife." The detective grinned, and small creases appeared at the corners of his gray eyes, which now sparkled like polished silver. "She eats dinner with me every night," he continued, "and then stretches across my lap, as if she were a tiny kitten, and goes to sleep. Fifteen pounds and she snores loud enough to drown out the TV."

"Really? How funny." Jan found she was smiling, relaxed. Forgetting for a few minutes was nice. "The children have been bugging us to get a cat, but Jeff's allergic to fur." She turned her hands, palms up.

Uh, oh. I'm getting a little too cozy with this man. I'd better back off. After all, he's the one who turned our house upside down, brought men and guns in here, and hauled Jeff off to jail.

Yet, just knowing the detective cared enough to come out late on a cold wintery night to check on them made him her hero of the moment.

He would be leaving shortly, leaving her to fight her fears. No, she couldn't think that way anymore. She depended on Jeff and look what happened. She needed to take full responsibility for their safety.

"I think I've told you everything I can remember, and it's been a long day." Jan yawned, even though she was fueled with caffeine.

"Yes, of course. Sorry to keep you up so late." He drained the last from his cup and set it in the sink. "Thanks for the pick-me-up."

"Here." She wrapped the remaining muffins in foil. "Take these."

"Really? Wow. Thanks. I'm not sharing with the troops, either." His face went serious. "We'll be keeping an eye on your home, and once the taps are installed, we'll be monitoring them. Call my cell at the slightest sign of trouble."

"Yes. Will do. And, Detective, I plan to be at Jeff's arraignment tomorrow."

"Good. I'll keep you informed of any changes in the court agenda."

"I'd appreciate it. Well, good night, then."

The moment Jan shut the door and heard Andy's cruiser drive off her shoulders dropped, bearing the full brunt of her responsibilities. There would be trouble about the missing drugs and the money owed. Knowing the police would be patrolling the road gave her a degree of comfort, but they wouldn't be here every minute of every day. She and the children needed to continue with the routine of their lives. With them in school and her at the bakery during the day, they'd be vulnerable. Staying tough through all this would be the hardest thing she'd ever done.

She started for her bedroom and realized she didn't dare leave the children unprotected. Grabbing a blanket and pillow, Jan bedded down on the floor between their beds, afraid to shut her eyes.

Chapter Twenty-Five

In the morning, Jan was pulling out of the garage with Mae and Billy in the backseat when her cell phone played the happy little tune she'd programmed in. Putting the car in Park, she delved into her purse to retrieve her phone and to check the caller ID.

Andrew Hoskins.

"Good morning, Detective."

"Jan, we've hit a snag here. Your husband tried to escape last night."

"Escape? Where is he?" Her voice rose an octave.

"Back in his cell being treated for minor injuries."

"Why? How?"

"Not sure. He didn't get very far. Our men went after him and found him in a heap on the sidewalk a couple of blocks down from our station. The officer in charge had been conked senseless, and Mr. Simmons's cell door was open. He's not talking about how he got out of a locked cell."

"So what happens now?"

"Well, it's a felony. An escape counts as a second offense against him. His arraignment will be moved to the next available date at the Superior Court. In the meantime, the officer in charge has him under close watch until we can get him into a more secure facility."

"What's going on with Daddy?" Mae asked, once Jan clicked off the call.

"He…uh, he won't be seeing the judge today. Nothing to concern you, sweetie."

"How can you say that, Mom? He's my father. It's your fault he's in jail. You didn't help him. You could've done something. He…he probably tried to escape so he could come home to see us."

Billy began to bawl. "I want to see Daddy. I want a wheelie."

Shaken by Mae's comments, Jan got out of the car and pulled open the back door on the side where her daughter sat, red-faced and sulking.

Stooping to Mae's level, Jan twirled her pigtail. "Come on, honey. I'm sorry. I should have been more thoughtful about your feelings."

Billy stopped crying to listen, sniffing back his tears.

"Here." Jan handed him a tissue. "Give that cute little nose a good honk."

"Of course you miss your daddy," Jan continued," but I can't bring him back to you right now. In fact, the police are so mad at him I doubt I can get in to see him for a while. Tell you what." She tipped up Mae's chin. "I will ask that nice detective if he will allow your father to call you so you can speak to him on the phone."

Mae's shoulders sagged and her face relaxed. "Really?"

"I can't promise, you understand, but I will ask. Now, let's get you guys off to school. Okay?"

Mae nodded. Billy looked confused.

Once Jan drove out from the shelter of the garage, they were subject to the full brunt of the weather. Pellets of rain or sleet, it was hard to tell which, covered her windshield. In the rearview mirror, Billy sucked his thumb and Mae's face remained stony. Surely, the word had spread about Jeff. Facing their friends at school would be hard for her children, but they had to do it sometime. Jan hurt for them, yet there was little she could do to protect them from the gossip.

At the bus stop, Jan parked behind Diane's car. From the back seat of Diane's car, Kelly and Tara exchanged waves with Mae. Over the long weekend, the girls had made peace with Jeff's situation. Knowing Mae would have her allies with her gave Jan a degree of comfort.

Seeing her, Diane turned off the engine and stepped out. Pulling the hood of her jacket over her head, she slipped into the passenger seat of Jan's car.

"Just checking. How's everything going?" Diane squeezed Jan's hand.

She cocked her head toward the back seat. "A bit of a blowup but hopefully it's settled."

"I get ya. With this cold weather, we've been disconnected. I've been getting so many orders my fingers are sore from beading. Look…callouses." She turned over her hands showing reddened fingertips. "But I'm selling, and that's good."

"It's great all your hard work is paying off."

Her gaze went to the backseat. "I know you don't want to say much now, but I'm home this afternoon. If you have time, come by and we'll have an old-fashioned coffee chat."

"I'd like that."

"Good. I'd love to show you some of the new stuff I've been working on. Oops. I hear the bus. Later, ya hear?"

Diana and Rana had been super, but Amy still wouldn't talk to her. Jan turned her cheek for a goodbye kiss from Mae before she slammed out of the back seat to catch up with Diane's girls.

Once the bus pulled away, Jan drove out of Charming Way onto Devil's Hill, the road ahead of her slick and shiny. Morning traffic was light on the one lane road.

As if out of nowhere, a car appeared close behind her. Driving conditions weren't the best, so she was traveling under the speed limit.

"What's your hurry, mister?" Jan muttered under her breath.

The high side of the mountain was to her left, while the steep low side was to the right. Many a car had jumped the restrictive fence and tumbled down the sharp incline. Jan traveled this skinny road so much that she had each switchback memorized and drove it by rote. She depressed the gas pedal, upping her speed to the limit hoping to put a little space between her car and the dark sedan tailgating her.

A glance in the rearview mirror revealed two men—one wearing a brimmed hat and the other bald and wearing sunglasses, despite the dark skies. The sleet beating at her back windshield blurred their faces.

"Back off," Jan shouted, smashing her palm against the horn and alarming Billy, who began to cry.

The sedan should have eased off at the blast, but it remained, riding Jan's bumper. It occurred to her the driver could have brake trouble, which meant the car was a runaway until it reached flat ground.

"Billy, you're clipped in, aren't you?" Jan's son had the propensity to pick at the harness.

"Uh, now I am, Mommy."

"Good boy."

Jan's thoughts flashed to the dark car that had parked in front of their house the past night. It would be silly to think the vehicle behind her was the same one. Black was a popular color. She scanned for a place to scoot over to allow the car past. She wanted it off her tail, whether it was a runaway or just an impatient driver.

Drat, this part of the road has no shoulder, and there's a nasty switchback coming up.

Tapping the brakes, Jan approached the curve. Her rear wheels screeched.

The car spun out and *crunch.*

The vibration shot her forward. Jan's chest strained against the seat belt.

Jamming the shift in Neutral, she let the car continue in idle while she caught her breath.

"No-o-o-o!"

Jan leaned on her horn at the black car coming at her from the side.

Pow!

The left front end of her car shimmied.

The sickening crush of metal sounded.

Something puffy exploded.

Jan's back went flat against the seat. Her hands flew from the steering wheel. "What the…"

Oh, God, that smell. Jan coughed and sniffed trying to get away from the acrid substance burning her throat and coating the inside of her nostrils. Her head spun in dizzy circles. She had to move. Do something. The faraway sound of a child's screams brought her to her senses.

"Billy! Are you okay?" To her clogged ears, her raspy voice seemed muted. Quickly, Jan put the gear in Park, shut off the engine, and then cracked open the car door to go to him.

My car's angled into the lane, have to move it.

Stink. Another car coming.

"Billy!"

Jan closed her door. Rigid with tension, she squeezed her eyes shut waiting for the second jolt, the sound of metal against metal.

Nothing.

When she ventured to look, a sleek silver car had parked to the side of the road in front of them. The car door opened, and a man wearing a felt hat and a heavy overcoat emerged.

Frank. It's Frank DiGiorno.

Jan unrolled the window as her neighbor approached the car. Allowing in fresh air helped with the smell. Her nostrils and throat still burned with whatever stuff that airbag had inside, and her skin itched.

"Frank. Thank God it's you. I s-spun out, then this car s-smacked me…and kept going." Jan's hand went to her forehead, which now ached. *Fresh blood on my knuckles.*

"Ya got some damage to the front end, and looks like your back side made love to a telephone pole."

Billy's screams pierced Jan's ears, causing her shoulders to hunch with renewed tension. Her hearing was back, and she wasn't sure she was ready for it. Jan moved to get out of the car.

"Sit tight, Jan. I'll get him for you."

With a rustling sound, Frank removed Billy from

his car seat. "Come to Poppa Frank, son."

Billy's screams subsided to snuffling and hiccupping, as he caught his breath.

"There, there." Frank held Billy to his chest patting his back. "I think he's just scared."

Pushing open her car door, Jan swung her knees around, so she sat sideways in the seat, and held out her arms to take Billy. The cold, wet sleet stinging her skin seemed refreshing. Why couldn't she stop shaking?

Control, Jan. You're not hurt. Billy seems okay. You were lucky. This time.

"I n-need to report this to the police." With her free hand, Jam rummaged for her purse on the seat next to her. It lay on the floor, its color dulled by that dusty substance. "I can't reach…"

"It'll keep," Frank said. "I almost rammed your car. First, ya got to move this tub. Did you, uh, get the plate of the car that hit ya?" Frank's face transformed. His eyes got squinty, and his lips went tight.

"No, my side mirror was beaded with moisture. All I saw were two headlights coming at me. The car was black, but it could have been dark blue. It was hard to tell."

With a shaky hand, Jan flipped over the key in the ignition. Thank the Lord the engine roared to a start. *Whew, at least I can drive the car.* She glanced around. Even if she straightened the car, she would still be blocking the road.

I have to go home. Yes, home, where I can lock my door and be safe.

"My daughter, she's at school."

"Your little girl will be safe."

"How do you know that?"

"Trust me. No one will harm you or your children." His words were sincere and brooked no argument.

Jan wasn't sure why she would trust Frank enough to believe him, but something about the assertive way he stated their safety as fact made her feel protected.

"Why don't I take Billy out of this mess and follow you home?"

"Go home, Mommy." Billy sniffed and then brushed at his tear-filled eyes.

He'd stopped crying and clung to her, his face and clothing dusted with the acrid powder covering Jan's body and the front section of the car.

"Billy, look at me." Jan sat him back on her lap. "Do you want a ride in Poppa Frank's fancy car?" The DiGiornos seemed like simple people. Jan didn't get how they could live in a middle-class neighborhood yet afford such an expensive car.

Billy's gaze went to the shiny sports car in front of them.

"We'll go slow," Frank said. "How about it, son?"

Billy nodded but didn't smile. He was shaken and, Jan was certain, dealing with the backsplash of the same burning powder she was.

"He'll need his car seat," she said to Frank.

Once she and Billy were locked inside their house, Jan examined her son for injuries. The car seat had done its job, and he seemed physically unharmed. Yet, he was too serious for a little boy. It turned out she had only a scrape on her knuckles, which must have whacked against the window. Once both of them were showered, and wearing fresh clothes, Jan dialed Detective Hoskins to report the hit and run and to plead a phone call for the children.

"Hit and run is a crime," Andy said. "Where is the vehicle right now?"

"In the garage. I drove it home. It was blocking traffic. I was afraid…"

"Jan, slow down. You did what was right for you and your boy. I need to look at the car and then check out the scene of the crash for clues. My tech is scheduled to wire your phone for the tap about two this afternoon. I'll stop by then."

"Sure. Okay. I guess I'll be here."

Even though Frank seemed to think Mae would be all right at school, she was Jan's daughter. She couldn't bear for her to come to harm. Yet, Jan was in no condition to navigate Devil's Hill. "Mae's in school, her first day back. I planned to pick her up."

"If you drive your car, it could contaminate evidence and, given what happened, it could be risky."

"Right. I hadn't thought of that. Maybe one of my neighbors can get her. I'm sure the accident has something to do with the money Jeff owes his dealer. I need to speak with him to see if he can pay them off so they will leave the children and me alone. I know he's restricted, but…"

"It's against regulations, but I will allow it as long as I can monitor the call."

"No problem. I understand."

After a few clicks and pauses on the line, Jeff picked up the transferred call. He spoke as if he had a mouthful of food.

"How badly are you hurt?" She couldn't help but ask.

"Jaw, a few teeth missing," he mumbled. "Be careful, Jan."

"Be careful? That's all you have to say?" Rage welled inside her. She clamped her lips shut to keep from spewing it out at Jeff. This was not the time, especially with Andy listening in. "I need to know. Do you have the money your buddies are after?"

"I'm broke. Dead broke, unless I can sell the stash the police have. Maybe you could talk to that detective who's been sniffing around you…"

"I don't think so." Jan jammed the "off" button on her cell phone.

She could have said much more to Jeff, but she didn't. He wasn't worth the effort. One would think cooling his heels in a jail cell for a day or so would give him time to think about the harm he'd done to their lives, rather than saving his own sorry hide.

Obviously, it hadn't.

Andy called Jan back. "I heard what your husband said. It's possible whoever broke him out of our jail expected him to pay them off. It makes sense now, why he was beaten, and why you and your family are their next target. If you are willing, we could set up a sting to nab them."

"Sting? You mean I should risk my life?"

"We'd be there all the time, ready to catch whoever shows up for the money."

"I don't have the money."

"Fake money, then."

"Let me think about it."

As Jan hung up from the call, her gaze landed on Billy. If something happened to her, who would take care of him and Mae? Her parents, she supposed. No, she couldn't bear to put Mae and Billy through one more trauma. They've already lost one parent. She was all they had. Yet, until this was settled, they were in danger. Jan ran her fingers through her son's hair. She never did get him to Frank's shop for a trim. He'd been clinging to her since they arrived home, only allowing her out of his sight for those few minutes when she ran under the shower.

Mae. Jan needed her home, but she knew she shouldn't drive her car.

She punched in Diane's number.

Chapter Twenty-Six

Jan never gave Andy an answer on the sting idea. She kept hoping the issue would solve itself without her involvement. Because of his attempted escape and the additional charge against him, Jeff had been placed in tighter security at the Enfield Correction facility, with his hearing at the Superior Court in ten days.

Jan blocked further thoughts of the Jeff situation with the beauty of the day. New fallen snow coating the trees and bushes made her view from the living room window a fairyland. She watched the Greenburg police car drive down Charming Way, around the *cul de sac*, and then back up the road. They'd been passing through a couple of times a day this week and, as far as scary incidents go, she almost felt safe. No more threatening calls or close encounters.

She checked the time. Loreen expected her at the shop in a few hours. Today, she needed to bring along Mae and Billy. Much to the children's delight, the school had called a snow day. The town plow had taken a swipe at the street, but it remained slick with matted snow.

It was nice to see the children in their bright puffy parkas, warm hats, and mittens building an igloo of sorts—they called it a snow house—on the part of their yard edging the street. Diane's girls were outside, as was Rana with her toddlers.

Jan squashed down the mother's guilt that nagged at her for leaving Billy to play while she ran inside to find dry gloves after shoveling the front walk and scraping the worst of the snow from the driveway. He seemed to be doing fine, with the older girls keeping an eye on him, but she wasn't sure how much longer Rana would stay outside. Carrie was probably due for a nap.

A green car, much like Jeff's company car, crawled down their road, scattering the children from the street up onto the lawn. Jan's lips curved into a smile. Mae and Billy knew the rules.

Uh oh, it just turned up my drive.

She wasn't expecting anyone from Klean Kare, and surely the police hadn't released Jeff's car. Certainly, the men who drove that sleek dark car who spied on them and sideswiped her car wouldn't go undercover in a coupe splattered white with road salt.

Two men wearing overcoats emerged and headed for Jan's front steps. From what she could tell, they looked harmless enough, but these days looks were deceiving. She would have felt better if Mae and Billy were inside, barricaded behind the door with her.

I'll get rid of them.

When the doorbell chimed, she braced to answer, not knowing who they were or why they were here. Setting the safety chain in place, she cracked open the door and peered out at two clean-shaven men, one sandy-haired and the other partly bald.

"Yes. What can I do for you, gentlemen?"

"I'm Gabe Cotter, and this is Pat Rice," the taller of the two said. "We used to work with Jeff. The boss sent us to pick up the car and his company computer. Nancy at the office was supposed to have called you about it."

"No, she didn't call. If she had, I would have told her to save you men the trip. The police have confiscated just about everything from Jeff's office and they also have his car."

Jan looked to the street, checking on the children, now engaged in a snowball fight using their snow house as a refuge. Diane's girls were still there, and Tara, being eleven, was decently responsible. Rana, though, wheeled the stroller toward her driveway. Certainly, she expected Jan would be out directly.

"Our boss is a barracuda, and he's going to be pissed when we don't come back with the goods. We've got a new hire coming in this afternoon," Pat said.

"I can't help you, but you can check with Detective Hoskins about the status of the car and any other Klean Kare property that may have been confiscated." She raised a finger in the air. "One sec. I'll grab one of his business cards for you—I've amassed several."

Jan raced to the kitchen, snatched Andy's card off the counter, and then handed it to one of the men through the crack in the door.

"Thanks for your help, Mrs. Simmons. Give our best to Jeff when you see him."

She managed a smile, knowing the next time she saw Jeff would be at his final hearing—and she wasn't planning to spend time shooting the breeze with him.

Once the men cleared the porch and headed to their car, Jan opened the door completely and called out to Mae and Billy. "Come on, kids, that's enough now. Time to come inside."

Stink. They're ignoring me. She jammed her feet

into her sodden boots and grabbed her coat.

The coupe backed down the drive and turned up the street just as another car approached.

A black one.

"Billy, Mae, kids. Now! Right this minute! Inside."

Jan's heart pounded with urgency. She flew out the door and down the steps toward the street. Her feet skidded forward. Next thing she knew she was on her back, gasping for air.

She managed to sit, her bottom soaked through with snow.

"Mom, Mom!" Mae shouted, running toward her. Kelly and Tara were behind her.

Rising, Jan brushed the snow from her backside, and looked for Billy, who must be lagging behind.

"They took Billy!"

"What do you mean? Took Billy? Oh, God help me." When she stood, her legs wobbled like jelly. She pressed a hand on her daughter's shoulder for support.

"The men in the long black car came at us. We ran on the lawn to get out of the way," Tara, Diane's oldest, sucked in a breath then exhaled. "Then they backed up and drove away and…and…Billy wasn't there anymore."

"No. No that can't be." Jan squelched her first instinct to berate Mae for not watching her brother and ran down the lawn. She might've slipped and fallen again. She couldn't say. All she knew was she had to find her son. He must be around here. Billy wouldn't get in a strange car willingly. He knew enough not to.

Jan pushed past the girls and ran, screaming, "Billy. Where are you, honey? Come to Mommy." The girls were with her, stopping to help her up each time she slipped on the packed snow.

The deadness of the silence that answered was freaky.

At the base of their driveway, Jan reached into the pocket of her jeans for her cell phone and dialed 911.

An operator answered at once.

"My son has disappeared. He was playing outside our home. Forty-six Charming Way. His name is Billy, and he's four."

"How long has he been gone, ma'am?"

"About five minutes."

"I see. Have you checked—?"

"You don't understand. I've been threatened. A car sideswiped me just yesterday, and now they've taken my son."

"We don't take a kidnapping lightly, ma'am. No need to be defensive. I will put out an Amber Alert immediately and send a squad car over."

"Detective Hoskins at the Greenburg station. Please let him know. He's been working on my case."

"Yes, yes. Of course. I will do that right now."

"Good. Now I have to get off the phone and search for my son."

"But ma'am—"

Once Jan hung up, she worked to be rational about the situation. Maybe the car had nothing to do with Billy's disappearance. It was common for cars to come down the street only to find it dead-ended, then turn around to leave.

But the girls said the car was black, the same color as the one that sideswiped me.

Her heart pounded inside her chest. She tore at her hair.

"Mom." Mae tugged at Jan's sleeve. "Do you think he went in that car?" We were supposed to be watching him." Her lower lip quivered. "I thought he was right behind me when we ran up onto the lawn, but when I looked back he wasn't."

Mae, Kelly, and Tara were upset as it was, no need to have them panic. Like she was doing. She hid it well. Jan sucked in a deep breath to calm herself before answering her. "I don't know, honey. Maybe that car didn't really take Billy. He may have decided to play hide and seek. You know how he loves games."

It was a stretch, but plausible. While he was pretty well behaved, occasionally, Billy would rebel, and she'd end up scolding him. Jan wanted to believe so badly that he'd strayed she convinced herself of it. She did a quick scan of the wooded area at the cap of their street. His parka was a boyish navy blue, new this year, but not exactly visible against the darker areas of the landscape. He was growing so quickly that she hoped it would last through the season. The sleeves were already too short.

"Billy," Jan yelled, "you can come out now. Hot chocolate!" She half smiled thinking of the brown mustache he always had when he finished his drink. She usually put an ice cube in their cups so the cocoa would be cool enough to drink sooner and the children wouldn't burn their mouths. He always ate the marshmallow first.

No response.

"Quick," she said to the girls, "run ahead and see if you can find out where he's hiding. Maybe behind your snow house or over by those trees." Jan's voice was calm as she directed them. Her insides quivered with nausea.

It's taking the police a long time to get here.

Keeping down the kind of panic that made her want to run through the streets screaming like a maniac, Jan forced herself to take controlled steps around the rim of the *cul de sac*, checking the snow for small footprints that led away from their yard.

Nothing.

Only two sets of tire treads from cars that had just come down the road. One set was deeper than the other, indicating a weightier car, she supposed.

"Girls, keep to the grass," Jan called, not wanting to destroy the only proof she might have of a possible crime.

Okay. Think. Rana's. Maybe Billy followed her inside and was sitting at her kitchen table having hot chocolate.

Circumventing the tracks, Jan made her way down Rana's drive and knocked on her back door.

"Jan. Hi. Come on in. I was going to call you to come by when I saw you had company."

She peered around Rana into the kitchen. Carrie was in her highchair, and Derrick was munching on some sort of snack.

"He's not here. Billy. Have you seen him?"

Rana clutched her arm. "He was playing with the girls when I left, and I saw you at the door watching. I figured—oh, my God."

The build-up of the past few days welled up inside her, and she burst into tears. "I think he's been kidnapped. He's disappeared. My baby boy."

"Oh, no." Rana came over to hug her. "I should have stayed outside until you came out. Carrie needed a diaper change."

"My children aren't your responsibility. Those men came to the door and distracted me. I should never have left my son, even for a minute. What am I going to do if he doesn't come back to me?" she wailed.

"Why would you think someone took him? He's got to be somewhere. I'll pack up the children and come check the neighborhood with you."

"It's a long story. I called 911," Jan said, sniffing. "The police should be here any minute. You have your hands full."

"Send Mae in. She can stay here while you figure this out. It's the least I can do."

"She feels responsible, and it's better if I keep her with me."

"Did you check with the DiGiornos yet? I saw Mr. D outside not too long ago."

"Good idea. Billy loves to be around Frank. Maybe he snuck over there when the girls weren't watching." *You're grasping at straws again, Jan.*

"I'll let you know if he shows up here." Rana smoothed Jan's hair. "Don't worry. He'll turn up."

"I hope so." Her voice wobbled.

Outside, Mae and Diane's girls waited for her at the top of Rana's driveway.

"He's not in the woods or anywhere around the front yard. We split up and checked. He's not answering, Mom?"

"Don't cry, Mae. We'll find him." Jan tried to make light of the situation for her daughter's sake, even with her stomach so cramped she was hard-pressed to remain upright.

"Mrs. Simmons, Tara and I are going to check our

house for Billy. I'll tell my mother," Kelly said.

"Good. Thanks."

Clasping Mae's hand tight against her, they went next door to The DiGiorno's. The walk had been sanded, and the driveway cleared, indicating Frank may have indeed been outside.

Jan pressed the doorbell, jittery as all crap. If her son wasn't here, and he wasn't at Diane's, she'd be totally screwed. She forced herself to remember Tara's exact words.

Billy had been *taken*.

Who would snatch a little boy? She knew of course—the possibility gave her the creeps, but before going into a total panic, she had to rule out other possibilities.

The curtain covering the long rectangular window on the left side of the door moved. Jan heard the clicks of locks being undone, then the inside door opened.

Mae and Jan must've been a sight huddled together, their faces tear stained and their noses red, because Tina opened the storm door at once and beckoned them inside. From somewhere in the house, a baby cried. *That's right, their daughter's staying with them now, and I'd heard their son-in-law was in an accident*. Baby Frank fascinated Billy.

"What's the matter? You and your little girl are crying." Tina's mouth went tight and furrows formed on her otherwise smooth forehead.

"My son. Is he here?"

"Billy?" She shook her head, then her eyebrows shot up. "He is missing?"

Jan sucked in a sob. She didn't know this woman well enough to all out bawl. Although she had always

239

been kind to them.

"Come in. I will make coffee."

"No. Thank you, though. I have to find my son."

"One moment. She turned and yelled, "Frankie!"

A male voice answered in an annoyed tone.

"Please don't disturb him."

"No." Her expression hardened. "It's okay. I ask him." Turning her head, she shouted, "Billy is missing. Was he outside with you?"

"Why. What's a matter?' Frank ambled to the door wearing baggy sweats and bedroom slippers.

"His momma's here. Says he was playing, and then gone."

"We think a big black car took him away," Mae said.

"Now, Mae, we don't know that for sure."

Frank rubbed the stubble on his jaw. "I ain't seen him, Jan. But I'll ask around the shop about that car. Did you see what kind it was?"

"It was dark, like the car that ran into me yesterday."

His lips went tight, and the twinkle in his droopy eyes went dead. "I'll see what I can find out. That ain't right."

"You're darn tooting it ain't right," Tina said to Frank. Her hands were on her hips, and fire was in her eyes.

Frank seemed to cave under his wife's glare, but only for a moment before straightening to his full height and towering over her. "Enough." His voice was firm.

Jan saw another side of Frank. A man in charge.

Turning, Mae and Jan plodded down the steps and

out the drive. She held herself together for Mae's sake, resisting the urge to fall on her knees and pray. She would pray, but not here. Not now.

Even though Jan was sure Billy had been taken, her heart leaped with the hope he would pop out at them from wherever he might've been hiding all this time. Billy loved playing Hide and Seek, yet he was too young to realize that the older girls used the game to have a few minute's peace from him pestering them. *Come out, come out, wherever you are*, they would call. Billy seldom showed himself at once, as he was easily distracted. Last summer, he decided to pick Jan a bouquet of flowers. The girls found him amid a pile of dandelions.

"Mom. Over here." Mae raced toward Candy's front porch, leaving a trail of tiny boot prints in the snow.

Jan tried to follow her but gave up when she landed on her knees and settled for walking up their cleared and sanded driveway.

Mae ducked behind the hedge bordering the front of Candy's house, then disappeared from view like Billy must have.

The extra anxiety sent her insides upside down. Jan couldn't breathe. She couldn't move, fearing if she did, she could lose Mae too. Ridiculous, she knew. The clock ticked in her head. One second, two seconds.

"Mae," she yelled.

Her daughter emerged from behind the snowy bush, thank the Lord, cradling Candy's orange cat. She was safe, for now.

"He's not here, Mom." Mae laid her cheek against Arnold's fur before she allowed him to wiggle free and run off.

Finally, Mae and Jan made it to their house and the empty, echoing room, where Billy's toys lay about like sleeping pets, where Bob waited on his empty bed to be hugged and loved.

She knew what she had to do next.

Chapter Twenty-Seven

No sooner had the door shut behind the neighbor lady and her kid when Tina zeroed in on him. "Now, Frankie, I know that look. Calm down. You can fix this."

"Yeah. I'm gonna strangle someone, that's how I'm gonna fix it."

"No violence. You promised. We have enough trouble with poor Vinnie being crippled, and my God can that man eat. That double batch of lasagna I made for dinner last night? Gone."

Frank held up his hand. "Stop complaining. You love men with a good appetite."

"Yeah, I sure do." Tina's hand smoothed over his cheek, and she kissed him. It was a sweet kiss, not a seductive one. But he liked that kind of kiss, too.

"I'll talk to them. Just talk. I promise."

"Ooh, I love you." She pinched his cheek. "On your way home, pick up a loaf of nice fresh bread at the bakery. We're having sausage and peppers for dinner— if you're good."

"Oh, baby, I'm always good. Now, let me be. I gotta make a call, then throw on my business suit."

Ten minutes later, Frank backed out of the garage and shot up the street toward the corner of Fifth and Grove, where Louie was to meet him with Jeff's handler. Broad daylight, right out in the open, men talking business. Nice and clean.

Before parking, he did a drive-by to be sure they were waiting for him. They were. Frank parked in the lot behind the theater and made his way to the sidewalk on Grove. Piles of once white snow crushed against the curb in dirty heaps and remnants of brown grit covered the walk. He passed a woman carting a shitload of plastic supermarket bags, and two teens that eyed him as if he were fair game. Just try it, he thought, and you'll get a surprise.

Louie turned as he approached and cocked his head toward the man Frank recognized as Wheezy, third cousin on his mother's side. The guy was a good-for-nothing with a big mouth and no action. It surprised Frank he had the guts to pull off a kidnapping.

"Louie, you tell me what's going on here. I'm not gonna deal with this shrimp," Frank said.

Louie scratched the back of his thick neck. "Seems your neighbor got caught dealing and we don't have the drugs or the money. He stiffed us. Wheezy thinks he's got the money but won't give it up."

Wheezy stuck out his puny chest. "Yeah. He owes me ten big ones. I want my money."

"*Your* money? How does it all of a sudden get to be yours?" Frank pulled the man up by the lapels of his jacket.

Wheezy's eyes went scared. The man's muscles stiffened under him.

"The deal is we share." Frank let go of Wheezy's jacket. The man slumped as if he'd dropped him. He shoved at his chest. "What's the matter with you fooling with the wife? She ain't got squat. You can't squeeze juice out of a dried lemon, *Capiche*?"

"But the money…" Wheezy fished in his pants pocket for his inhaler and took a hit.

"Fuck the money. It's peanuts."

"Not to me," Wheezy replied, lifting his chin.

"Wait a minute. Something's not adding up here. Louie, you set this up for Vinnie. What do you know?"

"Nothing, boss. I gave it over to Wheezy here. He's late on chipping into the pot. Now I know why."

Frank squinted at Wheezy through the slit in his droopy eyelid. "You're hiding something from the family, you little runt." He grabbed the man's nose and twisted hard, "Spill it, or I'll cure your asthma for good."

"Ow, let go. You're hurting me."

Frank released his fingers, and then wiped the snot on Wheezy's jacket. "Give, you disgusting prick."

"I'm into some bucks with Bruno. I got a family. A wife, three kids…."

"*Madonna mia.* You goons never learn."

"He'll kill me."

"No, he won't. He'll deal. Get him on the phone for me. Now."

Wheezy's rheumy eyes shifted from Louie to him.

"Go ahead, do it," Louie said.

Frank grabbed Louie by the throat and squeezed. The man's eyes went scared. "I give the orders here. You work for me until Vinnie's in shape to take over."

"So-o-rry, boss," Louie croaked out.

Frank released his grip, allowing Louie to bend over and gasp for breath.

"Got Bruno." Wheezy handed Frank the phone.

"Good, Wheezy." He took the phone. "The kid, Bruno. Get him back to his mother."

"What kid?"

"Don't play stupid with me. I got Wheezy here by the balls, and I'll be after yours next."

"I don't answer to you. You're retired, and Vincenzo is laid up. The only person you got to rely on is Louie, and he ain't got the guts to go against me. I'm my own boss now, and Wheezy's thinking of coming over with me."

Bruno's words were a punch to the gut. No way was he bending over for that asshole. The kid, he had to remember. This call isn't about Frank DiGiorno; it's about Billy.

"Don't tempt me to get nasty with you. I still got clout to arrange for your dead body to end up in a gutter. Now, let's cut out this bullshit and talk business. The kid's father owes ya ten grand for the stash the police took. I give you a chit for the bucks, and you return the kid and lay off the mom."

"No good. The cash or the kid dies."

"Ooh, getting ballsy on me, huh? How about I write ya a check and give it to Wheezy here. It'll take time to get that much cash without arousing suspicion."

"Sure, and the check goes *boing boing*. Cash for the kid, or bye bye kid."

The phone went dead.

He'd ignore Bruno's insult, for now. But Bruno just moved to the top of Frank's elimination roster. Vinnie was improving every day, and once he was back in fighting shape they'd clean up this mess but good.

Meanwhile, Frank had a problem.

"Wheezy, you're gonna tell me where Bruno's got the kid stashed."

"I'm not sure."

"Then get sure. Go check his house, then the places he hangs out. He must have someone taking care of Billy."

Frank adjusted his derby hat, straightening the brim so it fit just right. "I want to hear from you in a couple of hours. *Capiche?* Good, now get outta my sight."

"Louie." Frank nudged the man's arm. "Follow him. Call me for orders as soon as that asshole finds the kid."

"But what about the money, boss?"

"You ask too many questions."

Chapter Twenty-Eight

Billy wouldn't have gone willingly. He never even cried out, according to the girls. That didn't surprise Jan. Whenever Billy was scared, he froze like a wooden statue. In such a state, it would have been a snap for someone larger to pick up his small body and get it inside a car. Maybe the man put him on his lap or maybe the snatcher sat in the back seat so there would be room to maneuver—room to hold her son down; to gag him if he were crying, to tie his hands behind his back as if he were some criminal.

The image made Jan's insides clutch. She couldn't know what actually occurred because she hadn't been there. If she had, Billy might be home sitting on her lap this very minute.

Dwelling on it wasn't helping her to be strong for Mae. Her little girl had been crying non-stop since they'd walked into the house, blaming herself. Nothing Jan could say consoled her. Until Diane's gang arrived to break the mood, the two of them had been huddled in the corner of the couch clutching, hugging, and sniffling.

The distant whine of sirens commanded the air, growing louder as they approached.

"Oh my God." Jan clapped her hands over her ears, "It's real. Billy is really gone." From deep in her gut, a sob wrenched out of her. She crumbled into her chair.

Diane, who had come over with Ted and the girls, rubbed Jan's back, which soothed her a little. "They'll find him, Jan."

She nodded, too choked up to reply. She had to pull it together for Mae, for Billy. The police would want to talk to her, and she needed to provide precise information without being a blubbering idiot.

"The sirens have stopped, and the vehicles don't seem to be driving this way," Ted said. Shoving his hands in his pockets, he ambled to the window and peered out. The girls, including Mae, joined him but remained silent.

Jan lifted her head.

"I'll bet they don't want to muck up the scene with a bunch of tire tracks," Ted said.

"Yes. Tire tracks." Jan rose. "I saw two sets. One was from the Klean Kare people but the other…" her voice wavered. "The black car. The evil black car that stole my son and tried to hurt us yesterday."

Black. The color of death. Jan's face dropped into her hands.

"Here, Jan." Diane handed her a tissue. "Blow your nose. Let's see if anything's going on outside yet." She took Jan's arm and walked her to the picture window as if she were a cripple needing assistance.

A Congo line of men and women streamed down Charming Way, walking to the side and keeping to the grass. Within minutes, several people worked to cordon off the end of the *cul de sac* with yellow crime tape. Techie types crawled over the area toting photo equipment, notebooks, and cell phones.

"Here comes the detective now."

Grim-faced and purpose-driven, Andy plodded up

Jan's driveway. Relief poured over her. He knew Billy. He knew their situation, and he supported her every time she needed him. She trusted him to do whatever was necessary to find her little boy.

Jan ran to the door to let him inside. "Thank God you're here."

"Mrs. Simmons," Andy said, as she led him into the living room. "Let's get down to business. Have you located a recent picture of Billy?"

She grabbed the one she had selected off the end table. "This was taken when…"

Andy took the photo from her shaky hand and laid it flat on the table. Drawing out his cell phone, he snapped a picture. "Give me a second to text this to the precinct."

Jan worked to keep her voice steady. "How long do you think it will take to find my son?"

He shrugged. "Hard to tell, but the more people watching for the car and the boy, the better our chances of nabbing the kidnappers. An Amber Alert has gone out, and our men are doing a preliminary investigation of the scene while we wait for the FBI to get here."

"The FBI?"

"Yes, they handle all kidnapping cases, but I'm here to work locally." The detective touched Jan's arm in an assuring way. "If you turn on your radio or TV," he continued, "you'll hear the Amber Alert for Billy." He tapped the photo. "This will help identify him better than the physical description I sent in. You said he wore a blue and white hat, a bright blue jacket, navy pants, and boots?"

Jan swallowed hard, envisioning her little boy dressed for play. Smiling and happy, until…*oh, God.*

What's he doing right now? Is he calling for me? Are they hurting him? She sucked in a breath to hold back the urge to burst into another crying jag. Crying wouldn't get Billy back.

Jan raised her chin, not caring that she looked a red-nosed mess. "Yes, that's right. A knitted hat I made him. He loved to pull it down over his eyes and pretend he was hiding from me. The jacket is quilted, a parka with a hood, and he wore waterproof snow pants to keep dry." Briefly, she shut her eyes, blinking back tears. "I forgot to tell you. His boots are black with fur lining. Because he didn't want the brown boots that were on sale, I paid full price for them. And mittens. Handmade. Red. The kind attached with a string underneath his jacket." As she spoke with her wobbly voice between sniffs, Andy typed the information into his phone for instant transmission.

"Mrs. Simmons, the best way to handle this is to interview each of you separately. We have set up a command post at the station, but we can talk here where everyone is comfortable. This procedure will take a while." He glanced over at Diane, Ted, and the three girls. "Can you and I speak privately, maybe in another room? I have a set of questions for you, and then I'll need to interview everyone here."

"What about Rana? She was outside just before it occurred," Diane said.

"When I stopped over, she was at the back of the house feeding her children lunch," Jan told her.

"This person lives…"

"Across the street."

Andy noted the name and exact address in a notebook he carried. "We'll make sure she and the children are questioned."

"Should we leave?" Ted's brow furrowed.

"If you could stick around, it would save our men from coming to your home."

"Why not take everyone into the family room? Turn on something the girls might enjoy. Please. Not the news." Jan wasn't prepared to see her son's picture facing her from a TV screen.

"I want to stay with you, Mom." Mae's arm went around Jan's shoulders. "Don't worry, Billy will be such a pest that those bad men will want to give him back."

She managed a weak smile at her. "I hope you're right."

Bzzzz.

"Someone's at the door." She peeked out the window. "Oh, no. There's a van from WCTZ parked out front."

"Those idiots. How did they get past the blockade?" The detective spoke into his radio. "George, get up here to the Simmons's front door and tell the reporter, no interview."

Jan's hand went to her mouth. "Everyone will know about Billy?"

"The media's always hungry for a good story. You don't need to talk to them now. When you're ready, let me know, and I'll allow it."

"My parents…."

"Where do they live?"

"Southern New Jersey."

"That's about…"

"…at least a three-hour drive."

He checked his watch. "With traffic, I doubt the

kidnappers have gotten that far, so maybe the FBI will hold off on issuing a Tristate Alert until they've assessed the situation locally."

Jan ran her fingers through her tangled hair. "Forgive me, Detective. Please sit." She indicated the sofa, then sat adjacent to him on a hardwood chair. She didn't seek comfort, just her son.

Mae, who had been drinking all this in crawled onto Jan's lap holding Blankie to her nose.

"I'll put on a pot of Java," Diane said. "Come on, Ted, let's give Jan privacy, and wait in the kitchen."

Once the Harper crew moved from the living room, the detective cleared his throat. "Does Billy have any identifying scars or moles, or does he have medical issues?"

"I'm afraid his only blemishes are freckles, and he's in good health."

"What about his emotional state? Did Billy seem depressed or upset lately?"

"Of course he's been upset. He misses his father and so does Mae." Jan hugged her daughter closer. "But he wouldn't just run away. He's too young."

"Maybe he tried to go to his father. You did bring him to the station a few days ago. He's a bright kid. He may remember how to get to our place."

Jan exhaled. "It's possible but unlikely. Why, moments before he disappeared he was laughing with the girls out front, wasn't he, Mae?"

"We were playing snow wars. Did you see the house we built?" Mae said.

Andy leaned over and tipped up Mae's chin. "I'll bet you and your friends can help us find your little brother?"

"We have to find him." Mae's eyes filled.

Jan hugged her close, resting her chin on Mae's head.

"We will, sweetheart." Andy tugged at her red braid like her father used to do.

Mae pulled away from him as if she'd been stung and hopped off Jan's lap. "I'm going in the kitchen with Tara and Kelly now."

"Did I offend her?" Andy asked.

"She's sensitive about Jeff being imprisoned."

"I understand. Can we continue?"

She sighed. "Let's get this over with."

"Jan," he held her eyes, "sitting here answering questions may be frustrating when you want action. Rest assured, as we speak, our men are searching the perimeter of the abduction."

"He's not here, Detective. I looked everywhere and even checked my neighbors' houses."

"You did the right thing. Now we need to dig deeper into Billy's disappearance. Our men will interview your neighbors and check every vehicle on the street. Often folks see something but don't realize it's important until we question them. Even the smallest piece of information can help us recreate what happened here."

"My son couldn't have gone far in the snow with his short little legs." Jan squeezed back a sob. His boots would be soaked through, and his nose and cheeks would be so chapped she'd have to smooth on aloe to heal them. When they found him.

They *would* find him. She had to believe that to stay sane.

"With the wiretap in place, we're monitoring any

calls you receive. If you will permit us, we'd like to search your home from top to bottom to be sure Billy isn't here."

"If he were at home, I would know it, Detective."

Andy held up his hand. "We're just being thorough. You said yourself, no one actually saw Billy get into that car."

"Yes, you're right. That's why…never mind. Detective, go ahead. Do your thing, but don't mess with my knitting again."

"Ma'am, it's not that kind of search. We wouldn't expect a child to hide in your knitting basket."

"I suppose." She suppressed a smile at the vision. "But the dark sedan. What are you doing about that?"

"From yesterday's examination of your car, we retrieved a paint sample of the vehicle. An alert is out for a black car with gray paint on its right front fender. If we find the car, we can trace it to the owner. It's possible it's the same car that parked at your house the other night and was here on your street this afternoon."

"What do we do now?"

"We talk to people. Every detail counts."

While Andy interviewed the children individually, Jan paced the floor, checking her watch every few minutes. Two hours ago, her son had been laughing and in the throes of a snowball fight, yet it seemed like two days. What were those men doing to him, and why hadn't they called her about a ransom?

A wash of guilt came over her. She should call her parents and let them know what's going on, but why put them through this? No, she'd wait until Billy was safely home. Besides, she wasn't in the mood for being accused of not watching the children closely enough.

"What if they don't call? What happens to my Billy?" Jan clamped her lips shut to keep them from trembling. Time for logic, not emotion. Emotion won't get Billy back any sooner.

"They will, Jan," Andy said. "As a follow-up to the call you received last night, we interviewed your husband. He confessed he purchased a double order on credit. These people are determined to get their money. We found five pounds in your husband's car, that's a little more than two kilos, so we're talking big bucks."

"A few weeks ago, I discovered a significant amount of cash in Jeff's desk, but it's disappeared. He claims he no longer has it, but I wouldn't put it past him to lie to me."

"We grilled him about that situation this morning," the officer assured me. "He planned to pay for the extra marijuana with the profit, once it was sold."

"But it won't be sold because you have it." Jan glared at Andy. "Maybe those men will be just as happy getting back their drugs?"

Andy raked his hand through his dark curls. "I'm afraid it doesn't work that way." With these guys, a deal is a deal. They can get nasty when things don't go their way."

A shiver ran up Jan's spine, remembering the chilling voice on the phone. Would men heartless enough to sideswipe a car carrying a woman and a child care about hurting a little boy?

"The FBI is pressuring your husband to identify his drug contacts as we speak."

"He didn't take Billy…"

"We know that, but he has crucial information about the people who might have been involved, which could lead us to your son."

"Of course he would, but what would those men do to Jeff if he ratted on them?"

"Jeff is behind bars in a patrolled area. He's safe."

"Safe? Sure he is. I've heard stories about men being killed while in prison. If those men could track me down, they can get to Jeff. Are you forgetting he escaped? He didn't manage that on his own. He wouldn't know how. Someone let him out so they could get hold of him for the money. Why else? Look, Detective, Jeff may have committed a crime, but he's my children's father. If harm comes to him, I couldn't forgive myself."

"Don't take on the blame for what the man has done. It's not your fault. None of this is."

Not my fault? It would always be my fault that I didn't see what was going on with Jeff in time to get my children safely away. She should have known.

Andy touched Jan's arm in a reassuring way. "While your house phone is being monitored at the command center, I need to check on the results of our neighborhood search and any news on the black sedan."

"Yes, of course."

"If it would help, you can wait with my people at the command center in the station's conference room."

Jan wrapped her arms around herself, suddenly chilled. "I need to stay here in case somehow, someway, Billy comes home."

"Very well then." With a nod, he left to join his team.

"You shouldn't be alone." Diane's comforting arm cradled her shoulders. "Rana's coming over to stay with you."

"Diane," Ted said, "you stay here. I'll take Kelly and Tara home and give them supper." He turned to Mae, who was intent on restyling Tara's curls into an updo. "Hey, girlie girl, you coming with us?" Mae shook her head and ran off to her bedroom. The door slammed.

Jan knew her little girl was hurting. Staying in control in front of her friends had to be hard. Jan fought off the urge to follow her, to throw herself on her bed and cry her eyes out without having to answer for it to anyone. She'd held back her emotions, and now everything inside her cried to let loose.

But she couldn't let go. She was the mother. She had to hold it together. Poor Mae was alone in her room. She needed to convince her to go with Ted and the girls. Getting out of this place for a while would do her good. Ted would keep her little girl safe.

Chapter Twenty-Nine

Frank slid behind the wheel of his million-dollar sports car and zoomed out of the parking lot. *Power. I still got it.*

Buzz.

He pressed a button on his console to pick up Tina's call.

"How did it go, Frankie? Did you get Billy?"

"I'm working on it, Lovie. What's going on home?"

"The street is crawling with police. You can't come home. The FBI is here, as well as the local cops. Someone could recognize you. In fact, the street is blocked off, and they're only letting in residents. I'm scared they'll find out about us. What if Jan's husband tells the police about our Vinnie?"

"Tina, stop crying. Jan's never met Vinnie. Her husband and that Mike think his name is Greg. Besides, all Vinnie did was give the guy a throwaway cell phone number for Louie, who set up the deal. His hands are clean, and Wheezy should have had enough common sense not to show his face."

"The police came to our door. I had to let them in. Lucille made Vinnie stay put. He's been moving around, and I was sure once they saw him they'd figure it out. I don't want you to go to prison."

"Calm down. Nothing's gonna happen to me. What

did you tell the police?"

"Just that I saw nothing, and the mother and her daughter came asking after their son. That's all I know. It's on the radio, Frankie, and a bulletin with Billy's picture just interrupted my soaps."

"Look, you're not gonna like this, but I need you to go over to Jan's house and find out if the kid is home, or if anyone has called her about him yet."

"I can bring her some sausage and peppers. What about you? Will you be okay?"

"I got a fridge and a cot in the back room of the barbershop. I'll hole up there until the fuzz clears out of our street."

"I'll miss you, Frankie."

"Miss you already, Lovie. Now, call me after you check on the mother."

Chapter Thirty

Five hours, and the men who took Billy hadn't called her. Jan had seen enough police shows on TV to know the longer Billy was gone, the less her chances were of seeing him returned safely.

What did they want with him for so long? What were they doing to him? Did they even feed him dinner? He must be crying, missing them. Wanting to come home and snuggle Bob. She could tell Bob missed Billy too by the way he slumped over the kitchen table in Billy's chair, where she'd placed him so as to not deal with seeing her son's empty seat.

What if they plan to sell him? Lots of childless families would pay more than a measly ten thousand dollars for a smart, adorable little boy they could call their own. Then, there was white slavery. Or rape!

Jan's heart beat five thousand miles a minute as the evil thoughts set in.

Oh my God.

She crumbled into the kitchen chair. She might never see her son again. Hold him in her arms. Read him *Goodnight Moon* at bedtime. Shivers racked through her body, releasing a huge, gushing sob.

"Darn you, Jeff."

Jan stared at the kitchen phone. "Ring. Call me." They *had* to call to arrange to get their money. Billy for the bucks. That would be the deal, so it wasn't likely the thugs would harm him just yet.

Somewhat calmed by the reminder, Jan dialed Andy to see how the investigation progressed from his end. Texting would have been so much easier, had she a smartphone.

Andy picked up immediately and spewed out an update. "Our techs have identified the tire treads, but I'm afraid that won't be much help. They are a common brand. We know the color of the car is Blue Black, which is offered by Chrysler, so that's a start."

"If only I had paid more attention I might've at least contributed something more. Has my husband divulged anything helpful?"

"Not really. According to the FBI interrogation, your husband was provided a phone number, now disconnected, and given a pickup/drop off point for the exchanges. Our man posted at the location has reported no activity."

"Stink. Do you think Jeff's telling the truth? Someone may have gotten to him when he escaped. Threatened him."

"Hard to tell, although if *my* son were kidnapped, I'd certainly do whatever I could to help find him."

"I suppose you're right."

Jan's hopes were pinned on Jeff being able to name the person who got him selling drugs, certainly not a robot. With Jeff being gone so much and his propensity to gamble, this drug thing might've begun with some low-life at one of the casinos.

She hung up the phone, feeling no more encouraged than she been moments before. At least she wasn't alone. Friends, what would she do without them?

"I feel guilty stealing you away from your families," Jan said to Rana and Diane.

"They'll survive for one night without us," Rana said. "Larry's pretty good at taking over, especially when he has help. Mom's been a blessing. While I bathe the kids and get them settled for the night, she's been making us dinner."

"Ted's taken the girls out for Mexican food, and then they're going for ice cream. He just texted me. The girls want Mae to sleep over."

"It's up to her. Did he say how she's been doing?" Diane punched in a note on her smartphone. "I'll ask him."

"Here." Rana set a cup of chamomile tea in front of Jan. "This will help calm your nerves."

She inhaled the familiar herbal aroma that had comforted her since babydom. "It's after seven. You two must be hungry. Why don't you dig into the food Tina DiGiorno dropped off for us?"

"That was sweet of her." Rana lifted the foil off the pan, which Jan had set on the counter. "Maybe I'll have a little. Diane?"

"What is it?"

"Hmm let's see, onions, green peppers and"—she picked up a small brownish circle and popped it into her mouth—"sausage."

"Pork? I don't do pork. It comes from those cute little pigs." Diane surveyed the casserole. "Maybe I'll just take some peppers."

"What's that noise?" Jan leaped up.

"Relax, it's the back door."

"Who?"

Diane peered out through the glass, then stepped

back as it opened.

Amy rushed in, her arms wide, and embraced Jan. "I was driving home from a late meeting when I heard Billy's name on the radio. Oh my God, Jan." She leaned back and cupped Jan's chin. "What happened?"

"It's a long story." Rana and Diane came up behind Jan. Her defenders—they knew about the rift. She and Amy had much to discuss, which she couldn't deal with just now.

"She's waiting for a ransom call," Rana said.

"Five hours, it's been, Amy. *Nada*."

"What can I do for you?"

Jan squeezed Amy's hand. "You being here is enough. If you haven't had supper, there's food on the stove."

"That can wait. In my religion, when someone is very sick or hurt, we find a prayer circle helps." Amy took Jan's hand and Rana's. Diane closed the circle.

"Good. Now everyone focus on Billy and pray in your own way for his safe return. If we pray at the same time, the plea will be strong."

As the three of them bowed their heads, it seemed a divine presence joined them to listen.

Closing her eyes, Jan envisioned Billy in the center of their circle hugging his favorite toy and smiling. She prayed with all her heart for his safe return.

After a few minutes of silence, the circle broke up.

"Does it work?" Diane asked Amy.

"Sometimes it's miraculous. At our church, a group of us prayed over a woman with terminal cancer. Now, she's in remission."

"Thank you, Amy. I'm glad you're here." Jan drew her aside to the living room. They sat on the couch facing each other. Rana and Diane remained in the kitchen, knowing it was time for them to settle things. That Amy had come here in Jan's time of need was enough, yet, Jan owed Amy support as well.

"Tell me about Stevie. What's going on?"

Amy's lower lip trembled as she held back a sob. "He's expelled from school. Most of his friends have abandoned him."

"How awful for you, and for Stevie too. I've been guilty as crap about being blind to what was going on between them. If I had paid more attention, I might've noticed Jeff and Stevie's relationship went beyond golf mentoring."

"It's not your fault. Mike and I discussed how we've neglected our son. I'm thinking about resigning my job so I can be home more for him. Working sure takes a toll on motherhood."

"My parents almost split when Will got involved with drugs."

"I remember you telling me about that." She touched Jan's shoulder. "You've had a hell of a time."

Jan handed Amy a tissue. "Here, I'll share these with you."

Plucking one from the box, Jan wiped her eyes and then blew her nose. She should have been fresh out of tears by now, but at the slightest reminder of this whole sordid business, they just kept coming.

"I can't say being home makes a person a better a mother. Look what happened to Billy right under my nose."

"I should have never shut you out, especially when you needed my support. Some friend I've been. Thank the Lord you had Rana and Diane to fill in for me while

I sorted things out."

"I knew you weren't gone forever. You needed time to deal with your son. What's going to happen to Stevie now?"

Amy wiped her eyes. "We scrounged up bail money, so Stevie is home, and we found a good criminal lawyer to plead his case. With luck, the court will let him off easy given his age and that it's a first offense." She held up her crossed fingers. "I'm hoping my son won't be sent to a juvenile detention center. Even thinking about him being thrown in with scum makes my skin crawl. If only I could whisk him away somewhere where no one can get to him, or turn back time so that Mike and I could have found out what he planned and stopped him."

"Maybe the judge will let him off with doing community service. You know, talk to other kids about his experience and prevent it from happening to them."

"He'd be good at that."

"I'll bet you wish you never recommended we move to Charming Way."

"What I'm sorry about is that Jeff turned out to be a corrupting bastard and that your Billy is missing. But never you." Reaching forward, she brushed a tear from Jan's wet cheek. "I love having you nearby, and I've missed having you as a friend. Mike doesn't feel the same, I'm afraid. He's forbidden me from having anything to do with you and the children."

"That stinks." Jan's gaze went to the phone. "The darn thing won't ring. Whoever has Billy should be calling to make a deal for his return. Why haven't they called?" she started blubbering all over again.

"I don't know what to tell you, except I can't

fathom why they wouldn't contact you. They are looking for money, right? A ransom?"

Jan nodded and blew her nose.

"They might be holding off to get you good and upset, so you'll cough up when they ask."

"They don't need to wait. I've been good and upset for hours. My stomach's a mess, and I've got a splitting headache." Jan's hand went to her forehead.

"Maybe if you lie down and shut your eyes…"

"I tried. It just makes it worse. Because then I think about Billy and what they could be doing to him. Are they torturing him? I don't know, I just don't know."

Taking a minute, Jan pulled herself together. *Calming breaths, Jan. Let the police system do its thing—while you wait in anguish.*

Amy's eyes brimmed. "I love that little guy, too."

Jan waved off Amy's comment, her moment of calm ready to explode. "Don't do this. I can't talk about Billy right now. So, let me ask you a question that's been on my mind. Did Mike know anything about what Jeff was doing? They were so close once."

Amy shook her head. "No, but he suspected something was going on. After Stevie's arrest, we tried to figure out where things went wrong. Mike said Jeff had been acting standoffish toward him ever since that poker game at the DiGiorno's. You know that Jeff lost a substantial amount of money there, don't you?"

"I figured as much, but I stupidly never grilled Jeff about that night. I should have because he wasn't acting himself. I knew something was wrong, but I let it go, just like everything else. Hmmm. Now that I think of it, that's when the phone calls began and when Jeff began going out at odd hours. He was turning kids into drug addicts and dealers to make fast money. Using Stevie. Oh, Amy, how could Jeff be so self-serving?"

"I wondered why Stevie went along with it. I thought we'd raised him to be honest. He's not the kind of kid that would hurt others like that, especially his friends. When I asked, he blamed it on peer pressure. You know Stevie has always felt insecure at school. He's quiet, doesn't talk much. Well, he said having the kids come to him to buy pot made him feel important. Older kids sought him out. Suddenly he was a big shot around the school. Look what it got him. He's not such a big man now."

"Stevie's an innocent corrupted by an adult who should've known better. It's Jeff's fault, not yours; just like it's Jeff's fault my Billy is gone." Jan burst into tears, big sloppy tears that poured from her eyes like a rainstorm.

Amy took Jan in her arms. "It's going to be okay."

Somehow, someway, she knew Amy was right. Amy was always right.

As if on cue, Rana and Diane came into the living room. "We wiped up the dishes for you and stuck the casserole in the fridge. Maybe you'll want some for a snack later," Rana said.

Jan shrugged. She doubted her stomach would handle such a spicy dish. "Thanks for coming over, guys."

"Oh, no you don't," Diane said. "You can't get rid of us that easy. Move over."

The next few hours went by without a phone call. Rana, Diane, and Amy refused to leave Jan to go home to their families. To pass the time, they moved to the family room, got comfortable, and found an old movie on TV.

Jan paced the floor. Eleven p.m.—no call from those awful thugs, and no news from Andy.

"Jan, you need to relax, or you'll wear out that spot on the carpet," Rana said, yawning.

"It's old anyway. As soon as I'm flush, I'm going to replace it." She wrung her hands. "What if they never call? What if I never see my son again?"

Amy stood from her perch on the couch and grabbed Jan's shoulders. "Stop it. You're sending negative vibes out to the universe. Think positive. They will call. Billy will be home soon. Whoever took him won't get far because every cop and every passenger car is on the lookout for their vehicle. Your boy's picture is being shown everywhere—on TV and by investigators. Trust they will find Billy. Envision his safe return. Now." She pushed Jan into Jeff's old lounger. "Sit." Picking up Jan's knitting basket, she handed it to her. "Keeping your hands busy will help calm your nerves."

Jan took a deep breath. "Yes, you're right. I'm not helping by being agitated."

Once her hands were in motion, working on Billy's sweater, her tension eased. As she completed each loop, she felt closer to her son. Jan wasn't sure when or how, but the details didn't matter. He was going to put this sweater on. She worked faster. She had to finish the sleeves and then sew everything together so it would be ready for him when he came home to her.

Using the remote, Jan shut off the TV. She wasn't watching it, and Rana, Diane, and Amy seemed to be dozing off. She focused on her fingers, pushing needles into loops and wrapping new yarn for the next stitch.

All the while, imagining the raucous sound of the house phone breaking the silence, bringing her hope.

The phone was going to ring. It had to. What she couldn't understand was why the kidnappers would wait so long to set up a time and place to exchange Billy for money.

Jan must have dozed off because she woke with a start to a jarring sound.

Finally. The call.

No. Not the kidnappers. Her cell phone was ringing.

Knocking her knitting to the floor, she grabbed the phone from the end table and pressed *answer.*

"Jan, Andy here. We…ah…found the vehicle."

"The car. Billy." Jan sat upright in the chair, wiping the fuzziness from her eyes.

"Not in it."

"Where did you find the car?"

Andy hesitated. "You know that mountain road up by Singleton?"

"Yes, it's narrow and treacherous. Oh my God."

"A call came in about a vehicle seen rolled over down in the ravine. Our men checked it out. Blue-black sedan with gray paint on its right fender. Likely the vehicle that rammed your car. The man inside was dead. We don't know if Billy was in the car at the time and ran off, or if the man had been alone. We're examining the car for DNA and searching the area for Billy."

"If Billy was with him, he might be injured. It's dark; he'll be scared and cold."

"With night vision goggles, our men are equipped to spot him."

"The man. Who is it?"

"We're running an ID now. Will keep you updated."

"Please."

Within seconds, Jan's team of friends encircled her, their faces frowning in concern.

Amy knelt in front of Jan and took her hands. "They'll find him, Jan. You've got to believe that."

Rana handed Jan a glass of water.

Why do people always think when you're upset you're thirsty? "No thanks." She pushed it away. Tears slid over her cheeks like a waterfall and her nose filled making it hard to breathe. "What I really need is a tissue."

Diane found the box and held it in front of her so she could pluck out a few sheets.

"The car was at the bottom of Singleton Ravine. The driver was dead. Billy was nowhere," Jan said between sobs. She blew her nose again and wiped the wetness from her cheeks.

"He may not have been in the car at all," Rana said.

"It's possible. The police are searching the area for him, just in case."

"So we wait," Amy said, "and we pray."

Amy, Rana, and Diane held hands, making a circle around Jan. Once again, they bowed their heads in silent prayer.

They're not just praying for Billy. Their prayers are for me.

Chapter Thirty-One

Bah. At night, the back room of the shop is a prison cell. Nothin' to do except watch the stinking little TV he put in here to check the odds. Frank broke off a hunk of the bread he'd bought for Tina, stuffed it in his mouth, and chased it with a slug of wine—at least it wasn't water. He could be home dunking it in the juice of Tina's sausage and peppers. Maybe she put hot sausages in this time, even though they give Lucille the farts.

The place was too quiet at night. He missed the activity. Marilee and Irene weren't flitting around, and the music wasn't playing.

To kill time, he phoned Tina. "Did ya go see the mom?"

"She was with the neighbors; you know Rana next door and Diane. Everyone was so upset. I was glad to get out of there."

Frank envisioned Tina twirling a stray hair around her talented fingers, one curvy hip thrust against the kitchen counter. He could be there right now, with his hands on those hips. "I know, but what did ya find out?"

"No word on Billy, yet. They're parked by the phone waiting for a ransom call. You never told me what you did about the money, Frankie."

"You don't need to know. It's business."

"Dirty business."

"I did what I had to do for the kid. Why do I feel the only one suffering is me?"

"You poor baby. When this is over, I'm going to give you The Special."

"The Special?" His balls ached, and little Frankie perked up. "Oh, Lovie, don't tease me like this."

Tina giggled, which made him smile. He loved the tinkle of her girlish laugh.

"Frankie, no one said you had to stay at the shop."

"True, but if the cops are still patrolling the street, they'll be on the lookout for anyone coming down the road. I'd better stay here tonight until this blows over. Ta kill time, maybe I'll stop at O' Brien's. Have a glass of cheap wine and mingle a bit."

"Stay away from that pool table. You know how you are when you're hustling."

Tina knew him too well. "I got to get off the phone. I'm waiting on a call. Talk to ya later." He made a kissing sound into the phone and disconnected.

Taking a sip of his fine Chianti, Frank paced the small area between the tiny refrigerator and the card table in his back room. Eight bells and not a peep from Wheezy. No surprise there. The man had the memory of a fly and was easily distracted by a neon sign hawking naked babes.

Louie hadn't reported in either.

"Fuck this waiting."

Frank speed dialed Louie. "Whatcha got for me? Where's the kid?"

"Not sure yet, but making progress. That asshole Bruno won't be bothering us anymore. I squeezed the shit out of him, but he wouldn't talk."

"Bad move to off him. Now we're stuck depending on Wheezy. Nice move, Louie."

"Not to worry, boss. I'm still on Wheezy's tail. He's been checking houses, so he's doing what you asked. I been all over Connecticut and now we're in Rhode fucking Island. I think he's seen me."

"Then he'll behave."

"So, boss, what if I find the kid? What do I do with him?"

Frank rubbed his jaw. Bristly. He'd have to shave, or Tina would hold back on The Special.

"I'll spell it out for ya. Find the kid, then phone in a tip to the police and tell them the location so they will come and get him. Use one of them throwaway phones so they can't trace you. Easy as pie. Oh, and he's a smart kid. When you're snooping around to make sure he's there. Don't let him see you."

"What am I supposed to do if he spots me?"

"*Madonna mia*. Tell you what, pick up one of them cheap Halloween masks. Nothing scary, mind you, and put it on so he can't identify you."

"Me, wear a mask?"

"Exactly."

That situation handled, Frank shrugged into his overcoat and strolled over to O'Brien's for a little action. He arrived to find the joint jammed with locals celebrating the TGIF thing. Lots of suckers waiting to be parted with their money.

A couple of hours later, Frank rolled over in the skinny cot in his office and groaned. His back ached, and his head pounded from all the cheap wine he downed. A sulfite headache. *Bah*.

He swung his legs over the edge, his bare feet

cringed at the feel of cold ceramic tile, and the stale smell of cigar smoke assaulted his sensitive nose. After flipping on the light switch, he kicked the poor excuse for a bed. He hoped to hell he was done sleeping here. Someone's gonna pay for this inconvenience.

He should have never got involved with helping Billy, yet the kid who called him Poppa Frank and loved to visit managed to wedge his way into his heart. He hadn't been around kids much until Lucille had baby Frank. The problem was the kid didn't do much except poop, eat, and cry, with the occasional giggle. In a year or so, the kid would be walking and talking like little Billy.

Frank ran his fingers through his thin, and at the moment, greasy hair. A hot shower would feel good about now, except the backroom of the shop didn't have one. If he was smart, he would've kept a clean shirt here, at least. He sniffed his armpits. Not good.

Picking up his pants from the floor, he put them on. The front pocket bulged. Reaching inside, he dug out a wad of bills so fat it had popped his money clip. Nice take last night. A bunch of newbies. No IOUs this time. Cash on the line or Frank no play. He had them going. He played the poor old man part, and they bit. One by one.

The best part, the bucks didn't have to go into the family pot. Escape money for him and Tina. It was time to blow outta here and head to Europe. Visit Tina's family for a while, maybe buy a little farm and start a vineyard and make some wine. If he had his way, Lucille, Vinnie, and the baby were coming along, at least until things cooled down. Louie was pretty good at taking charge. He was young and strong and knew the rules cold.

Louie. Why hadn't he called? These goons today. Ya had to coach them every step of the way. No accountability.

He felt for his cell phone in his pocket. Not there. Got to be. *Ah*, he picked it up off the floor. Must have fell out during the night.

Louie picked up when he called him. "Nothing yet, boss. I lost some time. Wheezy slipped away from me."

Frank's stomach clenched. "I knew I couldn't trust that asshole. We're done with him. Got that, Louie?"

"Yeah, I'll put him on my list."

"The hit list."

"Got you, boss. The good news is I found Wheezy naked in a brothel. He said Bruno had a grandma out in the sticks. I got an address out of him. I'm headed there now to check out his story."

"Ya must be tired. Long night, day actually. Christ, it's four a.m. Gonna be light soon. All right, assuming Wheezy gave it to you straight, you'll have the kid soon. Did you pick up a mask?"

"Nah, nothing's open now."

"What about that ski mask you wore for the bank job?"

"Oh, yeah, good idea. It's in the trunk."

"Madonna Mia, you left evidence in your car? What were you thinking? Never mind. Good, then make sure you wear it when you look for the kid. In fact, pull over, and get the mask out now, before you forget." Louie was tough, but he wasn't the brightest bulb in the chandelier.

"Yeah, yeah. Will do. I'll call you."

"Make it soon. This stunt is dragging on."

Chapter Thirty-Two

As night turned to day, Jan's hopes of recovering her son deflated like an old balloon. The search of the ravine was ongoing; but, really, how far could Billy have traveled on foot? If he were injured, he wouldn't be far from the crash site, and they would have found him. In a way, she was encouraged the police found no tiny boot prints leading from the crash. Maybe he was safely inside a warm place waiting to come home to her.

She'd shooed Rana, Diane, and Amy home to their families early, with a request that Ted walk Mae home right after breakfast.

"Where's Billy?" Mae asked as she came in the back door. She scanned the kitchen in anticipation.

"He's not home yet, sweetheart, but that nice detective is making progress. Today's the day," Jan said, faking a perkiness she didn't feel.

"I can't stop thinking about Billy. Oh, Mom, what if we never see him again?"

Jan did her best to block the horrible thoughts she'd had about him being sold into slavery. She chucked her daughter's chin. "Of course we'll see him. I'll bet right this minute he's on his way back to us."

If only that were true. Jan was ready to bargain with the devil to make it happen—the devil being the kidnappers who never even called. If they were so hot for their money, why hadn't they made an effort to contact her?

She pulled Mae to her. "I'm happy I have you, darling. I would be lost without you."

"Mom, come on. It's going to be all right. I'm going to take a shower and change. I've been in these clothes since yesterday. I feel icky."

"Go ahead, honey. I suppose I should do that too."

Jan toyed with the idea. She didn't dare, even if she took the cordless into the bathroom while she showered, she might not hear it ring over the rush of water. No, a shower would have to wait until all this is over. If it would *ever* be over.

Jan struggled from the chair. She needed fresh air. Something. She'd been closed in since yesterday, yet she didn't dare leave the house in case the kidnappers called. Maybe they had fallen asleep and planned to call this morning. It was only eight, but Billy would be awake now. If he were home, he'd have toddled from his room clutching Bob and sucking his thumb. She would feed him some cereal and then turn on cartoons to keep him busy while she got Mae going. At the thought, Jan's eyes watered. *You'd think my tear ducts would have run dry by now.*

When the phone rang, her heart stopped. It had to be *them!*

Reaching over to pick up the call, Jan's hopes plummeted. The screeching of a siren at the other end of the call tore at her ears. Bad news from Andy.

"Oh, no. Please don't tell me he's—"

"We've got Billy. I'm with him in an ambulance headed for Hartford General. Meet us in the emergency room," Andy said.

Jan wavered in place. "Are you sure? Really? You've got him? My son?" Her voice went up an octave with each word until she found herself smiling through tears of joy.

Wait. Emergency room? The tension in her body let go. Her knees crumbled under her, smacking the floor with a painful clunk. Reaching for Mae, who had come at hearing the call, Jan pulled her daughter close.

"He's hurt, my baby?" Jan choked out.

"He seems okay, but it's standard procedure to run him through a medical check before releasing him. Someone called in a tip. We picked him up in Rhode Island. One of our men found him wandering on the road."

"In the road. He could've been hit by a car…"

"Mommy?" Billy's voice was flat, devoid of emotion.

"Oh, my darling, Mommy missed you so much. You are safe with Andy. Mae and I are on our way to see you." A fresh bout of tears spilled from her eyes.

"Okay."

Jan wrapped her arm around Mae's narrow shoulders, realizing she was crying tears of relief as well. Yet, Billy did not sound like himself, which scared her. What had those men done to her little boy?

Andy came back on the line and said in a hushed voice. "He's a bit disoriented and chilled to the bone. We've got him wrapped in a blanket."

"Thank you for taking care of him, Andy. We'll be right over."

When Jan and Mae arrived at the hospital, the nurse was quick to get them in to see Billy. They had him in one of those curtained bays. A man in a medical coat blocked their view of her son, although she saw Billy's feet dangling from the side of a cot. Andy sat in a chair to the side. He rose when they entered, his face serious.

Dragging Mae by the hand, Jan dashed in between Andy and the doctor and took Billy in her arms. She hugged him to her, reveling in the feel of his warm little body against hers. "I'm never going to let you go, my darling."

Billy lay against her like a limp rag, emitting a small moan.

"What's wrong?" Jan asked the doctor. "Tell me."

"He's still in shock, ma'am," the doctor said. "Give him some time, and he'll be fine. He checks out okay physically, although he refused to take off his clothes so I couldn't examine him as thoroughly as I'd like. Once you get him home, check him over for surface bruises, and perhaps follow up with your pediatrician."

"Bruises? Did those men hit you, honey?" Jan pushed back so she could examine her son. She smoothed his cheek, dirtied with something sticky and brown. His eyes were glassy, and he couldn't seem to focus on her. He clutched the white and blue hospital blanket draped over him as if it were a lifeline. "Answer me. Are you hurt?"

Billy shook his head, then his face scrunched, and he burst into tears. "I want to go home, Mommy, and I want pancakes."

The tension in Jan's shoulders released. "There's my little boy." She kissed his forehead. "You're going to be just fine, sweetheart."

Mae took Billy's hand. "I've got lots to tell you."

"Your son is a brave young man," Andy said.

She'd almost forgotten he was still here. "We aren't sure who called in his location. For all we know, it could have been one of his kidnappers. We need to take him back to the station. The FBI wants to interview him to find out what he knows so we can put out an APB on the kidnappers."

Billy grabbed Jan. "No. Home, Mommy."

"The FBI can go to—sorry. Andy, my son is exhausted and upset. Can't interviewing wait until he's at least had a good night's sleep?"

"I'll see if I can put things off."

"You do that." Jan kissed the top of Billy's head. "And no FBI. My son won't want to talk to strangers."

"Got it," Andy said. "Suppose I drop by in the morning?"

"That should be okay, but no pressure. Understand?"

Andy saluted her. "Got it, ma'am."

Once her son was clean and settled in his bed, Jan left him with Mae reading him a story and made the dreaded call to her parents. As far as they were concerned, the biggest issue was Jeff's imprisonment. Since then she had dodged their calls and held back information that would upset them further, even Billy's kidnapping.

Because he had been located and returned to her within twenty-four hours, Jan hoped the news of his kidnapping hadn't reached Jersey. If it had, her parents would have been at her doorstep waiting along with her, which would have been comforting to her but would have put them in possible jeopardy. These thugs seemed to know everything about her family, which gave her the creeps; her mother and father would have made two more targets for their threats.

During the call, the information Jan divulged hit her mother like a baseball bat. She went quiet. Jan heard a loud thump.

"Mona, Mona!" Her father spoke to his wife on the open phone line.

"Mom, Dad, what's going on? Are you all right?"

Finally, her father picked up the phone. "Your mother just collapsed."

The call disconnected, leaving Jan's heart beating like a bongo drum. Her mom's high blood pressure was common knowledge, but she'd been under a doctor's supervision for years.

What if she's had a heart attack?

Now, more than ever, the pain of being so far away jabbed at Jan.

Her first inclination was to grab the children, jump in the car, and get to Jersey. *Deja vu* for all those nights she tried to walk out on Jeff. The reality of picking up and leaving never quite met the expectations of the dream. She would need to wake up Billy, who had just gone through a trauma, and disturb Mae. Traffic would be horrendous, as always when driving through New York City, and they'd most likely arrive in the wee hours of the morning.

By the time she got there, the children would be upset, and her mother might be fine. In fact, she may have collapsed for reasons other than her heart. Her mother had a flair for the dramatic.

Jan took a deep breath to calm herself and then dialed her parent's phone number.

It rang four times before her father picked up.

"Sorry, honey. I was just going to call you. Mona's

come to. I'm going to have her doctor check her over anyway, but if you ask me the sudden shock made her blood pressure go down."

"You *do* understand. Everything's fine now. Billy is home and safe."

"You never explained why, Janice."

"It's a long story. I don't want to upset Mom or you any further, especially with everything under control."

"We can come up in the morning."

"Not tomorrow. I expect to be out most of the day. I…uh…need to see Jeff, and find out what's going on with his hearing, but soon. Maybe this weekend. Okay?"

"She's coming to see us, Mona," Jan heard him say.

The happy lift in her father's voice warmed Jan's heart. This time, she *wanted* to spend time with them. She and the children needed a break from this depressing environment. Maybe they'd stay a week—or forever.

****

Morning came, bringing sunshine into the bedroom where Jan slept, both children cuddled against her. She eased out from between them, trying not to waken them.

"Where are you going, Mommy?" Billy clutched her nightgown, drawing her back down.

She turned to him and kissed the tip of his nose. "To put on a pot of coffee. How nice to have you back home, sweetheart."

Mae sat up in bed and yawned. "I like your bed, Mom. It's more comfortable than mine is."

"Don't get used to it. Tonight, both of you are going back to your room." *So I can get some rest.* "But I promise you will be safe there."

"I didn't dream of the monster last night," Billy said, his brow furrowed, "but the lady in the bathrobe kept telling me to go to sleep, but I couldn't."

Billy hadn't said anything yesterday about what happened to him once he left Charming Way in the black sedan, but it was obviously on his mind now.

"Is that where those men took you? To a lady's house?"

Billy nodded.

"And she wanted you to sleep? Did she give you food?" Jan couldn't stop touching him to make sure he was really there. She had many questions for her son.

"Just chocolate." Billy climbed out of bed, dragging Bob with him by its arm. "I have to tinkle, now, Mommy."

Okay, it was a start. Little by little, Billy's story would come out until all the pieces were in place.

Mae must have sensed her brother's need for privacy last night because even she held back on drawing him out on his experience.

Jan was slow to move this morning, feeling as if she'd run a marathon. She hadn't, of course, but the stress of the past week took a toll on her energy. With effort, she washed up and dressed, knowing Andy would be by soon to try to talk to Billy.

Half an hour later, Billy and Mae sat at the kitchen table waiting for Jan to produce breakfast. The doorbell buzzed.

Mae leaped up and ran to the window to check who it might be. "It's Andy, Mom. Should I let him in?"

"Of course. Bring him in the kitchen, where we can talk." Soon Andy would begin questioning Billy. She wondered how the detective planned to handle the procedure.

Andy walked in appearing rested and dressed in his usual business suit. "Morning, all." He held up a large bag bearing an emblem like the one on the bag she'd found in Jeff's drawer. Except this bag was bigger and emitted an aroma that made Jan's stomach rumble.

"I picked up breakfast at the drive-through on the way over," he continued. "If your children are anything like my Ollie is, they love Mickey D's breakfast sandwiches—and so do I." He grinned.

"Good timing, I've been trying to get up the motivation to make the children eggs." They'd had pancakes oozing with butter and syrup for dinner, last night, per Billy's special request, and she needed to get some protein into them this morning.

Mae took the bag from Andy and began unpacking it, placing the sandwiches on the table. "Look, Mom, there's even yogurt for you."

Jan tipped her head to the side. "You remembered about my gluten issue. How thoughtful."

"No problem." He set down a cardboard tray holding drinks. "I picked up coffee and shakes to go with the food."

"Please sit down." Jan gestured toward Jeff's chair at the head of the table.

"Can we eat now, Mommy?" Billy hugged Bob to his chest. "My tummy hurts."

"Of course, darling, but why don't you set Bob down so you don't get food all over him."

"He's hungry, too, aren't you, Bob?" Billy tipped

the toy's oversized, boxy head forward in a nod.

"Very well." Jan wedged an extra chair between Andy and Billy. "He can sit next to you."

Without further ado, Billy plunked the toy in the seat and unwrapped his sandwich. After taking a bite, he shoved it at Bob's painted mouth.

"It's nice that your friend Bob could join us," Andy said to Billy. "Have you told him about your big adventure?"

For a minute, Jan thought Billy was going to clam up. He pursed his lips and studied his sandwich. Then he turned his head toward the toy. "Bob, you won't believe what happened."

Jan's attention perked, yet she continued stirring her yogurt so as not to interfere.

"What happened is you got into a car with those strange men." The words spewed out of Mae's mouth like a pent-up volcano. "Why did you do it, Billy? You know better." The tears streaming down her freckled cheeks belied her attempt at anger.

Jan hugged her daughter close. "It's all right, honey. He's here now, and that's what matters."

"But he should have known better, Mom."

Billy's face went sad. His lower lip quivered. "It wasn't my fault."

"Of course it wasn't, honey." Jan picked him up and set him on her lap.

Billy stuck out his tongue at his sister. "I wasn't talking to you anyway. I was talking to Bob."

Jan looked at Andy and shrugged. "This is going to be harder than I thought."

"Give it time. I, uh, moved in too quickly."

The room was quiet, except for the sounds of

munching and slurping until Billy finished the last of his chocolate shake and set his cup on the table. "I had a lot of chocolate yesterday, a whole bag I didn't have to share."

"The lady in the bathrobe?"

Billy nodded.

"Do you remember how you got to her house," Jan asked cautiously.

Billy reached for his toy.

Andy passed it over to him.

He held it close, resting his cheek on top of Bob's flat head as if it were a touchstone.

Jan smoothed her son's hair. "You don't have to talk about it if you don't want to, but if you can tell us what happened, Andy might be able to find the bad men and put them in jail."

"With Daddy?"

"Yes, with Daddy."

Billy worried his lower lip, seeming to absorb the concept. She waited for him to talk more about his father, surprised that her son would associate his father with those thugs. Yet, was Jeff much better? He'd endangered young children and his family.

Billy sat upright and began to speak. "An arm came out of the car, and *boom*. I was inside. A big man held me on his lap. Tight. Like this." He demonstrated by squeezing Bob hard enough to make the pillow toy flatten at its middle. "He said I had to do what he said, or he would get my sister, too. I wanted to save you, Mae." Billy sniffed back tears that had begun to leak from his eyes.

Jan hated to put Billy through this, but better he talked about it than kept it inside.

Mae looked down at the table. "I'm sorry for being mean to you."

"Did he talk funny?" Jan asked, thinking of the man with the raspy voice who had threatened them.

"He sounded a little like Daddy does when he has a bad cold."

Andy had settled near Billy at the table, his gaze intent. "That's good information, Billy. Can you remember where they took you?"

Billy's brow wrinkled. "I saw trees and then the man carried me into the house."

"One man?"

"No. A man with a hat drove the car. I was in the back seat with the bald man."

"Would you recognize the house if you saw it?" Andy continued.

"It was white, and there was snow on the grass, but no one made a snowman."

"Billy," Andy said. "Think hard. What happened next?"

Billy toyed with Bob's skinny arms, wrapping them into a knot, and then undoing it. "The man gave me to a lady who looked really old, older than Grandma even. She pinched my cheek and said I was cute. She gave me candy and then put me in a bedroom. She shut the door. I tried to open it, but I couldn't. I banged at it and cried, but the lady didn't come until it got dark. She brought me macaroni and cheese. Not the good kind you make, Mommy. This was orange and sticky."

Jan couldn't help but smile. Her son, all of a sudden a connoisseur of mac and cheese.

"Did you eat it?" Mae asked.

"Yes. I was so hungry. I drank my milk too,

Mommy."

"So, Billy"—Andy set down his coffee cup—"what happened next?"

"The lady said I had to stay so I might as well go to sleep. I think it was her bedtime. She had on her bathrobe and slippers and a funny thing on her hair. I tried to sleep, Mommy. I needed a bedtime story, and Bob was home. I can't sleep without Bob." Billy squeezed his toy.

"Now, Billy," Andy said. "I'm wondering how you managed to get out of that bedroom. The police found you wandering in the road."

"I went out the window."

Andy's brows went up. "That was a very brave thing to do."

"I jumped and landed in a prickly bush. And I remembered to put on my coat and boots before I tried, just in case."

"What a smart little boy you are," Jan said, all the while horrified at the vision of her son climbing out a window in a strange place in the dark. Yet, she was relieved to learn the bruises she found on his buttocks and the back of his legs were from a fall, not from a sexual assault.

"When you were outside, was anyone around?" Andy asked.

"Just trees. I saw a light far away, and I walked toward it. It was good I wore my boots because the grass was wet."

"That was exactly the right thing to do," Andy said.

"A car was coming. It wasn't black like the bad man's car. I think it was white. White is good, isn't it, Mommy?" He turned to Jan. "Good guys have white cars. I was going to hide just in case, but I was cold and scared, so I just stood there. The car stopped."

Mae's forehead wrinkled. "Another strange car. You didn't get in this time, did you?"

"Shush, Mae, let your brother finish," Jan said.

"A man dressed like a policeman said, 'Get in, Billy.' He knew my name, Mommy. How did he know my name?"

"Someone called in at the station and said they knew where you were. We sent that car out to find you," Andy said.

"Oh. That was good. I'm done." Billy climbed off Jan's lap. "Bob said he wants to play in my room."

"Good job, sport." Andy ruffled her son's hair. "Glad you are home and safe." The detective slid back his chair and stood. "I need to get back to the station and see how they're doing identifying the men who took Billy."

"I'll walk you to the door, Detective."

Jan escorted Andy as far as the porch, where they would be out of Mae and Billy's earshot.

"The children and I are grateful for your support," she said, crossing her arms to ward off the cold. "There is so much I don't understand about what is going on. You've been kind enough to keep me informed and respond whenever I call. That means a lot right now."

"Just doing my job, ma'am." If he had a hat, he might've tipped it.

"One more thing." Jan posed the concern that continued to haunt her. "Do you think we're safe?"

Andy replied with a raised eyebrow and then turned to head down the steps to his car.

Jan stood at the door until he drove off. The man

had been a godsend through a crisis she knew was hardly over. Billy's escape foiled the kidnapper's chance of holding him for ransom. Yet, she questioned why they held him most of the day without making their move.

The car, of course, with the dead man inside must have had something to do with it. He had been garroted, mob style so the rollover couldn't have been an accident. Andy claimed no proof, other than the man they'd found was in the car identified as the one that sideswiped hers the other day.

Two men, one possibly dead, and a debt still owed.

They were not safe.

Not Billy, not Mae, not me—nor Jeff.

How easy would it be for someone to hide in the back seat of Jan's Ford and offer her life for the money? She'd seen how quickly a child could be snatched up. Billy and Mae were prey no matter where they were. Even locked in this house, like prison, with the right mindset and equipment a person could get inside.

Mae came alongside her and squeezed Jan's hand. "It's going to be all right, Mom."

Her chest went tight, and she gulped back a sob. She wanted to reassure her daughter, but she couldn't.

Joy Smith

Chapter Thirty-Three

The men in black, the gangsters in the black car, still haunted Jan. On Thursday morning, a few days before Jeff's trial, that awful man called again. His wheezing, the voice scratchy and abrupt, she would know it anywhere.

"The brat got away, but youse ain't off the hook. I know where you live, where you work, and where the little redheaded girl goes to school. I got friends inside with orders from the top to squeeze your husband until he coughs up the dough. One way or another, I'm gonna get what's coming to me. Call you tonight with details."

"Leave us alone!" Jan shouted into the dead phone.

Not knowing what else to do, she called Andy.

"You must be fed up with me by now," Jan told him, "but I just got another call. Is the tap still on my house phone? It was the raspy man. He wants his money. Jeff's in danger, and so are we."

"We haven't removed the wire yet, but I'm not sure it's still being monitored. Hold on, I'll check."

Cradling the phone, Jan listened to dead air for at least ten minutes before Andy came back on the line.

"I've got an officer reviewing the tape right now. Any chance of a trace?"

"I doubt it. The call was short like the others. The man is supposed to call me tonight to let me know where to take the money." A giggle escaped. What money? She barely had enough to buy groceries this week. "These men don't fool around; their next step is action. I can't go through it again. I just can't." Tears welled up in her eyes. Her children, her home. They were open to anything those thugs might plan. They could be captured and tortured, killed even.

"Have you reconsidered the sting we spoke about earlier? Typically, they'll name a drop off point where you would leave the money. The dough would be fake, but our men would be positioned to nab anyone who came to get it."

"What if it goes wrong? Fake money will only make them angry. Angry enough to nab me as I'm leaving. I don't like your plan, Detective. I can't risk my life and leave my children without a mother. They've already lost a father.

"Is there any way you can get a loan?"

"Not right away. Maybe they'll be satisfied with less, a down payment. That man never stays on the line long enough to negotiate." Jan thought of the five-thousand-dollar check she'd ripped up. If she asked, she was sure her father would write out another, but she couldn't bear to ask them. Besides, she'd still be beholden to those men and their awful threats for the rest of it."

"That's tough. I'm not sure what to tell you. Technically, this debt is on your husband's shoulders. He's been moved to a high-security area if that's any assurance."

"I know, and I appreciate all you are doing. Would it be possible for me to visit Jeff? I need to speak to him about our finances face to face. And I have some questions to ask him about the source of his debt."

"The FBI…"

"…Obviously hasn't learned anything from him. He will talk to me, though."

"I'll arrange it, but you'll have to wear a wire."

A wire. Just like in TV shows. She'd need to make sure their conversation wasn't too personal. Yet, if she could get information out of Jeff, where the FBI failed, maybe they'd catch the men who have been after her, and she'd be able to sleep nights again.

"I'll do it, Andy. I'll…need to take the children with me to make sure they are safe. I don't dare leave them with anyone. I even kept them home from school today."

Andy was silent for a minute and then said, "The Enfield facility won't allow children under twelve in. I plan to be at the Greenberg station this morning, though. When you come here to be wired, plan to leave Billy and Mae with me. I can't promise I'll have time to entertain them, but they will be safe in my office."

"That's very kind of you, Andy. I'll pack up a bag of books and quiet games. I don't expect I'll be gone more than an hour and a half."

"Good. I'll notify the agents of our plan. Does ten o'clock work for you?"

"Deal."

At Enfield, after submitting to all the entry rigmarole, a guard ushered Jan to a private visiting room to meet with Jeff.

"Billy. Is he all right?" Jeff asked at once.

"Yes, no thanks to you. Our family is still not safe. I received another threatening call about the money, Jeff. It won't stop until we pay these men off or the police find them and lock them away."

He wiped the perspiration from his face with the hem of his orange prison coat, even though the visiting room was air-conditioned. "I told you. I don't have it. I only get paid when I sell the weed, and you know how that went this time. Can you get a bank loan?"

"Oh, sure. Our credit is good as gold. The last time I went in to cash a check I got the fish eye from the teller."

"How about your parents? They must have a good chunk of dough saved."

"You mean their retirement money?"

"Yeah, what do they need it for?"

"I'm going to make believe you never said that. My parents are not involved in your mess, and I plan to keep it that way. It would help if you could nail the men so we'd be off the hook for your debt."

"Look, I did talk to the police, but I could only tell them what I know. Squat. That's why I'm not worried about these guys coming after me. The fact is I can't identify anyone I haven't seen."

"This isn't all about you, Jeff. They're coming after our children and me, too. How did you get involved with such scum?"

Jeff tilted his head. "I shouldn't tell you because you probably won't believe me."

"Try me."

"Remember the night I went to the DiGiorno's for poker?"

"Go on."

"I ran out of money and ended up with an IOU to that Greg guy, Frank's son-in-law. Big dude." He motioned upward with his hand.

"So Frank DiGiorno started this?"

"No, he cut me off and folded the game. He wouldn't give me a chance to win back my money. Do you believe that?"

"Seems to me he did the right thing."

"Yeah, but not for me."

"How much did you lose?"

"About eight grand."

"Did you pay that Greg guy back?"

"I couldn't. I was short funds, and he wouldn't wait the two stinking weeks until my paycheck came in. Greg gave me a phone number and said to call it for a loan."

Jan sat forward in her chair, her chest heaving from the anger growing inside her.

"When I called, the contact made me a deal I couldn't resist. It was easy, pick up a supply—the weed was already in small packs—and get someone to sell it. I didn't have to do anything except fill the orders and collect the money."

"You lazy son-of-a-gun. What possessed you to get our godson involved?"

"The kid was whining about his allowance. He wanted a smartphone and all the stuff the rich kids had. I felt sorry for him. I did him a favor. Stevie got a nice cut." Jeff leaned back in his chair, his face smug.

"Are you proud of yourself? I hope so because that pride's going to come down a few notches when they lock you up with hardened criminals looking for your sweet cheeks." Jan shocked herself at the way she spoke, like some street tramp. Yet, the words spewed out and darn if she didn't feel a whole lot better for it.

Jeff's face flushed, and fresh perspiration beaded

on his face. "You've got to help me."

"I don't 'got' to do anything."

Jan signaled the guard. "I'm done here."

She seethed the whole drive back to Greenberg. How had she ever gotten involved with such a heartless jerk? She saw what she wanted to see. A handsome guy who seemed to care about her and made her parents feel better about losing their son. Marrying him seemed like the right thing to do at the time. Until now, Jan hadn't accepted the real Jeff. The Jeff hiding beneath the nice-guy shell was truly a bastard.

At the Greenberg station, Jan handed the tiny digital device used to tape her conversation with Jeff over to Andy. She had expected a real wire, but it seems that technology is obsolete.

Among the pile of folders on his desk, one laid open. With his tie and jacket removed and his shirt sleeves rolled up, the detective seemed more relaxed than normal. Billy and Mae, who worked at a small table placed in one corner of the office, glanced at her and then continued their projects.

"Thanks, I'll get this over to the agents," Andy said, dropping the device into an envelope.

"Don't you want to know what's on it?"

"I'll take a recap."

Jan leaned over and said in a hushed voice, "Greg. He's the DiGiorno's son-in-law. They live diagonally across the street from us."

"Hmmm. Greg? No last name?"

"Jeff claims he doesn't know it."

"We'll call on your neighbors and see what we can learn."

"You don't think Mr. DiGiorno's involved, do

you? He and his wife have been so sweet to us."

"Hard to tell, but if we can ID this Greg, we can get a lead on the kidnappers."

"That would be a relief."

"Can we go now, Mom?" Mae said. "I'm done with my homework."

"Look." Billy pushed a paper at her. "I drew a picture of Andy at his desk."

Jan smiled when she saw Billy had drawn the sun in the corner of the page. Andy was but a stick figure with some brown scribbles where his waist should have been." It's wonderful, honey." She kissed the top of his head and passed the drawing to Andy.

"Looks just like me," Andy said with a smile at her son. "In fact, I'll tack it up on my bulletin board."

Billy's big grin made Jan's heart sing.

She shook Andy's hand. "Thanks for watching the children. Will you let me know what happens with this Greg investigation? I still have that call about the money hanging over my head."

"You say he'll be phoning tonight?"

"I don't know what to tell him."

"With your new information, we've got a good shot at nabbing your man before he can harass you further."

"But what if you don't?"

"Then go along with it. Agree to whatever he asks." Andy put a hand on Jan's shoulder and caught her gaze. "If it comes to that, we'll put you and the children in a safe house while we activate a sting. Emma's about your size. We'll stick a scarf on her head, and they'll think it's you dropping off their money."

"I trust you to keep us safe, Detective."

"I'll do my best."

Chapter Thirty-Four

Frank languished on his king-size bed with his wife hovered over him licking off the maple syrup she'd rubbed over every inch of his body. Her hair was tousled like a wild woman's, her lips swollen. *Ah, The Special.* He'd only had it one other time with whipped cream. Not sure which he liked better.

"Oh, Lovie, what you do to me. Don't stop, please don't stop." He pushed Tina's head down on his erect soldier. His hands stuck to her hair. "Geez, you did my fingers too?"

Tina didn't reply, following the house rule of not talking with your mouth full.

"Oh, baby, you're the best." He lifted his hips and gyrated. "Oh God, oh, God." With a final thrust, he spewed forth in her mouth and then collapsed back onto the mattress.

Tina pushed up from his torso with a sucking noise, her size D boobs scraping against his thighs. "We're out of syrup."

"No problem. We ain't got company anymore so you don't have to be making French toast and pancakes every morning."

"It's lonely without Lucille and the baby here." She stuck out her lower lip in a pout and rolled off him onto her back.

Madonna mia, I finally get some peace and privacy

to fuck my wife, and she's lonely. Women. "Don't be. They'll be here every Sunday for dinner, as usual. And we can always take a fifteen-minute ride to Hartford to visit them."

"I suppose."

Bzzz. Bzzz.

"Your phone, Frankie."

"Fuck the phone. Come here." He pulled her close. "We're gonna need a shower, babe." He wiggled his eyebrows. "How about I soap you up and make sure you are very very clean?"

With a girlish giggle—he loved it when she relaxed and let go like today—Tina rolled off the bed and pulled him to a standing position. Her warm tongue attacked his nipples.

Thank you, Viagra. I'm ready to go at it again. Man, after twenty-five years of marriage, most women would be thinking about how they were gonna get the syrup outta the sheets.

Bzzz. Bzzz.

"Frankie?" Tina's gaze went to the phone on the dresser.

"It's Louie. I told him Vinnie's back in charge. If it's important, he'll figure it out. Come here you." Scooping her up, he carried her into the bathroom.

An hour later, Frank lounged in front of the TV dressed in his boxer shorts and a T-shirt. *Nice not having anyone else around.* He could strut around naked if he wanted to. He clicked the remote. He was up for a good cop show.

Nothing on.

He didn't know how Tina put up with all the crap on TV. Women jibber-jabbering about stupid stuff, like ways to avoid carbs and sneak vegetables in their kid's food.

"Bah, who needs this?" Tossing the remote onto the coffee table, he followed the aroma of pasta sauce to the kitchen.

"Smells good in here."

"I'm making your favorite, lasagna."

He nuzzled the back of her neck, pushing his erection between the crack in her juicy butt cheeks.

"Aren't you satisfied yet?"

"Never, as long as you're around."

She shook her head, but he could tell she was smiling. "Maybe you need to cut back on the Viagra. I'm gonna have trouble walking for days."

Ding dong.

"Did you hear something?"

Ding dong.

"There it goes again. The door. You go see who it is." He gave her a friendly shove. "I ain't dressed for company, but you look good enough to eat."

"Oh, all right, but at least put on a pair of pants. It's probably Jan. She always brings back my food containers full of something good. We'll need dessert tonight."

"Got whipped cream?"

"Get out of here." Tina brushed by him laughing. "You're like an elephant, you never forget."

"Only the good times, Lovie, and all of them have been with you."

In the bedroom, Frank was buckling his belt when he heard a male voice. "Who the hell?"

He strode from the bedroom to the entry hall, as Tina admitted two suits. Tina's face was pale and her lips clamped tight.

"I'll handle this," he said to her. "You go finish what you were doing in the kitchen."

"Mr. DiGiorno?"

"Yes, what can I do for you guys?"

One of the suits stepped forward and put out his hand. "I'm Detective Hoskins, and this is Petty Officer Diggs of the FBI."

The officer nodded.

Frank drew up his shoulders, ignoring the extended hand. "ID?"

"Of course." The fuckers flashed their badges.

"Can never be too careful these days. We just had a crime in this neighborhood, and my wife and I are leery of strangers."

"Yes, I'm the detective who's been working the Simmons' case. You know their son was kidnapped a few days ago?"

"Yeah, someone came by and questioned my Tina. Got her all upset."

"Sorry. The boy is back home, but his mother is still having some issues we're addressing. May we sit and chat for a moment?" The man's gaze strayed to the living room.

Madonna mia, fuzz in my house for the second time in a week, and now they want to sit and chat. This can't be good. "Sure, why not." Frank settled in his armchair and indicated the couch for the two dudes. "Now, what's this about?"

"We have reason to believe your son-in-law Greg is involved in this case."

"Greg? Greg?" Oh yeah, now he remembered. He'd used a phony name to intro Vinnie the night they played poker with the neighbors. "Your source is fucking with you, Detective. I don't have a son-in-law named Greg." Frank stood, conversation over.

"We're not accusing him of anything at this point, Mr. DiGiorno, but we need to interview him about a loose end involving the case."

These guys aren't gonna give up. Sooner or later, they'll put two and two together, and Vinnie's face will come up. If they show his picture to Jeff, *boom*, Vinnie would be nailed and so would he. *I gotta protect us.*

"Just a minute, officer. I think I know the guy Jeff might mean. When he was over for a little game, a friend stopped by with another guy. Greg, that's what he called him."

Can you provide us your friend's phone number?"

"Oh, yes, of course. In fact, I'll go you one better. I think I have Greg's number too. I'll jot it down for you. Excuse me a minute."

Tina waited in the kitchen, looking much too sad for a woman who'd been laid big time. "I heard. Who's this Greg guy?"

"Tell ya later. Got a pencil and paper? I know how to handle this."

After scribbling down the information, Frank returned to the living room. "Here ya go, Officer. Gregory DiPietro." Frank chuckled. "His friends call him "Wheezy."

The detective gave him a half smile and then tucked the paper in his pocket. "We appreciate your cooperation in this matter, sir. We'll let ourselves out."

"You do that."

Frank stared at the men until they got into their vehicle and drove off, then he locked and bolted the door.

"What are we gonna do, Frankie?" Tina's eyes widened. "They're gonna find out about our Vinnie?"

"No, they're not. I just solved a problem for us and did a nice thing for that lady across the street."

"Jan?"

He nodded. "But that don't mean we're in the clear. We're gonna get the hell out of here in case they made me. Call Lucille and tell her I'm flying everyone to Italy for a little vacation, and then book us on the next flight out."

"Now? You mean today?"

"Yes, now."

"But my lasagna?"

"Stick it in the freezer."

"I could bring it next door. Rana has her parents there. I'm sure she could use a night without cooking."

He cupped her chin. "Get this neighborhood out of your head. We don't live here no more."

Tina ran toward the bedroom, sobbing.

I'm such a bastard, but a man's gotta do what a man's gotta do.

Picking up his cell, he punched out Louie's number. "The fuzz just left. It's time to tie up our loose end and don't drag your feet. The cops are onto him."

"My pleasure, boss. I always hated that little SOB."

Chapter Thirty-Five

Leaving Andy's office, Jan was somewhat relieved. They had a solid lead on the person who might be threatening them. Holding the children's hands, she steered them around the icy patches that remained on the police station's parking lot.

"Who wants to go out for Mexican?" she asked, getting a round of cheers in response. "Good. Lunch, then we'll head over to the Sweet Shop. I have to work a few hours this afternoon, are you all right with that?"

"Oh goodie," Mae said. "Loreen lets me cut out cookies."

"And I do a good job on the sprinkles, don't I, Mommy?"

"Yes, darling." Jan squeezed Billy's hand.

An hour later, when the three of them, stuffed with burritos and such, arrived at the Sweet Shop, Loreen greeted Jan with a huge grin.

"You'll never believe who just called."

"Out with it. I can tell you are bursting with good news."

"You've, ah, heard of a company called, IBG?"

"International Baked Goods? They're *huge*."

"They called this morning."

"Well, go on. What did they want?"

"They are very interested in taking on our line of gluten-free cookies and cakes."

"You're kidding?"

Grabbing both Jan's hands, Loreen danced her around the back room. "We're in the money!"

"Hold up." Jan smiled, almost breathless. "What does this mean?"

"I'm not sure, exactly." Loreen's brow furrowed. "It seems the demand for gluten-free baked goods made them realize they needed to fill a gap in their product line. They are sending a representative to discuss producing our baked goods commercially."

"So they really want our recipes."

"Something like that."

"And our goods would be under the IBG label?"

"I would assume so."

Jan had to think about it. She wasn't sure about giving up everything. "What does that mean for us?"

"They want to hire us as consultants. Don't you see? This is perfect. We would continue doing what we are doing now, you developing and converting recipes to great tasting gluten-free desserts, and me selling them to our customers. Once a product is taste-tested as perfect, we would sell the new recipes to IBG for mass production in their kitchen."

"What did you tell them?"

"That I had to discuss this with my partner and we'd get back to them." She nudged Jan's arm. "I was very cool on the phone. You would have been proud of me."

"Hmm, we may want to negotiate getting a percentage of their sales on our recipes instead of actually selling them. That way, if things don't work out, we can pull away."

"You really have a good head for business, Jan.

Since gluten is your shtick, why don't you give this Lawrence Day a call and set us up a meeting to negotiate. Here's the number."

Jan took the paper and grinned. "Loreen, you've just made my day. I will call this man back in a day or so. I am still dealing with some issues at home, and this way we won't seem too anxious."

"Good thinking."

"Are we going to cook now, Mom?" Mae eyed the warm oatmeal cookies Loreen had cooling on a rack.

"We're cooking all right, honey, in more ways than one."

The afternoon at the bakery flew by, with Loreen and Jan each adding to a list of talking points regarding their prospective business deal. It wasn't until Jan and the children were in the car driving home that the onus of the demand for money descended on her, dampening her good spirits, and dragging her back down to living in fear.

She knew she should be home parked by the phone, but dreaded the thought. When they took Billy, they never called. What if the call didn't come?

It was only five, but dark outside. As Jan drove down Charming Way, the only lights glowing came from within the homes she passed on the way to theirs. Shortly, she, Mae, and Billy would walk into their dark house. She would reach for the light switch just inside the door, and nothing would happen. What if the man with the horrible voice had decided to break in while they were gone? Jan shuddered at the thought, even though she had left everything locked tight.

She was about to turn in up their drive when her gaze landed on their mailbox. She hadn't picked up the mail in days, and now the lid barely closed. Pulling the car alongside, Jan rolled down the window and took the stack of envelopes and magazines onto her lap.

Before they emerged from the car, she shut the garage door automatically. No sense providing an opportunity for anyone lurking about to get inside their home.

"I'm bored," Billy said as soon as he got inside the house. "What can we do?"

"You children need to entertain yourselves for a while. Mommy needs a break."

Jan piled the mail on the kitchen table. The flood of bills never seemed to end. She'd fiddled with due dates so everything wouldn't come due on the same day. Sitting down, she started opening envelopes.

Mortgage, electric, water, car loan, charge cards— the bills were endless.

Would she ever catch up?

Jan stopped at a slim white envelope bearing the Klean Kare return address. Although it was addressed to Jeff, as were all the bills, she ripped it open.

"We regret to inform you," it read, *"that your employment at Klean Kare is terminated, effective immediately. We hope the attached funds will carry you through to your next endeavor. Good Luck."*

Humph. Jeff's sure going to need luck. She flipped to the attachment, and her mouth dropped open.

"Look, kids, your dad's company just sent us a severance check." Jan waved it in the air.

"What's a severance?" Billy asked.

"It's three thousand dollars."

"I need new sneakers for gym," Mae said.

"And you'll get them, my darling girl."

Once the initial excitement passed, it hit Jan. If the police failed to nab her caller, at least she had cash on hand to fend them off for a bit. She clutched the check to her heart.

No, I'm not doing it.

She and the children had suffered from Jeff's failures long enough. This money would help tide them over until—she crossed her fingers—the IBG deal went through.

Chapter Thirty-Six

By eight, the children were tucked in bed and asleep. Collapsed in front of the TV with her knitting, Jan kept an ear out for the phone waiting for the details on the money drop so she could inform Andy to set up the sting. Even though she'd kept the line open, the phone hadn't rung all night. Maybe Andy located the DiGiorno's son-in-law and hadn't had a chance to call her.

Using her cell phone, she punched in his number.

"Andy, I'm still waiting for the call about the drop-off. I'm wondering if they're going to drag this out again."

He chuckled. "I was about to call you. I suspect you won't hear from the thugs. Is it too late to stop by? I'll fill you in."

"Why? I mean what?"

"We may have found your caller, who is possibly the man involved with abducting Billy."

The tension in Jan's shoulders let go. She collapsed back into the chair.

"Jan? Are you there?"

"Yes, just relieved. Please. I'm awake. Come by."

When the doorbell rang ten minutes later, Jan ran to admit the handsome Detective Hoskins into her living room to find out what went down. What went down? She was starting to think like a police officer—

and she wasn't sure if it was a good or bad thing.

"My neighbors are going to start gossiping about these late night rendezvous." Without thinking, Jan flipped up her hair up in a flirtatious move, tilted her head, and smiled.

When Andy laughed, the strain in his face relaxed into a grin, creating deep lines in his cheeks and revealing his adorable dimple. "Should I be flattered? It's not often I get to spend time with a beautiful woman and call it police business."

The compliment from a good-looking man took Jan by surprise. Usually, Jeff picked apart her appearance. She opened her mouth to object and then closed it. *You ditz. Just say thank you.* She didn't, but, as she turned away, her lips curved up in a closed mouth smile some might interpret as being coy.

"Come on in. I have a pot of coffee on. Do you mind the kitchen again?"

Andy followed Jan inside "My favorite place." Drawing out a chair with a scraping sound, he sat down while she poured their coffee.

"I don't have any fresh cookies today. The children made gelatin cutouts yesterday. Want some?"

"Save them for the kids. Coffee will do me fine."

After setting two mugs on the table, Jan joined Andy. "So?" With her elbows on the table, she rested her chin in her hands. "This must be really important for you to talk to me in person."

When Andy cleared his throat, Jan sucked in a breath. "It is. We found Greg, the man your husband named from the poker game, a couple of hours ago." He held up his hand. "Now, we haven't yet proved he's the one who called, but when we ID'ed the body…"

"The body? You mean?" Jan made a slashing motion across her throat.

"Yes, garroted like the man driving the black sedan was. Likely, a mob hit. Both men we've found dead have done jail time. Because of the identical MO's, and the ID on the sedan, we feel these two were involved in harassing you and abducting Billy.

Jan's hand flew to her mouth. "Greg is the DiGiorno's son-in-law. No, that can't be true. Billy calls them Poppa Frank and Momma Tina. We had coffee at their house. Tina brought me chicken soup after Jeff was arrested. The leftovers from her sausage casserole are still in my fridge. They seemed upset when I told them Billy was missing."

Andy made a clicking noise with his mouth. "There's something else you need to know. When I stopped at the DiGiorno's this afternoon, something about Frank was familiar. I'd seen his picture somewhere, only his hair was brown, and he wore a full beard. I had my assistant do some research. That sweet old man is Don Frank Carlucci, also known as "The Lid" because of his droopy eyes. He ran a small operation in Hartford. Word on the street is he recently stepped down and handed control of The Family to his daughter's husband, Vincenzo Rigatoni. Vinnie."

"The Family? You can't mean Family like in Mafia?" Jan's voice rose.

"Mafia, cartel, whatever."

"Here? On Charming Way?"

"Yes. My sources say Frank Carlucci is trying to clean up his act. He's opened up a barber shop in town and, so far, it's been legit."

"I planned to take Billy there for a haircut. Wait,

something's not making sense. "If Frank's son-in-law is this Vinnie, then who's Greg?"

"To protect his identity, Mr. Carlucci must have introduced his son-in-law using an alias. Gregory DiPietro is a distant cousin of the Carlucci's, street name Wheezy due to his asthma problem."

"Wheezy, the raspy voice. And he…he's dead now?"

"Yep. You won't hear from him again, not in this world, anyway. We suspect he and his partner, Bruno Pacello, may have tried to cheat The Carlucci Family."

"I can't believe Tina and Frank were involved in Billy's kidnapping. They doted on him. They were upset when I told them about it."

Andy's eyebrows went up. "We found a rap on her too. Prostitution charges. She went by Tina Tongue in her younger years. She's been clean for close to twenty-five years. Probably when she married into the Carlucci family."

Jan's body froze in shock. "We moved here because this was supposed to be a nice neighborhood," she said in a small voice.

"It is now. When we found Wheezy's body, I sent over a team of officers to pick up Frank Carlucci for questioning. Your neighbors have moved out of their house. I doubt if they'll be back."

"Frank and Billy were pals. You don't think he had anything to do with—no." Jan shook her head. "He wouldn't, no matter who he is or what his past. He was kind to me when I had that accident and helped get Billy home. Maybe he knew who did the job and talked to them. Maybe he even called in that tip about my son's whereabouts."

Andy stroked his jaw. "It's possible. He has connections. He can make things happen."

"What about Jeff's debt?"

"My guess is that's been handled. The two men who were after the money are dead. If you feel comfortable about it, would you allow me to show Billy a few mug shots so we can verify his abductors?"

"Billy's been waking up with nightmares of being trapped in a dark room. I hate to put him through any more angst. Although knowing he was safe from the men who captured him might help him move on. I'll ask him, Andy." Jan yawned, despite the caffeine she'd ingested. "Thanks to you and your team, I'm going to sleep very well tonight."

Andy took her hand and held it a beat too long. "I'm glad."

Jan's face heated, as she looked into his silvery eyes. *I could fall in love with a man like Andy.*

****

In the morning, the sun seemed brighter, and the air seemed to have lost its chill. For the first time in weeks, the oppressive cloud that hung over their family lifted.

Mae had begged to go back to school for days. Jan couldn't put her off much longer, so she drove her—not quite ready to put her on the bus—and walked her inside, taking Billy with them.

"I'm not a baby, Mom." Mae moved ahead of her.

Jan caught up with her. "Not so fast, young lady. I didn't get a goodbye kiss." When Jan moved to kiss her, Mae turned away.

"Not here. You're embarrassing me." She nodded to a group of girls and ran to join them.

"Pick you up out front at three," Jan called after

her.

"Can I go to school after we see Andy, Mommy?" Billy said.

"We'll see, sweetheart." In mommy talk that meant no way could she bear to leave him until she knew for certain he was safe. "It might take a long time to look at the pictures."

On the way to the Enfield facility, where Andy was to meet Jan with Billy to review mug shots, she passed through the drive-up window at National Bank and Trust and deposited Jeff's severance check. What a relief to have all that money available. Jeff's preliminary hearing was scheduled for this afternoon. Given the evidence against him, she was certain his case would go to trial. Andy agreed to sneak her in to see him beforehand.

With Billy settled in with Andy, the guard took Jan to a private visiting room where Jeff waited, seated on a straight-backed metal chair. When the guard shut the door, the room seemed to close in on them. Jeff's guard stood at the door, watching and listening. A private room without privacy.

"How do you stand it in here?" Jan asked Jeff. His face seemed drawn and pale against the orange prison-issued shirt. He was going to pay dearly for all he had done. She supposed she should be glad he was getting his comeuppance, but she couldn't help worrying about him.

"Don't have much choice. The worst part is the quiet. They have me in isolation."

"For your safety. In case you're interested, Detective Hoskins thinks they've found the men who abducted our son. Billy is looking at mug shots right now to verify this."

"Detective Hoskins. The guy who nailed me? You talk about him a lot." He cocked his head, and his face hardened. "You have something going on with him?"

"How dare you…" Jan rose to leave.

"Sit, Jan. I'm sorry. I've had too much time to think. I've lost so much—you, my children, my life." Dropping his head in his hands, he squelched a sob. "No one could love me like you do. I need you."

Jeff's hardened shield dropped away and inside, Jan realized he was a lost soul.

"Please." He reached for her hand, his eyes watery, pleading.

Jan let him hold her hand. The battle had ended and maybe this was a truce of sorts. As much as she wished she could respond to Jeff in kind, it wouldn't be right to give him false hope.

Easing her hand from his, Jan spoke bluntly. "Our divorce will be final in two months. I'm sorry it has to end this way, but you let me down. When we married, I expected us to be forever. I stood by you when you lost your job, lied to protect your image, and took you back after you cheated on me. I tolerated your actions in hopes you would come to grips with your problems and treat the children and me with the respect and love we deserve." She shook her head, her vision blurred by tears. "But you blew it. You hammered me down. I…don't love you anymore."

"God, Jan. I knew you were upset, but I didn't think you had it in you to hate me."

"I don't hate you, Jeff. I pity you."

"I've stopped drinking." He chuckled lightly. "Had no choice. But I'm going to stick with it when I get out of this place. Honest."

Jan rose to leave.

"You're staying for my hearing, aren't you?"

"No. You and your public defender can battle it out in court without me."

"Maybe I won't get convicted, or I'll be on parole soon. What about then? Where will I go?"

"That's for you to figure out. Good luck, Jeff."

As Jan followed the guard back to Andy's office, it occurred to her Jeff never even asked about Billy or Mae.

Billy, seated in front of Andy's desk, was waiting for her. "All done, Mommy. Detective Andy said I did a good job finding the bad guys. Look, he gave me a tootsie pop." He held the candy up to show her—"root beer"—then popped it in his mouth.

"Can I go to school now? You let Mae go."

Jan looked at Andy, who had rocked back in his desk chair. "What do you think?"

"I think you should get on with your life."

"Yes, you're absolutely right." Jan realized then how much she'd come to depend on Andy being there for her. "I'll miss our chats."

"I'll be around." He winked at her.

"So will I." In another life, she could have easily gotten involved with such a selfless man. In this life, not happening. She'd worked hard to claim her independence. Besides, what man in his right mind would want to be saddled with another man's children?

Giving Andy a gracious smile, Jan took Billy's hand. "Come on, let's get you to school."

Billy danced ahead of her all the way to the car. "Will I be late for show and tell, Mommy? I hope not because I've got lots to say."

"Be careful. Don't run with a lollipop in your mouth." What if he fell and choked and—*Stop it, Jan. He's fine, and you're fine*.

After leaving Billy in the hands of his teachers, Jan drove to the Sweet Shop. She'd left Loreen without gluten-free products for three days and expected on-line orders waited to be filled.

When she arrived, Loreen clasped both her hands. "My dear, you've been through so much."

"It's over. We're safe. It feels so good to be free." Jan washed her hands and pulled on a pair of surgeon's gloves. "How's business been?"

"I have a wait list for your Nutella brownies, and let's see." Loreen rifled through the orders. "Karen Jones wants a gift basket with an assortment of your treats for a friend who just had a baby. A boy."

"How about the on-line mixes?" Jan took down ingredients from the overhead cabinet—her pre-mixed gluten-free flour, spices, sugar, and the king-sized jar of Nutella for the brownies.

"The printouts are by the computer. Good thing we specified a two-week lead time."

"I can only put in four hours today. Tomorrow, I can stay till three, as long as you don't mind my bringing Billy in the afternoon."

"Of course you can." Loreen rested her hand on Jan's arm. "Are you going to make that call to IBG today?"

"Yes, of course. Where has my mind been? Let's do it right now."

With the IBG meeting scheduled, and the situation involving Jeff's debt settled, Jan picked up Mae at school and headed home. On the way, she sang along with the car radio—an old Helen Reddy song from the women's lib days called, "I Am Woman." So true. The world was opening up for her. She'd been caged for years. Finally, she was set free.

Catching on, Billy and Mae harmonized from the back seat with tra-la-las.

When Jan turned into Charming Way, the barren trees lining each side of the road that had looked so limp and dreary yesterday stood proud and stark against a blazing blue sky.

"I want to say hi to Poppa Frank, Mommy," Billy said.

"Momma Tina lets me have coffee," Mae added.

Jan knew she would have to tell them what happened in a kind and tactful way, but she couldn't bring herself to deal with it this minute.

"Not now, my dears. But look, Amy's car's in the driveway. We haven't visited with her in a long time."

"Stevie. I want to see Stevie. Can we see Stevie, Mommy?"

Jan hadn't seen or spoken with Amy since the night she came over to console her about Billy. She wasn't sure how welcome they would be. The rift Jeff caused had damaged their friendship. Amy had taken the first step toward healing. Now it was Jan's turn. She needed Amy to accept her back as a friend. Mike would be at work, so Amy should be alone.

Parking in her drive, Jan let the children out of the car.

Billy started for the back door.

She grabbed the back of his coat. "Not so fast young man. We're guests today. Taking both their hands, she led Billy and Mae to the front porch and pressed the doorbell.

They waited for a few long minutes, which didn't surprise her. In their neighborhood, friends came in the back way. She suspected Amy was as leery of strangers as she was. Jan raised her hand to buzz again when the inside door opened.

Stevie looked out at them through the storm door. His eyebrows went up and, for a moment, Jan thought he might shut the door on them. Instead, he lowered his gaze, as if embarrassed to look her in the eye, and then unlocked the door to let them inside.

"I missed you, Stevie." Billy clung to his legs.

"Me too," Mae said. "Why haven't you come to play with us?"

Stevie knelt. "I've been…very busy." He stood, shuffling his feet against the tiled foyer floor. "Uh, nice to see you, Mrs. Simmons. I'm sorry about what happened."

Jan hated that she considered her godson in a new light. He'd been handing drugs out to kids. Jeff's dirty business. But he was young and vulnerable, and Jeff took advantage of him.

"Oh, Stevie." Jan cupped his chin and made him look at her. "It wasn't all your fault."

"I had a choice. I made the wrong one."

"Will you be all right?"

He straightened up and pulled back his shoulders. "Yes. I can handle it. When I get out, my folks are sending me to a private school. I can start over. I'll make new friends. It's all good."

Amy came up beside her son and laid her hand on his shoulder. "Jan? Oh, Jan, I've been meaning to call you. Stevie, why have you let the Simmons stand in the doorway? Come on inside." Her gaze lowered. With a smile, she ruffled Billy's hair. "You've had quite an adventure, young man." Picking up Billy, Amy kissed his cheek.

Billy wiggled out of Amy's arms. "Can we play now, Stevie?"

Stevie grabbed his hand. "Sure thing, sport. Come on, Mae. Bet I can beat you at checkers."

"No, you can't. I'm the champion."

Amy and Jan watched the trio go off to Stevie's room.

She linked her arm in Jan's. "Coffee?"

"Of course."

Chapter Thirty-Seven

"What the fuck? Where is this place?" Frank steered the rental van he'd picked up at the Naples airport along the barren mountain road.

Baby Frank slept like a goddamn angel in the backseat, a godsend because the little shit screamed during most of the flight to Italy. Off and on for six fucking hours.

The grass and shrubs were brown with patches of melting snow. Cold, but not fucking freezing like winter in Connecticut. Every once in a while, they'd pass a homestead marked off with metal fencing and slide lock gates to keep in the horses and cows.

"We could have stayed in a nice hotel in Naples, but no, you wanted to visit your nana. Is she still alive?"

"Of course. My cousin would have written me if anything happened to her. I tried to call, but I don't think she has a phone."

"So we're popping in. All five of us?" Frank sighed. "*Madonna mia*, how did I get talked into this mess?"

"She'll be surprised to see me all grown up with a daughter and a grandson. Funny, I don't remember Faeto being this far up from the Amalfi coast."

"When was the last time you were here?"

"I was little, I think ten. My father went to

323

America, and then he brought Mom and me over. My brothers too."

"Da, I have to pee," Lucille said from the back seat.

"Didn't you hit the can at the airport?"

"Yeah, but…"

"There ain't no place out here. This'll have to do." He pulled off the road. "Okay, Lucille, go."

As soon as the car stopped moving, Baby Frank stirred.

"What do you mean *okay*? I don't see a bathroom."

"What do ya want me to do? This vehicle don't come with a built-in pee bucket."

From the back seat, Vinnie snickered. "Nice to be a guy, huh Pops? Just aim and shoot wherever we damn well please."

Frank pointed out the window. "See that bush, Lucille?"

"You want me to pull down my pants out here? What if I get a rash?"

"Squat."

Handing Vinnie the baby, Lucille pushed open the door. "It's chilly. I'll freeze my ass off."

Tina got out of the car. "I have to go too."

An hour later, they drove into the tiny town of Faeto, at the top of the mountain. Clean, thin, fresh air. If he was girlie, he might even call the place cute. Its pastel, red-roofed houses were jammed together and had metal balconies and hanging plants.

Tina pointed at one of the houses. "My aunt Sophia used to live there." Her hand had crept over and now rested on his crotch. The boys were hard as tennis balls.

"Yeah, nice, but where's your nana's place?"

"Keep driving. It's just down the road from here, in the country."

Tina's roving fingers had him thinking about pulling over at the small inn ahead and getting a room. Yeah, a little siesta. Didn't Europeans nap in the afternoon? But he had baggage in the back seat, Lucille, Vinnie, and the baby—who was suckling on his mother's tit with big slurping noises. With his elbow, he gently nudged Tina just under her plump breast. He'd like to do a little sucking right now.

He upped the speed. They couldn't be far away.

Finally, they came upon a large stretch of land leading to a house surrounded by trees and gardens, which weren't producing anything except brown leaves at the moment.

Forgetting her "job," Tina sat forward in her seat and pointed. "This is it." She pecked at his cheek, making him smile. "I love you. Thank you."

"You can thank me properly later," he replied.

Frank suffered through the greetings. The old lady, Nana, cried when she saw Tina, cooed over baby Frank, and then bustled about the kitchen setting out a mini-meal of cheese, Italian cold cuts, and bread fresh out of the oven. In a way, she reminded him of Tina, with her hair pulled back in a chignon, a housedress, and stockings. She hadn't been expecting them, yet she acted as if they'd planned this visit for months.

"Here." Nana handed Tina a bottle of red wine. "Open this so it can breathe." She turned to Lucille and tipped her chin toward one of the cabinets. "We'll need glasses, plates. Frank, you sit." She pulled out a chair at the head of the table. In older Italian families, men were king. He'd forgotten that.

By this time, baby Frank was due for a diaper change. Setting the opened wine on the table, Tina took the baby to the back bedroom. It seemed this house had rooms up the kazoo. Apparently, they housed workers here during the growing season.

Frank sat at the rustic-looking wooden slab Nana called a table. It was large enough to fit a dozen people.

Vinnie slid in at his right. "Nice digs, eh, Pops? Real country. No one out here but goats and chickens. We ain't staying long are we, because I gotta get back and take care of business." He pulled out his cell phone. "No signal. How's Louie gonna keep me in da loop?"

"You can't go home right now. You're tied to that kidnapping—and so am I, indirectly."

"Nice you got that little kid back home."

"Yeah, and I got rid of two bad apples at the same time. Wheezy was gonna screw us out of the money."

"Oh, yeah, the money. Are we square?"

"I took care of it." He patted Vinnie on the shoulder. "Sometimes, ya just got to do the right thing. It's only money, after all." Picking up the wine bottle, he checked the label. His eyebrows went up. "Hey, I know this wine. Costs a bundle back home." He poured a sample in his glass, waved it under his nose like he'd seen connoisseurs do, and then took a sip. "Smooth, with a hint of pear. Must of cost old Nana a bundle."

Vinnie laughed. "Pear? You kidding me?" Vinnie dumped some in his glass and took a slug. "Grapes, Pops? Not pears. You getting senile?"

Once the women returned, Frank dug into the food, ripping the bread apart with his hands and stuffing it in his mouth to smooth out the bite of the aged provolone cheese. Simple but authentic Italian food, like the little deli in Hartford he used to frequent.

He sipped at the wine. "This is an excellent wine, Nana.

"Just local," she said. "From the valley in Naples, Campania. Our wines are very popular abroad." She winked. "Big business."

"Big business, eh?" Frank gave Vinnie *the* look.

His meal completed, Frank stood. "Nana, you're the best."

The old lady smiled. She must have been pretty in her day. Her olive skin hardly showed a wrinkle, and he guessed Tina would age just as well.

He cocked his head at Vinnie. "Let's take a walk."

Leaving Tina talking old times with her grandmother and Lucille tending to the baby, they headed out the back door toward a small arbor. He examined one of the leaves. It was brown now, but a familiar shape. "Grape leaves. My father used to grow concord grapes in our backyard. He never did much with them, but we kids used to snack on them. The skin was tough, so we just squeezed the center out into our mouths and swallowed it whole, pits and all.

"Let me guess, Pops, you want to make wine."

"We could make a bundle here. I got investment money in the bank in Cancun. I'll buy up a winery, plaster on a bunch of fancy labels and up the price."

"Not *we*, Pops, *you*. I ain't sticking around here."

"But you and me, we can get things set up."

"What about the Naples gangs? They ain't gonna appreciate us cutting in on their takes. Besides, you've been makin' a big deal about staying clean."

He rested a hand on Vinnie's shoulder and leaned in. "Well, here's the thing. I miss the action. I tried it back in Greenberg. Boring as hell and shit followed me anyway. The way I figure, I might as well get a kickback. Now"—he rubbed his hands together—"where was I? Oh, yeah. No one needs to know, see. We keep this tight. Just you and me. We funnel the profits back home to the family treasury."

Frank squeezed Vinnie's shoulder and gave him a hard stare. "You in?"

"For now, but I get a cut off the top."

Frank whacked his son-in-law on the back. "That's my boy."

Chapter Thirty-Eight

As it turned out, Jeff's case went to trial. He was sentenced to three years for possession, plus an additional two years for operating in a school zone with a possibility of supervised probation for good behavior. That it was a first offense, and he had dealt in a low-end substance, rather than heroin or coke, helped keep his sentence light. This meant he would likely be in prison by the time their divorce hearing came up. No big deal. She'd handle it alone, just as she'd handled everything else, and be better for it.

Jan dialed her parents to tell them the news about Jeff and to remind them she and the children were coming to see them.

"Mae has early dismissal this Friday, Mom, so I figure we'll get to your place by suppertime."

"Oh, yes, about that."

Oh no, here it comes. "What do you mean? We're staying the weekend, isn't that what we discussed. The kids have school Monday, and I have to work."

"We know. Dad and I have been talking. You and the children have been through a lot."

"Yes, but—"

"Please, Janice. Let me finish. We agree you relocating near us would be a problem when your lives are in Greenberg. So, your dad and I are going to sell our house and move up there with you."

"*With* me? But Mom—"

"Did I say *with* you? Heavens no, your home isn't large enough for all of us. Besides, Dad and I like to have our own space. We looked online for condos in your area."

"Online? You have a computer?"

"Of course we do. As I was saying, we saw some delightful places advertised. We have an appointment with a realtor on Saturday."

"Saturday? Here? You want to move here? Oh my God, Mom, that's terrific." Tears welled in Jan's eyes.

"We can help you with Billy and Mae. You're all we have, you and the children. Dad and I are getting older. We've decided to retire and realized we have no reason to stay in Jersey. Our friends can come see us, and we'll make new friends. You *do* have a Catholic church in town?"

"Oh yes, and they're very active socially. And, Mom, Rana's parents just moved here. You and Dad will like them."

"Oh, Jan, I'm so glad you want us there. You've been a little distant lately, and we weren't sure."

"I love you, Mom, and Dad too. Billy and Mae will be thrilled." Jan snapped her fingers, tried to at least. "I know. I'll invite Rana and her parents to dinner Saturday night so you can meet them."

"Oh, dear, what shall I wear?' Do you want me to cook something?"

"Casual, Mom. Don't bring a thing. You can help me fix dinner. It's been a long time since we've cooked together."

Jan hung up with joy in her heart. The puzzle of her life was coming together. One by one, each piece fit perfectly. She was on a roll. She'd been through the worst, and now she was winning.

Yay for me.
For us.

****

Jan's parents moved quickly. The sale sign was up at their Jersey home by the time they arrived Friday afternoon. For Jan, her parents were changing their lives. She knew then just how much they loved and needed her and the children. She needed them too.

It appeared her parents were flusher than anyone knew. They were never lavish in their spending—no fancy vacations abroad. They were homebodies and lived well but simply. When they fell in love with a condo on East Street, Jan's father plunked down a deposit.

By the time her mother and father left Greenburg on Sunday afternoon, they had a closing date. One month. Just in time for Jan's divorce hearing.

While their families had split over Jeff involving Stevie, Jan and Amy snuck in visits when Mike was at work and met for shopping at the mall.

Jan hadn't entirely abandoned Jeff. They made their peace—had to. The children still loved their father and asked about him. Mae drew him pictures, and Billy made him pipe cleaner "toys" he could play with. Jan brought him books. Her parents visited him. After all, he had no one. Jan ran into Candy on one of her visits. She'd lost her spunk; dark roots showed she was growing out the blonde color. Like Jan, she'd been through her own kind of hell.

The DiGiorno's house remained vacant, as far as Jan could tell. No activity, except for the landscaping service that routinely arrived to mow and treat the lawn, rake leaves, and generally maintain the exterior of the house. She wondered if the DiGiornos planned on moving back one day. For her, the house remained a monument to the past, a reminder not to take their safety for granted; that people aren't always who they seem to be.

Next door, Candy and Bob's house sold quickly, and why wouldn't it? Realtors lauded the benefits of living in a good school district with lots of children and friendly, at-home mothers. Of course, they skipped over the fact that The Mafia once invaded the street, and that it was a mini Peyton Place.

Charming? Hardly. Nevertheless, to Jan, Charming Way was home, where friendships reigned over troubles.

****

On a Saturday morning about ten, a week before Jan's parents were to close on their condo, Mae ran in from outdoors, her cheeks flushed with excitement. Billy was behind her.

"Mom, a kitten. He's so cute. Please say we can keep him?"

Billy tugged at Jan's sleeve. "Please, Mommy, please."

"Calm down, honey. Start from the beginning? What kitten?"

Mae's eyes moved to the doorway.

"Andy." Her lips curved into a smile.

Jan hadn't seen the detective since they wrapped up at Jeff's hearing, but he looked good. Instead of his usual business suit, he wore jeans and a black leather jacket over a plaid flannel shirt. One hand held a small dark-haired boy who seemed to be Billy's age. The child, clad much the same as his dad, leaned against Andy's leg sucking his thumb. In his other hand, Andy cradled a fuzzy orange ball with frightened eyes.

"Jan, I don't mean to impose. Mae told me she's always wanted a kitten. Nellie just had a litter." He held up the wiggly little creature.

"Aw, come here." Jan took the kitten and cradled it against her like a newborn baby. "Why, she's shaking."

"It's a tom, a male. He needs a home where he will be loved. Six weeks old, weaned from his mama, and litter trained. If you decide to keep him, I have litter and food in the car."

"Can I hold him, too?" Billy reached for the kitten.

"Be gentle now, he's very fragile."

"I will, Mommy."

Jan eased the kitten into Billy's waiting hands.

Mae crossed her arms over her chest. "How come he gets to hold the kitty first?"

"No fighting, kids, or Detective Andy will take his kitten back."

"I wouldn't really." Andy pushed the shy little boy forward. "Meet my son, Oliver. Ollie, say hi to everyone."

The child replied in a small voice.

Jan took the little one's hand. "Billy, why don't you let Mae hold the kitten? I'll bet Ollie would like to see your new truck."

"Yeah. It's a fire engine with a ladder that goes up and down." Billy passed the kitten to Mae but waited to hear her decision.

"I'll take care of him. I promise," Mae said, holding the kitten to her cheek. "He's so soft."

"Of course we'll keep him. He's adorable, and he needs us. He told me so. Andy, don't just stand at the door, come and sit. I'll make a fresh pot of coffee."

"Sure, but first"—he knelt in front of Mae and Billy—"you two have a big decision to make." He scratched the kitten's head. "This little guy doesn't have a name yet."

Mae giggled and kissed Andy on the cheek. "Thank you for bringing us a kitty. I think we should name him after you."

"Detective Andy," Billy said.

"No, silly," Mae corrected. "That's too long. How about *Andy*."

"I'm flattered," Andy said to the children. Rising, he put his hand on his son's shoulder. "Billy, how about showing Ollie that truck while your mom and I chat."

"Sure, Ollie, it's in my room." He took the child's hand. "Come on."

Andy and Jan smiled at each other as the two boys scampered off.

"Ollie doesn't get to play with kids his age very often. He stays at my mom's. She's widowed and loves the company. Says he keeps her young. Her condo is in a fifty-five or over community, so no playmates."

"I'm glad you brought Ollie to meet Billy. There are no boys his age on the street here, either. That's one of the reasons I take him to pre-school."

"I'm trying to get him a spot in Fun for Tots for the spring session. It's close to the station. Mom doesn't drive, or shouldn't drive. She's dealing with cataracts."

"Billy goes there now. The teachers are wonderful. I'll put in a good word for your son. It's nice your mom can care for Ollie. My parents are moving here so the children and I will have family around. It's not easy being a single parent."

"Amen to that. So, Jan, I don't mean to pry, or maybe I do." He waved his hand. "Forget it. It's none of my business."

"You want to know what happened between Jeff and me. You're probably thinking I divorced him because of his crime, but our marriage was over long before that." She stirred her coffee, not wanting to look Andy in the eye.

"Jan." Andy tipped up her chin. "Look at me. It's all right. I suspected something else was going on. When I arrested Jeff at your neighbor's house, the woman clung to him, as if she were the wife, not you."

"You've got sharp eyes, Detective. By that time, I'd filed for divorce. Technically, Jeff and I were separated." Andy didn't say anything; he looked at her steadily. She babbled on. "Everything happened at once. I found out Jeff had been having a long-term affair with the woman you saw with him, and then the police came busting in. Jeff's involvement with narcotics sealed it."

"The man must've been blind. You're beautiful, and you have courage. Only a fool would've cheated on someone like you."

"Then Jeff's a fool, and so am I for having tolerated him for so long. My children will hate me one day for exposing them to the lies and deceit that went on in our home."

"They'll get over it and so will you."

"I'm doing fine now." Jan set her elbow on the table and rested her chin on her fist. "So, your turn. What's your story? You obviously were married."

Andy exhaled audibly. "Pretty much the same as yours, without the drugs and stuff." His lips closed in a wry grin at the mention. "I know what it's like to be cheated on. I found her in our bed with my partner. Whatever happened to death do us part? Are they just words?"

"They aren't supposed to be, but life changes people. And not always for the good."

"So true."

"I have full custody of Mae and Billy. The court agreed their father is a bad influence."

"My ex didn't want Ollie. What kind of woman doesn't love her own child?"

"The wrong kind." Jan took his hand. He seemed visibly upset. "All I know is I intend to raise Billy and Mae to be honest and to respect others."

Andy squeezed her hand. "I'm with you on that. I'm a cop, remember?"

He rose from his chair. "I'd better get Ollie and let you get on with your day."

Jan rested her hand on his arm. "I hope you'll stop by again. I've…we've missed you."

"I missed you all too, Jan." His eyes softened and for a moment, she thought he was going to kiss her.

Mae ran in holding up the kitten. "Mom, what do I do? Andy just peed on the rug."

The detective's hands went in the air. "Not guilty."

They all laughed, including Ollie who seemed to have fast-friended Billy.

"We're going to have to schedule a play date for our boys," Jan said to Andy.

"And one for us grownups too." Andy winked at her. "I'll call you."

A word about the author…

Joy Smith merged a successful career in nonfiction with fiction writing when she discovered making up stories and characters was more fun than sugarcoating facts. In addition to *Hear Me Roar*, Joy is the author of a romantic suspense and a children's book, as well as four how-to books and a cookbook.

When she is not glued to her computer or contriving plots, she might be out sailing with her handsome captain, at home crocheting shawls and blankets to donate to those in need, or at the gym trying to work off those danged extra pounds.

http://www.joysmith.net

Thank you for purchasing
this publication of The Wild Rose Press, Inc.

If you enjoyed the story, we would appreciate your
letting others know by leaving a review.

For other wonderful stories,
please visit our on-line bookstore at
www.thewildrosepress.com.

For questions or more information
contact us at
info@thewildrosepress.com.

The Wild Rose Press, Inc.
www.thewildrosepress.com

Stay current with The Wild Rose Press, Inc.

Like us on Facebook

https://www.facebook.com/TheWildRosePress

And Follow us on Twitter
https://twitter.com/WildRosePress